UNNATURAL
CAUSES

Peter Swan

In memory of dear departed friends, Fred Fisher, Bob Miller, Jerry Casby, Bill Rubidge, and John Powell.

ONE

Sunday morning

Garrison was the first of the men to enter the room. The top buttons of his Hawaiian shirt were undone and a gold neck chain just reached the dark mat on his broad chest. He had come to the room they were using as a card lounge a few minutes early to glance at his stacks of chips. He did not really think anyone would have shorted his stash from the night before, but why take chances? Satisfied that his winnings were intact, he went over to the credenza and mixed himself a bloody Mary. The morning sun filtering through the plantation shutters striped the green baize surface of the poker table.

Garrison took a pull on his drink and thought about how they had finally come back together. They had all once been friends of a sort. But events over the years had made many of them bitter and angry toward one member of the group. There were pairs among them who still enjoyed each other, but criss-crossing tendrils of distrust and grievances had ended general fraternization. They had not been together as a group for over three years until Eldridge proposed the poker game. Eldridge was surely not as guileless as he sometimes seemed. His invitation had been masterful. It mixed innocent good intentions – to relax together and move past perceived wrongs -- and an unspoken challenge to their Alpha-male inclinations to smash their rivals even if only in a high-stakes poker game. Garrison looked up as Bacon entered the room.

Bacon grunted and closed the louvers on the shutters, then used the dimmer to adjust the lights. He had not shaved and Garrison thought he seemed even more tightly wound than usual. "Drank too much," he offered with a slight shrug of his shoulders. "You had a hot streak."

Garrison nodded, "Yeah, and that big pot at the end helped. You see any of the others at breakfast?"

"No. I stayed in bed. You didn't eat?"

"I don't eat much in the morning. The coffee and Danish here will be enough. I took a walk on the grounds."

The door opened and Eldridge entered, wrinkling his nose. "Smells like a fucking smokehouse in here!" He fanned the door open and shut. Eldridge always looked fit and toned. Garrison wondered if he had done a three-mile run and twenty pushups already that morning. "Where are the rest of them?" asked Eldridge. "I saw Takimoto and McCaffrey and Kleidaeker all in the dining room, but they left before I did. "

Bacon looked at Eldridge with hooded eyes, "Maybe you'll have to round them up." At that moment, the three men entered the room. The one called McCaffrey nodded silently at the others and took his place at the table. He began to rearrange his piles of chips as he quickly surveyed the room. "Caughlin isn't here," he said.

"That son of a bitch is always late! Thinks the world runs on his time," said Bacon quietly as he pinched the bridge of his nose.

Eldridge headed for the door. "I'll check his room, make sure he's up."

He returned five minutes later. "His door's locked and he doesn't answer a knock. I telephoned from the registration desk and no one answered. I checked and he's not in the dining room. He must have decided to get some air. Screw it, let's start without him."

They settled into their chairs and Bacon dealt a game of seven-card stud. Eldridge had pocket sevens and won it with three of a kind. Garrison thought Eldridge was bluffing a straight and called his raise with two high pair. "Shit! You had them all covered up," he said as he watched Eldridge sweep in the chips.

The next hand, McCaffrey dealt jacks-or-back draw. He dealt himself kings for openers and then drew a pair of nines. Garrison, who had been dealt a pair of aces, did not improve and flicked his cards to the middle in disgust when McCaffrey re-raised him and won. They watched with amusement as Kleidaeker's pudgy fingers fumbled the shuffle and spilled a few cards on the table top. He had begun to deal the third hand when they heard a scream followed by running footsteps and a maid's tremulous voice calling to someone else.

"The guy in C-six is dead! Go tell the manager!"

Kleidaeker stopped in mid-deal and looked at Eldridge. "C-six. That's Caughlin's room!"

TWO

Tuesday afternoon

I had just wrapped up an investigation into an employee-theft ring at a large regional hardware chain. The client was satisfied to have stopped the hemorrhaging and the D.A. had enough to go to the grand jury. My bank balance is no longer running on fumes, but knowing that a healthy fee was on the way didn't hurt. I was spending the tail end of the afternoon paying some bills when the phone chirped. I picked up, gave my name, and heard nothing. I tried again.

"Hello? This is Rick Conwright."

"Mr. Conwright, this is Amanda Nelson. I'd like to make an appointment … this afternoon, if possible."

I looked at the clock on the wall. It was four forty-five. "It's almost five. Can we do it tomorrow?"

"I … I'd really like to talk to you right away." Her voice dropped. "It's taken me almost three days to decide to call you. I shouldn't have waited. I very much want you to take this on for me."

"Can you give me an idea of what I'd be taking on?"

"I want you to look into my father, Sean Caughlin's, death. They say it was a heart attack. If you will see me, I'll explain why I need your help with this."

I told her how to find my houseboat and twenty-five minutes later she was at my door.

After my wife left me two years ago, I converted the extra bedroom to a fully-equipped office. The window looked past my neighbor's boat and out onto Portland's Willamette River. I drew the blinds to keep the late afternoon sun from glaring into my guest's eyes and motioned her to a chair. She was in her early thirties and wore a beige linen dress and chocolate colored pumps. Her chestnut hair framed her face in a simple bob. She was nice looking without being head-turning and her only makeup seemed to be kind of a dusty-rose lip gloss.

I settled into the chair behind my desk and pulled out my notebook. "You don't think your father died of heart failure?"

She looked down and cleared her throat. "I don't know. He had a heart condition … even had a pacemaker. But … well, he was at this meeting -- a three-day poker game actually -- with some men he didn't altogether trust. My father was a businessman. Some would say a tough businessman. When I heard who was at this game, I remembered that my father had told me once that two of those men, Bacon and Takimoto, had some kind of grudges against him. I don't know why he agreed to play in the game."

"Did he tell you the reasons behind those 'grudges'?"

"No, and I didn't press him."

"Was there an autopsy?"

"No. That wasn't my call. There was no legal requirement to have one. His doctor signed the death certificate and his wife didn't ask for an autopsy."

"You said 'his wife'. She is not your mother?"

"No. A few years after my mother died, my father married GeorgeAnn."

"So your father went to play poker with some men you think didn't like him or did not wish him well. You think someone murdered him?"

"Look, I said I don't know. Maybe it was just my father's time to go and it happened in a strange setting. But I'd like you to look into it."

"You referred to your father as a 'tough business-man' and thought a couple of these poker players had grudges against him. Was he hard to get along with?"

"He and I did not have a close father-daughter rela-tionship … I often wished that we did. But he was never unkind to my mother or to me. Apart from our family he was … I guess you could say … a little aggressive in his interactions. I sometimes thought he only saw winners and losers and was damn-well not going to be one of the losers."

"I see. Have you talked to the police?"

"No. What could I tell them? If you find anything … well, then maybe I will."

"It doesn't sound as if you have any medical evidence about his death beyond the death certificate. The answers should be there … in the medical evidence. I'd have to see a copy of the death certificate and get permission to talk with his doctor. Then I'd need a list of all the people at this poker game and the location where the game was held."

"GeorgeAnn will have the certificate and her cooperation will be necessary with the doctor. We don't get along very well, so I can't be sure she'll agree."

"I can get a copy of the certificate from County Records, but it would be really helpful to speak with his doctor. Wouldn't the widow be equally interested in your inquiries?"

My would-be client hesitated. "Maybe. But my guess is she'll think I'm being paranoid and will not want to do anything to cast a lurid tone on my father's death."

I knew that the next week-and-a-half on my calendar was fairly open. This woman sounded perfectly rational even though her concerns seemed to rest on a scanty foundation. It would probably be a quick job and relatively easy money. After a few moments reflection, I decided to take the case.

"Okay. I'll look into it and do what I can, but you've got to understand that there may be nothing there ... just a death by natural causes."

"If that is truly what it was, I can accept that. But I don't want a superficial job. I'll gladly pay you to take a good, hard look at this."

"Fine. I'll need a retainer. Say, two thousand dollars." I handed her my hourly rate sheet. "If that's used up, I bill twice a month. My expenses are extra."

She scanned the rate sheet indifferently and then reached for her purse. "I'll write you a check right now."

"Thank you. Was your father wealthy?"

She finished writing the check and handed it to me before she answered. "Yes. He owned a very successful company. He manufactured industrial rubber-based products ... tires, shock absorbers, gaskets ... things like that. And he held some valuable patents."

"Did he leave a will?"

A slight sigh escaped her lips. "Not that I know of."

"Do you think your father was in good shape? Healthy?"

"Well, like I said, we all knew that he had a heart condition. But it seemed to be under control. He was watching his diet, he had lost a bit of weight ... but he was still too heavy. He walked most days ... just a couple of miles ... I wouldn't say he was in *poor* shape."

"What about enemies? Anyone you can think of beside these two men at the game you thought had grudges against him?"

She paused for a few seconds. "No one I can think of. I suppose I can't say he was well liked, but I have no reason to believe he had enemies who might want to kill him."

"Do you know why he went to this game?"

"Not really. The only time he mentioned it to me, he sounded like he wasn't even sure himself why he was going. I could tell he wasn't entirely comfortable about it, but he did say he was damned if he was going to be the only one who didn't show up. I think all of them were people that he had known over the years, but I didn't sense that he had much warmth toward them."

She gave me a list, as best she knew, of those who were playing in the game. We agreed that she would call Mrs. Caughlin to ask permission for me to question the doctor and that I would call her in the morning with more questions. I saw her to the door. After she left, I poured myself a Bushmills on the rocks and moved to a patio chair on the aft deck of the houseboat. I sat there watching a couple of yachts on the river and wondering what was there about a poker game – even a high-stakes one – that could cause a man's heart to stop.

⪡⪢

Wednesday morning, I went on the internet to look for bios of Caughlin and the three men that Amanda

Nelson thought were at the poker game. As Amanda had said, Caughlin was described as the CEO and sole owner of Rubber Master Products, Inc. He had a Bachelor of Science degree in chemical engineering from Purdue and a Masters from Cal. He was shown as being on the board of directors of the Chamber of Commerce, but, other than that, there was no indication of public service or personal association with any charitable causes. I could not access any financial information on Rubber Master because it was not a public company, but the company's website indicated it manufactured a considerable array of rubber-based products. Many were used in the transportation industry. Licensees of its patented process manufactured long-lasting recaps for truckers. The recapped tires were marketed under the "Rhino" brand. Other products were apparently supplied as components for larger assemblies and the company also made a line of tires for general aviation aircraft.

Stanley Bacon was listed in "Who's Who in Oregon". It showed him as the owner and president of "Pilot's Choice", a local supplier of equipment such as tires, avionics, and propellers for general aviation aircraft. He had chemistry degrees from the University of Washington and Ohio State and had been the Vice Commodore of the Columbia Yacht Club. Amanda had told me that he and her father had been partners in a business when she was in college. She said it was a tire recapping business, but she did not know what had become of the company.

The next name, Stephen Takimoto, was not in Who's Who. I tracked him down through telephoning The Oregonian, the newspaper where, in another life, I used to be an investigative reporter. It turned out that Takimoto owned three pharmacies in the greater Portland area. He was a graduate of the pharmacy school at Purdue. His pharmacies had, a couple of years ago, been under investigation by the State Board of Pharmacy, but no irregularities in his operations were ever found. The investigation had ended without any action by the Board. On the lighter side, Takimoto apparently was a fairly good amateur golfer and had won a couple of country-club-type tournaments.

The third name Amanda gave me was that of Paul Eldridge. She said he was some kind of a commodities broker and thought he had known her father for years. I could not find him on the internet, but I called a friend who imported bauxite and he knew of him. He told me Eldridge worked for Epsin Commodities. Amanda thought there were several more players at the game so I had some blanks to fill, but at least I had a few persons to contact. But before interviewing any of the poker players, I needed to speak to Caughlin's doctor. Even before that, I needed to check in with my client.

I punched in Amanda's number and she picked up on the third ring.

"It's Rick Conwright. How did it go with Mrs. Caughlin?"

"She was pretty resistant at first. She said it was a hard time for her and my getting in a dither about his death wouldn't help a bit. But, I said I wanted you to get started in any case and that you would be discreet. She finally seemed more or less resigned to it and said she would call the doctor and tell him he could talk with you."

"That should help. Thanks."

I told her I would report to her if there were any significant developments and hung up. I phoned Caughlin's physician, Dr. Lewis, and got lucky. He was in his office between patients and took my call. I asked him about the severity of Caughlin's heart condition.

"He had complained of how winded he got when he walked uphill. I gave him a thorough cardiac check-up. His heartbeat was too slow and it was serious enough that I convinced him to have a pacemaker implanted. But he seemed to be getting along quite nicely with it. Of course, he had a significant ongoing health risk and I had him in for further check-ups twice a year."

"Were you surprised that he died?"

"Well, I didn't expect it, but surprised? Not exactly. As I said, he was a person at risk."

"When did you see the body?"

"They had already taken Sean's body to the morgue by the time, Mrs. Caughlin called me. It was Sunday and I had no rounds, so I was at home. I think she called me from Seattle. I went directly to the morgue. I estimated he had been dead for approximately five hours."

"Did you examine the body?"

"Yes, of course. The Assistant Medical Examiner and I looked him over together. There were no signs of trauma or any indications of poison or toxins. He was found on the floor next to his bed with his pajamas on. He had no current symptoms of any disease. It was evident to me that it was a case of cardiac arrest."

"I understand there was no autopsy?"

"That's correct. The examiner and I saw no reason to perform one."

"Did his wife ask for one?"

"No. She asked me how it happened and I gave her my opinion. That seemed to satisfy her."

"You wrote on the death certificate that the cause of death was 'cardiac arrest due to acute myocardial infarction'."

"Correct. It was tragic, but not unprecedented. Despite good care, his improved health regimen, and the pacemaker, it sometimes just isn't enough even at his relatively young age."

"How old was he?"

"Fifty-seven."

I thanked the doctor and hung up. A few minutes later, I was walking up the marina gangway toward my Acura. I wanted to see the place where Caughlin had died. Amanda had told me that the game was held at a resort called "Hamilton's". It was on the east side of town and had its own golf course. When I got there, I saw there was a central building with five or six detached one–story buildings behind it amidst mature fir trees and rhododendrons. It looked like there were ten units in each of the out-buildings. I pulled into a stall in front of the main building. An eye-catching young woman wearing a royal blue blouse under a white vest with a Hamilton's logo stood behind the counter. Beyond the reception desk and off to the right, I could see white linen tablecloths and crystal on the dining-room tables. To the left, I saw an imposing door marked "Spa". I introduced myself and offered my business card.

"I've been retained to learn all the details of Sean Caughlin's death. You probably know he died at a gathering here last weekend."

"So what does 'learning all the details' mean?" she asked.

"The family just wants to understand the circumstances surrounding his death. To get closure, I guess," I replied. I may have stretched the point with a reference to the "family", but I wanted her cooperation.

"So how can I help?"

"I'd like to know where the group was housed. Where the card game was played. Which rooms the various men were in."

She looked dubious, but keyboarded a query into her computer. "All right, I guess I can write down the names and room numbers for you. You can prob-ably go into the entertainment suite if no one's using it, but some of the other rooms including the one Mr. Caughlin was in are occupied."

"That'll be fine. Do you have a map to show me the layout of the buildings?"

"Yes." She handed me a diagram of the property. "They were all in Building C just beyond the pool and toward the golf course from here. The entertainment suite is the larger unit at the end of the building."

"Thank you. I won't disturb anyone."

I doubted that the young woman had the authority to give out the names of each guest. But, by implying that I already knew all the names and merely wanted her to show me the room assignments, I now knew who all the players were beyond the short list that Amanda had given me.

"One other thing," I said. "That fancy gate that I came through ... is it locked at night?"

"Yes." She looked at me uneasily. I could tell she was starting to wonder if I was snooping around to lay the foundation for some sort of law suit. "All our guests are given a code to punch in if they need to enter after we close the gate at eight-thirty. The code changes every week." She sounded a little defensive as she continued, "throughout the resort we have installed cutting-edge security hardware and software for the protection of our guests. Why do you ask about that?"

I did not want to make her so nervous that she would ask me to leave. Besides, I might have more questions for her later. "Oh, someone had said that one of the players arrived late in the evening on the first night. I'm not even sure that's the case, but I was just wondering how he got in."

That seemed to mollify her. "I was on duty that afternoon. I'm sure everyone arrived well before dinner."

"Well thanks. That straightens that out."

I did not go directly to Building C. I wanted to reconnoiter a bit to see how the resort was laid out. The large pool had a structure at one end for the pumping/filtering equipment and lavatories. Tall evergreen trees rose from the manicured lawns surrounding the buildings. Each building was far enough from the others to give a sense of separation and quiet. At the golf course, I found a modest pro-shop, lavatories, and a shed for garaging the electric carts. The assistant pro told me that the lavatories and golf-cart shed were locked when he closed for the day. The entire property was enclosed along its perimeter by a four-foot high cyclone fence. Shrubs and hedges along the fence sheltered residential backyards on three sides and blocked off the city street on the fourth side. I headed back to Building C thinking the place certainly could be penetrated by a determined intruder, but there were few places to hide if someone came in openly during the day and then had to lay low somewhere until after midnight.

I crossed a wrap-around deck with small varnished logs for railings and entered the "entertainment suite" where the men had played cards. Four leather cigar chairs were arranged around a gas fireplace. There was a Pullman kitchen along the wall opposite the door and a credenza under the windows. A round table with seven straight-back chairs stood in the center of the room. A small table with an inlaid chess board stood against the inside wall between two more chairs. I found the poker table-top in a closet. There was a small lavatory next to the closet.

I sat in one of the cigar chairs and studied the list of room assignments. The room at the opposite end from the poker room, C-1, had been empty. From the empty room working back toward the poker room, the occupants were Stephen Takimoto, Ted McCaffrey, Marshall Kleidaeker, Carl Maitland, Sean Caughlin, Anthony Garrison, Paul Eldridge, and Stanley Bacon. Takimoto and Bacon were two of the names Amanda had given me, adding that she thought they might have borne grudges of some kind. Eldridge was the third name. The young woman at reception had said that all the rooms were laid out and furnished identically. She added that C-5 was presently unoccupied and gave me a key-card so that I could look inside.

I stepped off the deck of the entertainment suite and headed for unit C-5. Before I went in, I looked at the ground under the window and the door of C-6 where Caughlin had stayed. There was an eighteen-inch wide strip of mulched bark between the lawn and the building. I saw no footprints or disturbance of the mulch. Going through the door of C-5, I found myself in a sitting room with a desk, desk chair, couch, easy chair, lamp, and television hutch. Ahead, on the right, was a passageway to the bedroom. In the bedroom, the king-size bed and bedside tables were positioned against the left-hand wall. On the inner wall was the door to the bathroom. A dresser/TV cupboard and a built-in wardrobe were along the right-hand wall. The sliding door in the outer wall opened onto a patio with reclining lounge chairs. The front door had a dead-bolt as well as a card-operated lock for the handle. The patio door had a security peg in addition to the door lock. The bedroom windows were casements that opened, but they were backed by screens removable only from the inside. The telephone in the bedroom sat upon the dresser rather than on one of the bedside tables. Attractive reproductions of landscape paintings on the walls and fresh flowers in vases in both rooms completed the décor.

In addition to the fact that there had been no marks on Caughlin's body indicating trauma or injury, I could think of no way for anyone to enter his room if he had used the security features. I knew that Caughlin's room would be forensically contaminated by now because of maids, the morgue workers, and use by subsequent guests, so my visual survey of C-5 was probably good enough. I made a note to ask the maintenance man if there had been any damage to the window screen. Other than that loose end, I had seen nothing on the premises that shed any light on the cause of death. If something malevolent had occurred, I would never begin to see it until I talked with the poker players. Before I left, I used the telephone book in the room to get the numbers and addresses of the men that Amanda had not known.

THREE

Wednesday afternoon

It was mid-afternoon when I arrived at Paul Eldridge's office in downtown Portland. Epsin Commodities was located on the fourteenth floor of the KOIN Center building. Eldridge had been cool toward meeting with me, but finally condescended to see me after the markets closed. The receptionist escorted me past a bullpen full of computer monitors, though only a few traders remained in their cubicles. Eldridge was apparently senior enough to rate a private office. He came from behind a desk with teak cabinetry set in a chrome frame and capped with a beveled glass top to shake my hand. He was six feet tall, with prematurely graying hair and grey eyes flecked with blue. He wore a mid-gray suit. He gave me a penetrating look – the kind that lets you know he is taking your measure – before he gestured for me to be seated.

"So this is about Sean's death?"

"I've been retained by his daughter. She just wants a better understanding of how it happened."

"Well," he said, raising his arms palms upward, "wouldn't the doctor or a pathologist be able to provide that kind of information?"

"On the medical side, sure. She's just asked me to learn more about the poker game, the persons attending, whether he was under any kind of stress or ate any food that disagreed with him. "

"If it was a heart attack, I can't see that any other factors would be significant."

"Probably not. But anyway, that's the sort of thing I'm looking into."

"Are you implying there might've been foul play?"

"I'm not implying that at all. I've just begun and the presumption is certainly 'natural causes'. But surely you have no objection to helping me fill in the blanks about this poker weekend."

"Well, it was a private gathering, very private. I'd say it depends on the kind of help you ask for."

"Let's start at the beginning. Whose idea was the game?"

"Actually, it was mine. I thought it would be a fun way to get-together. You know, just a men's weekend. I called a few people and the idea seemed to have legs. It took a little while for me to find dates when everyone was available, but I finally worked it out."

"Did you pick the place?"

"I was prepared to hunt for a place, but Marshall Kleidaeker was one of the first persons I spoke to and he offered to take that on."

"Did you suggest Hamilton's?"

"No. Marshall came up with that. I'd heard good things about the resort, but I'd never been there. We decided it was best to pick a resort that was close by and Hamilton's filled the bill nicely."

"So no one offered their home?"

Eldridge hesitated for a beat or two, then said, "We thought a resort setting would be more relaxing."

"Did any of you golf or have massages?"

"No, we arrived late Friday afternoon and pretty much played cards until late at night and resumed playing around nine-thirty or ten in the morning."

"Where did you eat?"

"The resort has a good chef and a decent menu. We brought our own booze and snacks, but ate all three meals in the dining room."

"So everyone made their own drinks?

"Yeah. Oh, I guess the last round Saturday night, Stephen offered all of us some of his V.S.O.P. so he poured that but, otherwise, we fixed our own."

"Okay. What were the rules of the game?"

"Five or seven card, mostly one-winner games, no wild cards. Dealer could choose, but a lot of us dealt Texas Hold'em or Seven Card Stud. And we played some hands of Draw."

"And the betting rules?"

"You're getting pretty nosey here, Mr. Conwright." He paused, nodded. "Okay. Three raises, one-hundred dollar limit."

"And the buy-in?"

"How in hell can any of this be relevant?"

"Listen, I'm not a reporter or the vice squad. Private investigators know how to be discrete. I just need to get the full picture of how this weekend went."

Eldridge kept his gaze over my shoulder as he answered. "Yeah. Well, we each bought in for five thousand. There was one re-buy at two thousand if you needed it."

"Did anybody go broke?"

"I don't think that's any of your business. Everyone in the group could afford to play! But Sean was right about in the middle … not down, but not far ahead either … if that's what you're getting at."

He was starting to get irritated and it was time to change the subject. "I gather you decided who was invited. How did you choose the players?"

"We've all known each other over the years through business or social connections. It wasn't the first time we've played poker together. It was a relatively small universe to choose from and everyone I contacted said they'd come if I could work out the dates."

"After the game broke up Saturday night, what did you do?"

"What do you mean, 'what did I do'? I took a short walk on the grounds to get some fresh air. One of the guys had been smoking in the room. I wanted to clear my lungs. After fifteen minutes or so, I went back to my room and turned in."

"Were you alone on this walk?"

"I was, yeah, but what the hell difference does it make? I never saw Sean again after we left the game room!"

"Was your relationship with Caughlin just social or did you do business with him as well?"

"It was both. It started because I have brokered most of his raw rubber purchases over the years."

"Did you like him as a person? Did anyone in the group not like him?"

Eldridge suddenly stood up. "Conwright, I'm not sure what your angle is, but we're through talking! You say your client just wants the 'complete picture', but it sounds to me like you're poking around looking for someone to blame for his death. The man wasn't *murdered*! His fucking ticker just gave out!"

As I rode the elevator to the garage under the building, I felt quite sure that Eldridge had held a lot back. His professed umbrage at my last question might have been genuine, but it could also have been an act to avoid answering questions about possible motives. But I had to ask myself: motives leading to what? Even if one of them had hated Caughlin enough to wish him dead, you can't will a man's heart to stop beating!

Tony Garrison had agreed to meet me around five o'clock at his industrial metal-working shop. It was an easy drive across the Willamette River. His facility was almost under the East landing of the Hawthorne Bridge, just off Water Avenue. It was an area of older, two and three story brick buildings that housed light industry, trendy restaurants, warehouses, and upscale tile-and-granite outlets. At Garrison's shop, a worker sweeping the floor around a grinding machine pointed me to the rear of the building where I saw a stairway leading to a mezzanine office suite. A powerfully built man answered my knock and introduced himself as Garrison. I could not decide if his crushing handshake was a macho display for my benefit or if it was his normal greeting. He wore perfectly pressed clay colored slacks and his soft yellow open-throated shirt with a monogrammed pocket and gold neck chain made him look as though he was straight out of a GQ ad. His clothes seemed a little out of place in the factory setting, but I figured he owned the place and could dress as he pleased. I elaborated on what I had told him over the phone about wanting some background on the poker weekend. He nodded toward a campaign chair in front of his desk and we both took our seats.

"So maybe I can start by asking you how long you'd known Sean Caughlin?"

"We met when we were both in the Army. That was what? A little over thirty years ago. We kind of stayed in touch … played golf once in a while … the occasional card game … saw a Trailblazer game together maybe once a year."

"Did your wives know each other? Parties? That sort of thing?"

"No. I've been divorced for the last seven years. I know he remarried a few years ago, but I don't think I've ever met his present wife."

"How did Mr. Caughlin seem the evening he died? Was he in pain? Short of breath? Was his color off?"

"No. He seemed his normal self. At first, he was quieter than usual. But by Saturday he was the same old Caughlin."

"And that means?"

"Aggressive, bullying, taking names."

"It doesn't sound like you respected him much."

He frowned and pursed his lips. "What else do you want to know?"

"How about the others? Did they resent him? Any bad blood there?"

"Look, I thought you wanted to talk about Sean. I'm not going to speculate about how other people may've felt."

"Let's go back to you then. What did you have against him?"

"Who said I ....?" Garrison stopped and drummed his fingers on his desk. Finally, he looked at me and shrugged. "Four years ago he was promoting a start-up company, Health Analytics. It was a pathology-analysis lab that was going to seek out-sourcing contracts from hospitals and clinics. The business plan seemed sound. It *was* sound as written. He got me in for a half mil. What he didn't tell me was that there were a couple of schmucks running the company. I felt those two guys basically looted it. I questioned their burn rate and their salaries a couple of times and I tried to get more information about the indebtedness, but Sean and his buddies blew me off. Then the outfit went under. I told Sean they'd swindled me. He either knew or should've known what his friends were up to. I wanted my money back ... I didn't ask for interest, just my original invest-ment. Sean's rich as Croesus and his other operations coin money, but he would never take a cent's worth of responsibility. He told me to get a lawyer if I wanted to go after the corporate officers. I did consult an at-torney, but he said we didn't have enough to go on, that there was no real protection under federal law for ground-level investors in privately held companies, et cetera, et cetera. I went back to Sean, but he basically told me to piss up a rope."

"Did you ever recover any money?"

"No. The creditors got it all. I talked to a couple of the other backers, but there wasn't enough enthusiasm to mount a law suit. The CEO and CFO left town and went back east …New York, I think."

"So how long ago was this?"

"About two-and-a-half years ago."

"Had you seen Mr. Caughlin since the company went under?"

"Not really. We'd bumped into each other once in a while at some charity event or country club function, but that little fiasco had pretty much soured our relationship for me"

"And yet you came to this poker weekend?"

"Yeah. Weird, huh? Well, Eldridge had this idea we should all get together … I don't know, maybe to let bygones be bygones … or maybe just so he could watch us getting into a three-day pissing match. Whatever. He kind of talked all of us into showing up."

"Did it seem to make things better between you?"

"Oh, it wasn't all that warm and fuzzy for me. But most of us did go back a long ways. I guess it *was* sort of interesting to see everybody and to watch things play out around a poker table."

"So if Eldridge had to twist everyone's arms, the relationship between you and Caughlin wasn't the only one that had cooled?"

"Look, I told you I don't want to go there. Let's just say things happen, life goes on, but some people still have issues. Maybe more toward Caughlin than with others … I don't know."

"When was the last moment you saw Mr. Caughlin alive?"

"When we quit for the night … in the poker room."

"Where did you go after you left the poker room?"

"Straight to my room. I showered and went to bed. The next morning I slept in a few extra minutes and then got dressed and went directly to the game room."

I thanked Garrison for his time and I wondered if losing half a million dollars due to a sleazy stock promotion was enough to make someone want to kill a man. And that started me wondering how many others around that poker table had "issues" with the late Sean Caughlin.

⟫⟨⟩⟪

I picked up a sirloin on the way back to the houseboat and started the barbeque on the back deck. While the steak was cooking, I called my client. I gave Amanda the names of the other players at the game to see if she remembered any of them. She said Ted McCaffrey's name was slightly familiar. She thought he might have been a customer of her father's and that she may have met him once at a dinner party. Other than that, the additional names meant nothing to her.

After I finished my steak supper, I tried to line up appointments with the other players. McCaffrey, who was based in Chicago, was off on a business trip. I managed to wheedle his cell phone number from his wife. He must have had his phone turned off when I called and I did not want to leave a message. I would try to reach him again in the morning. Bacon flat out refused to talk to me. He sounded like he had already downed a couple of drinks too many. I reached Kleidaeker and he agreed to meet me the next day at his flagship tire store, Marshall's Tires, in the suburb of Milwaukie about seven miles south of downtown Portland. I could not find a number for Maitland in the phone book. I have a friend who plays on the same city-league volleyball team as I. He is a manager for the telephone company and has helped me out in the past by giving me some restricted information. But I did not want to ask favors of him too often, especially since he has had to bend a few company rules to help me. I would try to see if I could wangle Maitland's address and phone number from one of the other players. Stephen Takimoto did not sound thrilled to talk with me, but we set up a meeting early the next morning.

The paper had let me keep my password to the archives when they fired me. I guess they figured everything there had been published for the public to read so there was no harm in letting me occasionally browse the digital records. Or, maybe they were just throwing a small bone to a guy who had been one of their top investigative reporters before I got sucked into the Clifford Darmsfeld vortex. That's a long story, but the short version is I was sure that this big-time developer was bribing some local zoning officials to grease some of his more controversial projects. I turned up a fair amount of evidence and wrote some good articles, but never quite found the smoking gun I needed to bust the story wide open. Meanwhile Darmsfeld was threatening to sue the paper. I wouldn't let it go and the paper finally had had enough. A few months later, I started my private investigator business.

I logged into The Oregonian's archives and searched for stories about the bankruptcy of Health Analytics. There were only two articles. Garrison was not mentioned. Caughlin was identified as a "Portland entrepreneur" who "had been instrumental in attracting limited partners" for the venture. The cause of failure was attributed to the time lost in replacing a critical, state-of-the-art piece of equipment that was defective, to the deferral of two large contracts, and to the "inability to contain costs". A follow-up story ran eight months later. It said the creditors had largely been paid off and the company had been liquidated. There was an allusion to unhappy investors, but the piece stopped short of repeating any allegations of fraud or misuse of corporate capital.

When I finished checking the newspaper archives, it was almost ten. I turned on the television to watch the evening news. Angie Richards had been promoted to late-evening anchor and whenever I was home at that hour, I watched. Angie's career had brought her to Portland from Boise a little less than a year ago. My wife, now my ex-wife, had left me fifteen months earlier, in part over my obsession, as she called it, with the Darmsfeld story. A friend, another volleyball teammate, told me that his sister, Angie, had just come to town and he thought we would get along well together. I eventually asked her out and, as they say, the rest is history. Not that it was simple history. We were just getting serious when the Vince Langlow case landed on my lap. The kidnapping of a prominent Portland business man was bound to be headline news so Angie was chasing the story from her angle while I was desperately searching for the missing man. This very nearly ripped us apart as her objectives and mine often conflicted as the case progressed. But it all turned out fine. I managed to get shot in the process, but, in the end, I saved Langlow's life and helped capture the madman who had abducted him. That case gave a major boost to my investigation business and also gave Angie the chops she needed for the anchor slot. There were some tense weeks that followed as she and I tried to repair the damage to our relationship caused by that case. I guess you could say we succeeded. We still maintain our separate dwellings, but, as my friend, Julio, says, we're no longer an "item", we're "a couple."

Angie, as she always does to me, looked dazzling and the newscast went smoothly, but there was nothing happening of particular interest. At ten-thirty, I turned in as thoughts of poker games where friends weren't so friendly drifted through my brain.

FOUR

Thursday morning

I wanted to get started early so when Stephen Takimoto suggested we meet for breakfast, at Bertie Lou's, I immediately agreed. As I approached the gray-blue frame house that had been converted to a hugely successful breakfast place, I saw a slender, medium-height Japanese-American man wearing darkly tinted glasses standing on the sidewalk. Seeing him, I had two instant and opposite reactions. One of my best undergraduate friends was a Japanese-American and he and I remained close until his death from brain cancer at the tragically young age of thirty-four. But my warm and trusting reaction was, to some degree, offset by a story I wrote early in my journalistic career about an Asian drug dealer who habitually wore dark glasses. He was one sinister guy. I had to remind myself that an investigator's job was to dig truths out of facts and that emotional first-impressions and snap judgments were almost always counterproductive.

I gave a slight wave in Takimoto's direction as I came closer. We introduced ourselves and were shown to a table. Bertie Lou's was in the antique-focused Sellwood district. It was always crowded and we were lucky to get one of the tiny tables without a wait. The aroma of onions and sausage spurred my appetite as we took our seats.

After our coffee was served, Takimoto asked, "So why is Sean's daughter so interested in that weekend?"

"Getting closure, I suppose. I guess she thought the circumstances of your gathering were kind of strange … probably wondering how it might have affected her father. I'm getting the picture that you all have known each other for some time, but that it had been a while since you had all gotten together."

"You could say that. It was kind of a loose group, but we did play poker from time to time. Things were … well, there were some hard feelings out there. Anyway, it's true we hadn't gotten together for a while."

"So why last weekend?"

"Maybe to try it out … see if it was still fun."

"Did anyone come with an agenda, for better or worse?"

"I'm not sure what you mean. Paul – that's Paul Eldridge – seemed to want to get everybody back on track, but even he … "

I waited, but he did not finish. "Yes? 'But even he what'?"

"Well, I don't know what it was all about, but he and Sean damn near got into a fight a couple of years ago. So I guess I was a little surprised that he came up with this idea. I mean if he was going to get us together, he couldn't very well leave out Sean."

"Because?"

"Well, I think we all got to know each other through him, one way or another."

"Let's go back to that almost-fight between Caughlin and Eldridge. Did you break it up?"

"No. But it was almost all over by the time I arrived on the scene. They were on the lobby overlook at the Schnitzer Concert Hall. Several of us were there at a charity matinee for the symphony. I heard that Brad Talmidge was the guy who cooled them down."

It was a name I remembered from my newspaper days. "Isn't he the Talmidge of Beneficial Insurance?"

"That's the man."

"I noticed that you and Caughlin both graduated from Purdue. Is that where you got to know each other?"

"Yeah. We were in the same fraternity as undergraduates."

"Did *you* have any problems with your old fraternity brother?"

"Why is that any of your business? I don't mind telling you how the weekend went, but I'm not getting into personalities."

"How about Stan Bacon? Did he and Caughlin get along well?"

"I said I wasn't going to answer questions like that. All I'll say is that they used to be partners years ago. I sensed it didn't work out too well."

"What kind of business were they doing?"

"It was a good-sized industrial vulcanizing operation. I think they recapped tires, maybe even manufactured some truck and construction-equipment tires … stuff like that. I can't quite remember the name. It might've been Vulcan Rubber or something close to that."

"I know you own several pharmacies. Did you have any business relationships with Caughlin?"

"Again, I don't see how your client could care about that kind of information. The details of things like that are really none of your business."

"Sorry, Mr. Takimoto. I'm just trying to understand why all you people still had ties, still had feelings, good or bad, toward Caughlin. Your being fraternity brothers was a long time ago."

"Well, we both belong to Waverly Country Club and, yes, Sean did loan me some money for the purchase of one of the pharmacies."

"Sounds generous."

"Don't worry! The loan was at full market rates. And, it was quite a few years ago."

"Is the loan paid off?"

He shook his head in disgust at my persistence, but, after a few seconds, I got an answer. "No. Not yet, but it's still on schedule."

"Are you a pharmacist yourself?"

"Yes. I've hired others, now, to be behind the counter. I've had to become more of an owner-manager."

"I can understand that. What can you tell me about Ted McCaffrey? "

"He's some kind of an executive for Pacific Freightways. I think he heads up their procurement in the western states."

"You think Rubber Master was supplying Pacific Freightways?"

"Yeah, Caughlin was definitely selling recaps to Pacific, maybe new tires too."

"A tight business relationship, then?"

"I guess so. In fact, Ted once mentioned to me that he was under pressure from the Chief Operating Officer to spread the business around more."

"Did McCaffrey get into specifics?"

"No. We were just talking about stress at the office and he said his boss didn't like to have the company dependent on a single supplier and was giving him a bad time about always using Rubber Master. Something like that."

"Okay. Getting back to the game itself, what time did it break up Saturday night?"

Takimoto removed his dark glasses and slid them into the breast pocket of his navy blazer. His face was smooth, without creases, and it remained expressionless as he answered. "It was after midnight. Probably close to twelve-thirty."

"Did everyone leave the room at once?"

"More or less, yes. I think Bacon and Caughlin were still in the room as the rest of us left, but they were on their feet so I would assume they left soon after."

"Were they talking or just fussing with their chips?"

"No, they were talking alright. I couldn't hear, but the conversation looked sort of intense."

"What did you do after you left the game room?"

"It was late by then. McCaffrey and I went down the walkway together to our rooms. We each went inside. We were outside for no more than a minute. I watched five or ten minutes of TV and went to bed."

"By the way, who is Maitland?"

"Maitland?"

"Yes. Carl Maitland."

"Oh, yeah. Carl. He's Kleidaeker's factotum. I think he's really kind of a bodyguard."

"I see. Was he playing poker?"

"No. Sometimes he would hang around the room ... read a magazine, but he wasn't in the game."

"Why would Kleidaeker need a bodyguard?"

"Beats me. Marshall's kind of a weird guy. He's smart, but he seems a little paranoid at times."

"How did he get along with Caughlin?

"I'm not going there, remember? I would only say that Sean kind of looked out for him, but once in a while he'd turn around and make fun of him ... rip him in front of the rest of us. As for how Marshall felt toward Sean, you'll have to ask him."

"I'll do that. But you said Caughlin ripped Kleidaeker sometimes. Can you at least give me an example?"

"Well … once we were playing golf: the three of us and another friend of Sean's. After a few holes, Marshall happened to say something that was a little naïve – he *was* kind of out of it occasionally – and Sean got sarcastic and made it sound like he was really a stupid ass. Marshall was obviously embarrassed, especially since he had just met the other guy. Sean just turned and walked away. I happened to see Marshall's face and he had a real hateful look. Then he muttered to himself. I saw his lips move. I'm pretty sure he said 'some day, Sean, some day'."

We finished our breakfast with general conversation and parted on the sidewalk. Takimoto had been at ease and helpful to a point, but I was sure that he, like the others, was holding a lot back. From his reluctance to speak about it and his body language, I sensed there had been a rift between Caughlin and him, but I had no idea of its cause. I was getting the impression that my client's father had managed to antagonize almost everyone in the poker group. I needed to discover how deep and powerful those animosities were.

I decided to call the State Board of Pharmacy and learn a little more about the investigation of Takimoto's stores. I was told that the findings were public record information and that the evidence showed the complaint to be groundless. When I asked the exact nature of the complaint, they referred me to the investigating officer who was not then available. I did not have time before my appointment with Kleidaeker to drive to the state capitol and back so I asked that he call me on my cell.

In the meantime, I drove downtown and entered the Beneficial Insurance headquarters on Fourth Avenue. The executive suite was on the eighteenth floor of the U.S. Bancorp building. If I remembered correctly, Brad Talmidge was the company's Vice President for Underwriting. I gave the receptionist my name and hoped Talmidge would remember me from the upbeat story I had done three years ago on the company's digital security program. I said I would need less than ten minutes of his time. He was in and he did remember me. He said ten minutes was all he had, but he would be glad to help if he could.

I told him I was a private investigator these days, and came right to the point. "I'm working on a case where Sean Caughlin's name has come up. I was told that you broke up a fight – or a near fight – between Mr. Caughlin and Paul Eldridge."

He seemed to relax a little when it was plain my investigation did not involve his company. "Oh, yes, I remember that. At the Schnitz of all places!"

"Can you describe what happened?"

"Well, I knew Caughlin slightly from the Chamber of Commerce. We served on the same committee a few years back. Anyway, it was intermission at the symphony. There were maybe fifteen people at the east end of the balcony hallway. Some were chatting, some were looking down into the lobby below. Caughlin and this other man – you say his name was Eldridge? – were kind of off in a corner. My wife and I were entertaining a customer and his wife. The four of us were just walking toward the overlook. Suddenly Eldridge raised his voice and I noticed the two of them. Eldridge said something like, 'I know everything!' Then Caughlin sort of grinned and said 'It was just a little spur of the moment thing, Paul.' This really set the other man off. He gave Caughlin a good shove in the chest and yelled, 'If you ever go near her again, I'll fucking kill you!' or words to that effect. I thought they were going to start swinging at each other right there! I went over and got in between them. I told them to calm down. Eldridge was really worked up and he grabbed at me. He was strong and he nearly spun me away. Then the chimes sounded and the crowd that had begun to gather dispersed. I kept telling the two guys to cool it. About then a good looking younger woman came around the corner and walked toward Caughlin. Then Eldridge let go of my arm and turned away. That was it. It was over almost as quick as it started."

"So no names were mentioned in their shouting?"

"Not that I heard. Of course I don't know what they were saying before they raised their voices."

"Do you know Stephen Takimoto by any chance?"

"Yes. Not well, but we're acquainted."

"Did you see him at the scene of this argument?"

"No, but it heated up so fast, my only focus was on the two men. As soon as Eldridge left, I rejoined my group and we returned to our seats. It was all rather embarrassing."

"Thanks for filling me in. I appreciate it."

"Didn't I see Sean Caughlin's name in this morning's obituary column?"

"You may well have. He just recently passed away."

"So there are questions about his death?"

"I wouldn't say that. I'm just trying to run down some things for the family. Whether he was under any special stress, having any problems ... that sort of thing."

Talmidge was too tactful to question me further, but he gave me a worldly nod as we shook hands. My ten minutes were up.

I was still puzzled that the coroner had not ordered an autopsy and that Sean's doctor had not asked for one. I called Amanda Nelson to ask her when her father's memorial service would be held. Amanda was not at home. A woman who identified herself as a twice-a-month housekeeper answered the phone. She told me that Amanda and her husband had left ten minutes ago for the service which was scheduled for eleven at the First Presbyterian church. She gave me Amanda's cell phone number. I got through to them just before they arrived.

"It's going to be a small, private service," she told me.

"I still think there should be an autopsy," I said.

"GeorgeAnn has settled on cremation. I don't think there is anything we can do to stop it. I know my father would not have wanted it that way, but …"

"Why do you say that?"

"I guess it sounds kind of silly after he's gone, but he survived a fire in his aunt's house as a child and was always very nervous about fire. We had fire extinguishers and smoke alarms all over the house as I grew up. He even had a fire escape installed for the second floor. And the other thing is: he was raised on a farm. Several times in past years he told me that when he 'kicked the bucket', he wanted to be laid back in the earth. But GeorgeAnn probably wouldn't know those things and, once she makes up her mind, she can be very determined."

"Do you know which mortuary is handling the cremation?"

"No. But I can find out and call you after the service."

I thanked her and walked into a teriyaki shop on the ground floor of the building for a bite of lunch before meeting with Kleidacker. On my way out to Milwaukie, the investigator for the Pharmacy Board called me back. I told him I was a private investigator and needed to learn what the charges were against Takimoto's pharmacies.

"There were allegations of 'cutting' or diluting the compounds used in mixing the prescriptions," he said. "I did find one month where some inventory tracking entries got mixed up due to mistakes by a new employee, but nothing to suggest any sort of dilution or substitution of fillers."

"Why did the Board file the charges?"

"Oh, the Board didn't reach the stage of charges. I was just told to do a preliminary investigation. As I recall, it was a concern raised by someone who was a member of the Chamber of Commerce."

"Is that normal?"

"No. That would be quite unusual in my experience."

"How did the complaining party get that information?"

"Well, I did have to find that out, but that information's a bit sensitive. I can only tell you that the complaint itself came from an influential member of the Chamber. Even then, it turned out to be double hearsay ... supposedly passed on from a former employee of the pharmacy."

I could see that he was not going to give up the names of the Board's sources, so I had to bluff hoping to force the issue. "How did Caughlin come in contact with the employee?"

"He said he employs a nurse at his factory and she knew... '

He realized his mistake and stopped.

"And he said she was the go-between?"

"I really can't elaborate."

"Was the pharmacy employee credible?"

"I never could interview him. He had left the Portland area and no one, including Mr. Takimoto, seemed to know where he relocated. But I did find out he had been let go, so he may have harbored bad feelings toward Takimoto."

"Did Mr. Takimoto know it was the employee who had supplied the information?"

"Well, he knew I was trying to reach this guy, but I never explicitly said he was a source."

"Did he know that Caughlin was behind the complaint?"

"He shouldn't have known the name of the Chamber member, but a colleague of mine dropped the file folder on the floor while we were in Takimoto's office. Takimoto helped us pick up the papers and I think he saw the name."

Ending the call, I grinned inwardly at the investigator avoiding saying Caughlin's name as he tried to shut the stable door after the horse had run away. I now saw that Takimoto had grounds for despising Sean Caughlin. I could not understand why Caughlin had turned on his old friend, but that would have to wait because a large sign identifying Marshall's Tires had come into view.

A young man with the name "Bud" stitched on his coveralls took me through the showroom and down a short hallway to Kleidaeker's office. The owner finished putting some papers in the drawer of a file cabinet and turned to greet me. I saw a man of medium height who could really afford to shed thirty or thirty-five pounds. He had a sandy complexion and pendulous ear lobes. He seemed startled by my arrival despite our having an appointment and my being "announced" by his employee. As he moved back to his desk, I thought I noticed a slight limp. His deep-set, hazel eyes swept me from head to toe a couple of times like some kind of a security scanner. He finally spoke.

"Yes. Sorry about old Sean. Have a seat. What do you want to know?"

"Let's start with how you got to be friends."

"Yes. Friends." He let it lie there for a couple of seconds. "We went to a boys' boarding school together. Farmington. It's in Minnesota."

"So you were classmates?"

Kleidaeker reached into a desk drawer for a pack of Winstons and lit one. As a reformed smoker, my nostrils quivered and I wondered if he would offer me a cigarette. He did not and I got past the moment. After he inhaled deeply, he finally answered. "Not exactly. Sean was a year ahead of me."

"And you both came west to Oregon?"

"Yes. My first business was failing. Sean had been in the Portland area for four years or so. He said to come out. He loaned me enough money to buy a little cut-rate tire dealership."

"And that became Marshall's?"

"Yes. My luck was better the second time. I turned the business around, built up a good clientele, and started selling high-margin products. Now, I have three outlets across the state."

"It looks as though you sell heavy-duty, industrial type tires."

"Yeah. Tires for tractors, straddle-trucks, dump trucks, fire engines, semis. Specialized, but profitable."

"Tell me about the poker game. I understand you found the resort."

"Yeah. I offered to help Paul with that. I knew about Hamilton's and thought it would be a good place. My assistant was the one who actually made the reservations after Paul agreed with my suggestion."

"By your 'assistant' do you mean Carl Maitland?"

"Yes. Carl contacted Hamilton's and worked it all out."

"Tell me about Maitland. How does he assist you?"

"He drives me around. Takes care of details for me." He made a vague gesture with a fleshy hand. "He's not much involved in the business side. Mostly personal things."

"Someone described him as a bodyguard. Is that one of his functions?"

"What does any of this have to do with Sean's heart attack?"

"Well, as I told you over the phone, I'm just trying to get a full picture of what happened on the poker weekend, who was there, what kind of relationships people had with each other and with Mr. Caughlin."

His eyes gave me that nervous scan again. "You think there was foul play!"

"Nothing really suggests that, but his death was sudden, and amidst a somewhat unlikely gathering. I'm just trying to help the family get some closure on the whole thing. Anyway, is Maitland also your bodyguard?"

He frowned and hesitated, then gave a resigned sigh. "Yes. I was robbed last year. A meth-crazed hoodlum broke into my home. He pulled a knife on me. It was a scary situation. I live alone. I thought he was going to kill me. Luckily, my phone rang and he panicked. He took my watch, some cash, and a video camera and ran out. The police were of little help. I started looking for a bodyguard the next day."

"Does Mr. Maitland live in your house?"

"Yes. There's an apartment over the garage. It's connected to the main house by an upstairs hallway. He lives there."

"Can you tell me more about the other things he does for you beyond personal security?"

"Sure. Like I said, he drives me around. He does some errands for my business. He's even doing some remodeling for me on a rental I own in Rivergrove. I don't need him much around the store. It's mostly in the evenings or on trips that I like him to be with me. And he's improved my home security system. He's handy that way."

"Did you check his references?"

"Of course. He had previously worked on a technical crew for a touring rock band. After that he was employed at a horse farm in the hills between Sherwood and Newberg. They said he was very competent and clever. They let him go because he was hitting on the owner's daughter. That didn't matter to me. He's been no trouble to me or anyone else and he makes my life easier."

"Do you remember the name of the farm?"

"Pleasant Acres, if you must know."

"You're in the tire business. Did you have commercial dealings with Caughlin?"

"Certainly. All of my recap business goes through Rubber Master and I buy a few specialized tires from them too unless I'm willing to import those tires from Asia."

"And you haven't done that?"

"No. Sean was a quick and reliable supplier. It was … simpler … to buy from him."

"How did you get along with Caughlin, Mr. Kleidaeker?"

"You know, I'm starting to not like your questions, Mr. Conwright. We got along, but that's all I'll say."

I told him I also wanted to talk with Maitland and asked if he were on the premises. Kleidaeker said no, he was not at the store.

"Would he be home at the moment?" I asked. "I could get over there quite quickly."

"Yes. He should be home. He has no errands for me today and it's too early for him to have left to pick me up. I can't guarantee that he'll speak with you, but I won't object."

Kleidaeker called Matiland and told him I wanted to come over. Maitland apparently agreed because Kleidaeker gave me his address. Afternoon traffic was always heavy on McLaughlin Boulevard and it took me a good twenty-five minutes to get to the large colonial house facing Laurelhurst Park in southeast Portland. Maitland looked to be in his late thirties. He was a well-muscled six-foot-plus with black hair and a kind of rough handsomeness. He wore a black polo shirt and light chinos. I knew Kleidaeker had told him who and what I was, but he had not invited me inside, so I explained my purpose in wanting to talk to those who had been at the poker game. He looked a little puzzled, but finally shrugged his shoulders and said to follow him to the living room. Kleidaeker had furnished his home comfortably. Nothing looked new, but everything was fairly high-end. The groupings were somewhat eclectic and probably reflected his bachelor whims. I opened my small notebook on the coffee table before me and began asking questions.

"Did you know Sean Caughlin before the poker weekend?"

"Not really. I think I had dropped Mr. Kleidaeker off at his office once and at his home once or twice over the last half-year or so. I met Caughlin on those occasions, but I did not stay so we probably hadn't spoken a more than a dozen words to each other before the poker thing."

"Did you get into conversations with him at Hamilton's?"

"Well, I suppose so. A few words here and there. The weather, sports … all very short. I was obviously not an insider like the others."

"Were you present in that recreation unit while the rest of them were playing?"

"Part of the time. I would read a magazine over in the corner if I was in the room. I wasn't excluded, but I had no real duties there and I didn't want to seem to be intruding."

"Where were you the rest of the time?"

"In my room. Watching television, reading magazines. Once I took a walk around the grounds … kind of checking things out from the security standpoint."

"So Mr. Kleidaeker didn't feel he needed you in the poker room with him all the time?"

"No. We talked about that, but he knew he would always be with the others in the game room. We agreed there was no need for me to be there all the time. We both had cell phones and I was never more than a few feet away if I was wanted for any reason."

"How did the others act toward Mr. Caughlin? Any arguments? Outbursts? Did he anger any one?"

"Not that I ever saw. Why? What's your angle? Do you think somebody there had anything to do with his death! We just heard he had a heart attack!"

"I'm just asking everyone how things went … trying to see if there could be more to this than meets the eye. Very likely it's just as you said … a heart attack. Maybe even an attack triggered by some unusual stress from just being at the game. So what did you notice about people's interactions with him?"

"Nothing out of the ordinary that I could see. I kind of thought things were a little tense at first. I didn't exactly know how they all came to know each other, but it seemed like they'd done things together before. And later in the evening, things loosened up. They'd had more to drink, I suppose. Anyway, I didn't think anymore about it."

"Did you or your boss pick the resort?"

"Mr. Kleidaeker knew about it and I think he suggested it to the guy who organized the weekend and volunteered me to make the arrangements."

"How about at night, after the game broke up … did you hear any unusual noise or commotion from Mr. Caughlin's room?"

"No. I'm a fairly heavy sleeper, so I might have missed something, but I probably would've heard a fight or yelling."

"Did you or Mr. Kleidaeker have a card that would have opened all the rooms? Kind of like a pass key?"

"No! Of course not! Everybody got their own key card when they checked in. Mr. Kleidaeker asked for two cards for his room and gave me one of them, but that's all."

"And you were never invited into or went into Mr. Caughlin's room for any reason?"

"Absolutely not. I don't think he ever invited anyone to his room for drinks, but – even if he had – I wouldn't have been included."

I thanked Maitland for his willingness to let me talk to him. It was time to head for my own home. Kleidaeker and Maitland had readily enough answered my questions, but Kleidaeker – like the others in the poker game – had not been forthcoming about his feelings toward Caughlin. I decided to call the boarding school, Farmington, as soon as I got to my houseboat. It would be nearly six back there, but it was worth a try.

A man answered on the fifth ring and introduced himself as the headmaster. He said at this late hour, staff had already left for the day. I told him about Caughlin's recent death and said I was looking for background information. After explaining that I was working for the dead man's daughter, and settling the dates of Caughlin's attendance, I cut to the chase.

"I've learned that Mr. Caughlin was in the company of another Farmington graduate on the weekend when he passed away. That other person was Marshall Kleidaeker. Would anyone working there now remember either of those students?"

"As a matter of fact, *I* remember them. I was an older student here when they attended. I went on to take degrees in education and, twenty years later, I came back to Farmington as the Head."

"So they were pals 'way back then?"

"Well, I suppose you could say that. Actually, Sean was a year ahead of Marshall. There was a tradition of hazing, like there was at many private schools in those days. The sophomores were the ones who hazed the freshman. Kleidaeker, unfortunately, was a plump, soft boy. He had a mop of unruly hair and large ears and he was clumsy. Those characteristics quickly made him the target of pranks and ridicule. Caughlin was a bit of a bully to begin with and, during the autumn hazing, he singled out poor Marshall. I was a senior monitor for our corridor in the dormitory and I tried a couple of times to rein Sean in."

"Did you succeed?"

"Not totally. But something odd developed. Because the other boys sort of ostracized Marshall, he turned to his abuser for friendship. And Caughlin would help him in various ways ... even support him at times. It was almost like some sick co-dependency. In retrospect, I almost wonder if Caughlin wanted Kleidaeker to stay in school and maintain some degree of normalcy just so he would have someone to pick on when it suited him. And then there was the accident."

"Accident?"

"There was a vaulted attic over the dormitory building. It was used primarily for storage. Somehow, the sophomores got hold of a key to the attic. One night they were hazing some of the freshman up there. Caughlin apparently got the inspiration to make Kleidaeker swing hand-over-hand across a rafter ten feet above the floor. I should add that I was on leave that weekend and didn't even know they had an attic key. Anyway, Marshall lost his grip and fell. He suffered a badly broken leg. There was talk of expelling all the sophomores who had been in the attic, but powerful parents intervened. Between the parents and the school's concern about its reputation, the matter was glossed over."

"Did that end the love-hate relationship?"

"Well, I graduated in the spring, so I don't know what developed in the next few years, but their relationship the rest of that year took a curious turn. I don't know whether Sean felt guilt or what exactly was the reason, but he took Marshall even more under his wing after that."

"And Kleidaeker's feelings toward Caughlin?"

"As I said, I don't know what happened with them after I graduated, but I thought Marshall was kind of trapped. I mean nobody thought Sean meant for him to fall; it was only about twelve feet across. Yet there he was: badly injured by a stunt organized by his principal tormentor. But, at the same time, he was dependent upon Caughlin for minimal acceptance among the boys. It was sort of pathetic, I thought."

I thought about Kleidaeker's limp and about the loan from Caughlin to start him in the tire business. I was beginning to sense that deep and turbulent emotional currents must have swirled around that poker table.

FIVE

Thursday afternoon

It was nearly five o'clock by the time I finished my phone call with the headmaster at Farmington. I remembered that I had turned off my cell phone while I interviewed Kleidaeker and checked for missed calls. Amanda had called me back just after four. She left a message that the cremation would be handled by Taggert Funeral Service. I found their phone number and called only to hear a recording saying their hours were eight-thirty to four-thirty. I decided not to leave a message. I would have to get over there first thing in the morning. I was bothered by the fact that a man with a pacemaker implanted would die of heart failure. I knew next to nothing about pacemakers, but I figured they were supposed to ensure that the heart kept working normally. Could the battery have died? Could there have been a manufacturing defect? Could he have been so stressed by something that his heart overrode whatever signals the pacemaker was sending? In any event, I thought I should get hold of that pacemaker and have some expert look it over.

In the meantime, I went to my computer and accessed an armed services data base. I thought it might be useful to see if any of the men at the poker weekend had been in the military. I figured every veteran's rank and discharge information would be publicly available. I already knew that Caughlin and Tony Garrison had been "army buddies" and I saw that those two served in the same unit during the Viet Nam war. They had been lieutenants in an Army logistical unit. Stephen Takimoto had been a Navy Pharmacist Mate. All three had honorable discharges and none of them had entered the Reserves. There were no records of Stanley Bacon, Ted McCaffrey or Marshal Kleidaeker having been in the service. Carl Maitland had risen to a Specialist 2 in the Air Force, but then was discharged "for the convenience of the service." Paul Eldridge made the rank of captain serving in the Army's Special Forces. After the war, he went into the Reserves and finished, after getting in his twenty years, as a full colonel. At the end of the session, I had not learned anything earth-shaking: Caughlin and Garrison had probably handled paperwork and stayed out of harm's way; Takimoto knew drugs; Kleidaeker had probably been 4-F; Bacon and McCafrey may have had student deferments for graduate studies; Maitland may have had an honesty problem; and Eldridge probably had mastered six ways to kill someone quickly and silently.

I called Hamilton's before I knocked off for dinner. The Manager was still on duty and I asked her for the names of the maintenance person and the maid who had first discovered the body. She had obviously heard of my previous visit and was somewhat reluctant to let me talk with her employees, but I assured her that the questions I wanted to ask would in no way compromise Hamilton's. She finally confirmed that those two persons would be at work tomorrow and agreed that I could speak with them provided she was present. I told her that would be fine and that I would try to get there in the forenoon and would call when I was on my way.

I had picked up some beef brochettes at Zupan's along with an ear of fresh corn. I soaked the corn in the sink, then threw it -- husk and all -- along with the brochettes onto my barbeque. Those, a green salad, and a glass of Shiraz, made for a simple, but tasty dinner. Afterwards, I topped off my wine glass and punched in the number for Amanda Nelson. Her husband picked up and passed the phone to her. I began by telling her whom I had contacted and summarized the little I had learned.

"Now I have a question for you. You said on Tuesday that you didn't think your father had made a will. If he had, do you know which attorney he would have used?"

"I'm sure he would've gone to Del Crocker or, at least to Crocker's firm. He's used him for years when he's needed legal work done."

"Does Mr. Crocker do estate planning?"

"Hmm. Maybe not. I believe he specializes in business and commercial problems. But I know there are several other attorneys in the firm so one of his partners might. In any case, I think Father would go to Del first if he wanted to make a will."

"Okay. I'll see if Crocker will talk to me. Another thing: you inferred GeorgeAnn was quite a bit younger than your father. Do you know if they entered into a pre-nuptial agreement?"

"I don't really know. Father never talked about that. But I think they might have because … because I over-heard GeorgeAnn talking on the phone one day…" She stopped at that.

"And…?" I prompted.

"Well, they'd been over to our house for dinner and I guess her earrings were bothering her. She took them off and laid them on an end table in the living room. We all forgot about the earrings and I found them a couple of days later. I was out doing errands that morning and I was not far from their house – this was before they bought the condo -- so I just swung by unannounced to return the earrings. As I came to-ward their front door, I heard GeorgeAnn's voice from the side patio, so I just went around outside the house toward the patio. It turned out that the reason I heard her voice was because she was on her cell phone. Just as I came into her view I heard her say '… but there's that fucking pre-nup ….' She saw me and stopped in mid-sentence, then finished the call. I was more shocked at her language than at what she said, but afterwards I thought about it. I think she was referring to some arrangement between her and my father."

"After that day, did you ever discuss it with your father?"

"No. It wouldn't surprise me if there were such an agreement, but I never thought it my place to raise it with him. My husband and I are comfortable enough financially and, even though I'm not fond of GeorgeAnn, I don't think she would have tried to influence Sean to cut me off with nothing."

"How did you learn of your father's death? Did his wife call you?"

"No. She was up in Victoria with two women friends. Someone at the poker weekend remembered my name, probably Stanley Bacon. When the EMTs couldn't get GeorgeAnn at home, they called me. After I pulled myself together, I knew I had to call her. I had the names of a couple who were good friends of father and GeorgeAnn. I called their house to see if they knew where GeorgeAnn might be. It turned out that the wife was actually one of the women who had gone to Victoria with her and the husband gave me the name of their hotel. So I called GeorgeAnn there."

"Were you close to your father?"

"Close? He was a hard man to get close to, even for a daughter. He was a decent enough father during my childhood. After I grew up and married, we certainly saw each other from time to time. I loved him, yes. But I wasn't as close to him as some children are to their fathers."

I let it drop with that and said good night. I slumped back in my chair wondering if my own client saw herself as a rival to the widow: a rival who might inherit more by a statutory intestate share than if Caughlin had made a will or had entered into a pre-nup leaving everything to his wife. Would that thinking throw her into my pool of persons with motives to want him dead? But then why would she have hired me? I wanted her to be innocent … just a daughter confused and concerned about the sudden death of her father. And, unless and until I had irrefutable proof otherwise, that is what she would be … my innocent client.

I knew Angie would be at the television studio by then. She would not have a lot of time to talk with just a little more than an hour before her newscast, but I had not called her all day and wanted to touch base.

"Hi, Angie. How's your day going?"

"Hello, lover! The usual busyness right now, though there's no big, breaking story for the late news. How's your new case?"

"I'm still kind of muddling around. I'm turning up lots of people with motives to go after my client's father, but nothing beyond that. He was probably just an unpopular guy who died of natural causes. Are you coming over tonight?"

"I'm planning to. Will you still be up?"

"Probably, but I've had a long day and I might crash if you're not here by eleven-thirty. If I've fallen asleep, wake me up when you crawl in!"

Last year with the Langlow case, things were quite different. With Angie working the very same situation as an investigative reporter and with my client's missing husband the focus of her interest, I had to keep almost everything from her. Now we have reached the point where there is some pillow talk. We have an understanding about where to draw the professional and ethical lines, but – on a personal level – we share with each other what is going on in our lives. So Angie knew that I've been hired to discover if there was a malevolent cause of Sean Caughlin's death or if his unhealthy heart had simply given out.

We said goodbye and I got back on the internet and checked some records at the Secretary of State's Office. I was looking for whatever I could find about Vulcan Rubber. Takimoto had told me that he thought that was the company founded by Caughlin and Bacon when they first started in the tire recapping business. I did not find much. The two men were the incorporators of the limited liability company and the firm seemed to have operated for a little more than ten years before it was dissolved. Vulcan's physical assets were bought by a new corporation, Rubber Master, nine years ago. Bacon was not an officer or shareholder of Rubber Master and – as I already knew – Caughlin was its CEO and owned almost all of the stock. About two years after the sale of assets, Bacon's name reappeared as an incorporator and principal owner of his own company, Pilot's Choice.

I found it curious that Stanley Bacon had refused to talk to me. He was a former business associate of Sean Caughlin's and participated in the poker game. I wanted to know why the men were no longer partners and the answer might well lie in the final years of Vulcan Rubber. I tried to think how I could get beyond the sterile records. I remembered that our volleyball team's strongest rival had a player on their team who was in the trucking business. Max Shelby? Max Shelton? I could not quite bring his last name to mind. I did remember that he worked for a trucking company owned by his family that was based in Portland. I turned off the computer and reached for the phone book.

I finally found it in the business pages: Shellenby Transport. Then I looked Max up in the residential pages and placed the call. Max and I had shared a beer after the last match between our teams and he knew about my new career as a private investigator. I told him I needed some background on Vulcan

Rubber and asked if he knew anyone who used to work for that company. He said he did not, but that his father might and promised to call me back. Five minutes later he did.

"Rick, we used to take our tires to Vulcan in those days and my dad remembered the shop supervisor's name. Pete McCormick was the guy. Dad thinks he retired not too long after they wound up the company and it was reborn as Rubber Master, but I found his name in the phone book." He gave me the number. "What are you working on?"

"Oh, I'm just looking for some deep background on a business matter. Thank your dad for coming up with the name. I really appreciate it!" I knew his question was just based on innocent curiosity, but that was all I wanted to say. I called Mr. McCormick and heard a strong, alert voice on the other end. He said he would be home working in his garden and would be glad to have me drop by any time tomorrow. I thought it could be helpful that he was retired and I hoped he did not have any current relationships in the industry to inhibit his answers.

Just inside the front door of my houseboat is an authentic brass enunciator that I had picked up at a marine antique shop several years ago. Other than one heirloom chest that came from my grandparents, I do not own or collect antiques. But I was captivated by old enunciators from the time I first saw one. Mine once stood on the bridge of a Matson liner where it was used to convey engine orders to the engine room. With its circular dial and brass housing, it seemed perfect for our houseboat. My ex thought differently. To her, it was a costly indulgence and over-the-top for our little floating home. But I've never regretted owning it. It had been looking a little tarnished lately and I spent ten minutes with a can of Brasso giving it a fresh shine. That done, I put a CD in the player and listened to some vintage Brubeck as I stretched out on the couch with heavy eyelids.

The next thing I knew, I felt a soft hand on my shoulder and Angie was bending over to kiss me. Her naturally blond locks brushed my cheek as I came fully awake. I gazed up into her sky-blue eyes and grinned. "What a great wake up," I said. "Thought I'd wait up, but guess I conked out."

Angie laughed. "We had a short staff meeting after the newscast and it slowed me down a little bit getting out of there. Your intentions were good, Rick. Let's turn in."

By the time I stumbled into the bedroom, Angie had stripped to her bra and panties. As I drank in the view of this fabulous creature I had fallen in love with, I suddenly felt more awake. She came over and kissed me again and pulled my shirt over my head. Then we kissed again and I unhooked her bra. She loosened my belt and slid my slacks down as my hands caressed her breasts and my fingertips found her taut nipples. From there on, our remaining clothes were quickly shed. Kisses spread flushes of pleasure over all the best places on our bodies. With a soft moan of delight, Angie guided me to her and we began the slow climb to the top of the roller coaster of our ecstasy.

SIX

Friday morning

Angie rolled over and went back to sleep when my alarm woke me up. I jotted down priorities for the day in my notebook as I finished a simple breakfast of coffee, fresh-squeezed orange juice and a Danish pastry. I had to battle the morning rush-hour, but traffic was flowing well and I reached Taggert Funeral Service around a quarter to nine. A receptionist called the manager, a Mr. Tapley, and then escorted me to his office.

Tapley stood as I entered. He looked to be six feet tall and had a full head of silvery hair. His dark-brown suit was set off by a buttery yellow tie. "How can I help you, Mr. Conwright?"

"I'm a private investigator, Mr. Tapley. I've been retained by Amanda Nelson, the daughter of the late

Sean Caughlin. I believe you are going to handle the cremation."

Tapley cleared his throat and looked as though he was about to interrupt, but then only smiled and nodded.

"Mr. Caughlin's death was untimely and the daughter has asked me to clarify the whole situation," I went on. A slight look of uncertainty crossed Tapley's face, but the smiling and nodding continued. "Mr. Caughlin had a pacemaker. This is a little delicate, but it would be extremely helpful to my assignment if, before you cremate the body, you could remove the pacemaker."

Tapley cleared his throat again and held up a hand. "Well, you see, Mr. Conwright, Mr. Caughlin's remains have already been cremated. We do most of that work during the evening shift and that occurred last night. His ashes are already in an urn awaiting the family's disposition."

I am sure my face showed my frustration and disappointment. I mentally kicked myself for not thinking about the possibility of a night shift coming on after the mortuary's more public "business hours". If I had considered that, I could have rushed over and pounded on the door and made my request before it was too late.

Tapley continued, "However, we routinely try to remove all metallic or man-made objects before the process begins. If he had a pacemaker, it will have been extracted."

A wave of relief swept over me. "And you have it?"

"Well, we simply dispose of things of that sort. It will be in the trash I should think."

"May I have it then? Can we look for it before the trash is picked up?"

"I must say, this is unprecedented. But I suppose there's no problem. You say Ms. Nelson is the deceased's daughter?"

"Yes, I could have her call you if that would make you more comfortable."

"I think that would be a good idea, but let's see if it can be located before you go to that trouble."

Tapley picked up his phone and asked someone to see if the waste receptacle had already been taken out and emptied into one of the garbage cans outside. The answer was apparently "no" and he told the person to bring the receptacle and a plastic sheet to his office.

"Is the person who removed it from the cadaver last night still on the premises?" I asked.

"Yes. His shift ends in just a few minutes. It was he to whom I was speaking."

I called Amanda while we were waiting and told her that she should give her approval of my request to Mr. Tapley. She did so and Tapley made a note in his daybook. By then, the technician had arrived with a small covered pail. We spread the plastic sheet on Tapley's carpet and emptied the contents of the pail on the sheet. The pacemaker was easy to spot and was the only one in the pail. Before anyone touched it, I spoke to the technician.

"I understand you are the person who removed this device. Is that so?"

"Yeah. I removed it because it would melt in the furnace and might possibly damage our equipment."

"And after you removed it, you placed it, without manipulating it or damaging it in any way directly into this pail?"

The man looked slightly bewildered and shrugged his shoulders. "Yes, of course. Straight into the pail."

"And this device on the floor in front of us is the same device you removed from the body of Mr. Caughlin?"

"Well, it sure looks the same. I mean I didn't mark it in any special way, but what else could it be?"

"I see there is a tiny serial number stamped on it. Did you by any chance record that number when you removed it?"

"Hell, no. There's no need to do that. If we remove one, we just throw it away."

"Alright. Thank you, sir. It is possible that I will ask you for a written statement covering what you have just told me. Just to establish a chain of custody, should that ever be needed."

"Okay. I guess I can do that."

Tapley was now looking concerned. "A 'chain of custody' sounds awfully formal. Is there a real problem here?" he asked.

"No," I said, "There's certainly no problem at all with your services. This is very likely going nowhere, but an autopsy was not done. Everyone will understand the death better and get the closure they need if we can find out why his heart failed. Being able to check his pacemaker could be a big help in that regard. And if it's going to be checked, it's worth a little extra effort to be sure this is actually the one that was implanted in Mr. Caughlin's chest."

My little speech seemed to mollify Tapley. If he was wondering why, if understanding the cause of death was so important to the family, an autopsy had not been requested, he kept that to himself. I slipped the pacemaker into a small envelope, thanked Tapley and his technician and left the building.

My next stop was Hamilton's Resort. I checked in with the manager. She used a walkie-talkie to ask the maid and the maintenance man to come to her office. When they arrived, she made introductions. "This is Mr. Conwright. He's a private investigator and wants to ask you a few questions about the man who died in C-6 over the weekend. This is Rosa Velasquez and Jim Stauffer."

They looked comfortable with the situation and I assumed she had already briefed them that I would have some questions. "Mr. Stauffer, I had a look at one of the units and noticed the windows all had screens. With regard to unit C-6 immediately after Mr. Caughlin's death, was there any damage to any of its screens?"

Stauffer was a stout man in his fifties. His teeth were tobacco-stained and a cauliflower ear suggested that he might have once fought in the ring. His coveralls looked freshly laundered and his voice was firm and confident.

"No sir. They were intact … no rips, no holes."

"And you've not had to repair or replace any of them? No bent frames or anything like that?"

"Not recently … not since that man died. No."

Velasquez was a handsome woman in her early thirties. Her fingers were dancing in her lap and pushing at stray locks of hair as she waited to be questioned. She spoke English well with only the slightest accent.

"And Ms. Velasquez, were all the doors locked or unlocked that morning when you found Mr. Caughlin.?"

"The front door was locked, but not with the bolt. It would be that way if the person had left the room. But, in this case, the man must have forgotten to use it. Anyway, I had to use my passcard to get in."

"And the patio door?"

"It was locked too. I heard one of the gardeners outside and when I saw that man there on the floor, I ran to the patio door to tell the gardener to get help. But the door was locked. I just wanted to get out of that room as fast as I could, so I forgot about the gardener and ran back out through the front door. I guess I started screaming, then I saw Delores come out of another room and we called the front desk."

"Delores is another housekeeper?"

"Yes."

"Tell me, did you smell anything when you first entered the room? Any unusual odors, any fumes?"

"Well, yes, I did. We're always careful to notice if anyone smoked in the room. They're not supposed to, but some do anyway and then we have to air things out, use an air freshener … that sort of thing."

"So you're saying you smelled cigarette smoke?"

"No, not that. It was very faint, but more like … like when my son used to make model airplanes. The smell was a little like the dope he'd paint on his models. But I found that man's body right away. I always begin in the bedroom and the moment I walked around the bed, I saw the body. After that, I wasn't thinking about how anything smelled!"

"I understand. How about water or liquor? Any glasses partly empty or bottles opened?"

"I don't think so. When I came back later to clean the room, the two water bottles on the bedside table were full and unopened and I never saw any liquor bottles Saturday morning or when I came back to clean after … after they took him away."

"Alright. Let me ask any of you another question. I have only been in C-5. Are all the rooms laid out the same way? Furnished the same way?"

It was the manager who answered my question. "They are identically furnished, except for the recreation units, a few family suites in Building E, and perhaps some of the pictures on the walls. As for the layout, they are mirror images … you know, so the bathroom plumbing is in the same common wall."

"So there would be symmetry in the pairs of units?"

"Yes. One and two, three and four, and so on."

I left them each one of my cards and thanked them for their cooperation. It was time to have a talk with the retired Mr. McCormick. Before I could start the car, my cell phone beeped. I put it to my ear and heard my ex-wife's voice.

"Rick, it's Justine."

Her voice sent a small jolt through my body. "Justine! Well, hello. Where are you?"

"I'm in Portland, that's why I called. I was hoping we might have lunch."

I checked my watch. I could still catch Mr. McCormick if we had an early lunch. But did I want to see her? For months after she left, I had been hoping to see her ... even imagining random encounters with her ... to see if we could rekindle the spark of our marriage ... to see if my new occupation could allow me to bridge the gulf that seemed to have come between us. It had always been a bit of a tense marriage. Justine was an interesting and attractive woman, but her mercurial personality made for a high-maintenance relationship. The houseboat was her idea, but within months she was complaining that it was "depressing". She thought my work as a journalist was "exciting and stimulating" for both of us, but she became increasingly strident in objecting to my irregular hours. After she filed for divorce and the decree was entered, I had begun to put that part of my life behind me and had started over. In a strange sort of way, I was actually happier now, less guilty about my professional life, more free. We had never had children and that probably made it easier for me to move on toward a fresh page in the big book of life. And, of course, Angie had become a huge new factor in the equation.

"Well, I … my day is pretty full …"

"Oh. I know it is short notice. I had some business here and I just thought … I just thought it would be nice to see how you are doing."

I could sense the disappointment in her tone. I wondered if she had really come down from Seattle for business. I concluded that a quick lunch would be the polite thing to do. "Well, sure. I have an early afternoon appointment, but lunch would be fine. If you're downtown, how about Nordstrom's cafeteria?"

Justine agreed and twenty minutes later we had placed our orders. I knew the food would be good and I thought the busy cafeteria would be a comfortable, neutral venue. We exchanged information about our new careers and a few old friends. We had nearly finished our meal when she took a deep breath. Her cheeks were slightly flushed and she twice started to speak and then backed off. A couple of minutes later, she laid down her fork and looked into my eyes.

"Rick, I haven't been all that happy in Seattle. I've missed Portland. More than that, I've missed you."

I felt another slight emotional twinge. Was it renewed hope? Guilt? Pity? Fear of unfathomed complications? In the collision with the here-and-now, I could not be completely sure of my own feelings. I decided to take the high road.

"Well, this starting over business isn't easy. New city, making new friends. Maybe you should just give it a little more time."

"You sound like your new job suits you more. I read about the Langlow case even in the Seattle papers." Then she leaned toward me across the table. "Rick, I was too judgmental."

"I was pretty wrapped up in that Darmsfeld story. I have to admit I was probably losing my perspective on a lot of things, including probably, our marriage."

"Have you … are you seeing anyone?"

"Yes." I saw her hands squeeze her napkin into a wad. "We're … we're kind of together these last few months."

She looked at me with moist eyes, but shed no tears. She was still a damned attractive woman. I thought life was never fair, but it was a little late for might-have-beens.

"I suppose I was hoping otherwise." She smiled with a sigh. "The great clarity of hindsight." She stood and seemed to regain her composure. "I'll be at the DeLux Hotel for another day, then back up north. Thanks for the lunch, Rick."

I watched her walk across the room and tried to sort out my feelings. Then I glanced at my watch. Somehow, that simple action shoved me back to the larger scale of my present situation. It was time to dig further into the life and death of Sean Caughlin.

McCormick's directions were easy enough to follow and I located his house on Poplar Avenue in Ladd's Addition. Ladd's is a somewhat unique and once-prestigious neighborhood in southeast Portland. Its tree-lined streets radiating out from a central circle are still lined with well-maintained homes. Pete McCormick lived in a craftsman-style bungalow. No one answered the doorbell so I called his name as I walked through a gate leading to his back yard. He was indeed a gardener and I found him with straw hat and gloves amongst the last of his dahlias and chrysanthemums. He pulled off his gloves and lifted his glasses to wipe perspiration off his face before he greeted me. I handed him one of my cards, apologized for being a little late, and complimented him on his green thumb. He gestured for us to sit in a couple of weathered wicker chairs on a simple cement patio. He shambled a bit as he walked and I noticed that his head projected forward from his torso as if he were fighting the onset of scoliosis. Once I was seated, he climbed the stairs to his back door and returned with two cold bottles of Coors.

I took a swallow of beer and began, "As I said yesterday, I'm investigating a matter where I believe it will be very useful to understand the relationship between the late Sean Caughlin and Stanley Bacon. I know they used to be partners of some sort in running Vulcan Rubber. I've learned that you used to be the Shop Supervisor there. Anything you can tell me -- how they got together ... what roles they played in the company ... how they got along – would be most helpful."

"A business matter?" he asked with a slightly raised eyebrow.

"Not exactly. More like it's a matter of interest to Caughlin's daughter. Things that happened in those days may shed light on things I'm working on."

"Uh huh," he said. I could not tell whether my vague response had reassured him or simply amused him. In any case, he seemed willing to talk. "I'm not sure how they first met, but I think they may have worked for the same company for a few years after they finished their graduate studies. They started Vulcan together. Maybe with a formal partnership agreement, maybe just with ownership of the L.L.C. shares ... I don't know. I think Sean put up more money than Stan and Sean certainly called the shots."

"So how did they divide responsibilities in running the operation?"

"Well, they hired me for the day-to-day stuff, hiring and firing, job scheduling, ordering shop supplies, making sure machinery was properly serviced ... that sort of thing. Sean developed customers and probably made the important contracting and financial decisions though they had a bookkeeper for the accounts and billing. Stan did quality control, purchasing of inventory, and some product testing. That was before they got into their research and experimenting."

"What do you mean by that?"

"They were both chemists, you know. In fact, Stan was a damn fine one and Sean wasn't too bad either. Anyway, they got this idea that they could improve tire life by introducing certain additives to the vulcanizing process. That became their big interest. They turned more and more of the rest of it over to me. They added a nice little lab out behind the main shop and spent most of their time in there. They were pretty secretive about it, too."

"Did anything come of it?"

McCormick looked out over his garden and took a couple of swallows of beer before he answered. "Oh yes. I think you could say that. It led to the break-up of their partnership."

"How so?"

"They had been experimenting for almost two years. Stan was the more talkative of the two about their research, but even he wouldn't tell me much. I gathered that they had made a pretty important breakthrough and that they were starting to test some prototype tires. Then Stan got in an accident. He owned a cabin cruiser and there was a fire when he was on the boat working on his engine. One of his legs and one side of his lower torso were pretty badly burned. He finally came out of it more-or-less okay, but he was hospitalized for six weeks and couldn't return to work for another five weeks after that. About four months later, their idea looked to be very commercially feasible and Stan thought they should apply for a patent. It was then, I guess, that Sean told him he already had a patent."

"You said 'he' already had a patent."

"Yes, I did. It seems Sean had applied for a patent in his own name as the sole inventor and that's the way it was eventually issued."

"Christ Almighty! How did he dare?"

"I never knew all the ins and outs of it, but, from things Stan said, I gathered that Sean claimed a two-barreled justification. The first part was that Stan was more like an employee doing something called 'work for hire' than he was a partner or co-inventor. The second part was that, in any case, he, Sean, discovered the final step in the chemical process while Stan was in the hospital."

"Did Bacon ever contest it before the Patent Office?"

"I don't think so. I'm pretty sure he consulted an attorney, but I'm not aware there ever was a formal challenge. Maybe he couldn't afford to fight it in court."

"I see. I suppose that was what broke up the partnership?"

"I'm sure it was. They weren't even speaking after Stan heard what Sean had done. They folded up the company within a couple of months after that."

"Were Bacon's hard feelings ever acted out physically?"

"One evening just after we had closed the shop and the employees had left, I saw them almost come to blows. I was too far away to hear what they were yelling about, but it ended when Sean finally walked away."

I had to be delicate in my next question so I wrapped my words in feigned astonishment. "Wow! So Bacon made personal threats?"

"I wouldn't know about that. Like I said, I couldn't hear what they were saying."

"Well, maybe later?"

McCormick studied my face for a second before he answered. "Not that I know of."

"But Bacon felt his name should also have been on the patent?"

"Well, he never said that to me in so many words, but, yes, I'm sure that's what he felt ... that he was a co-inventor."

"Do you know if the patent really did have commercial value?"

"Oh, I'm quite sure it did. I think it made Sean Caughlin a very wealthy man. Do you know why Rubber Master has been such a successful company?"

"No, not specifically."

"Well, it manufactures, and probably license a few other companies to manufacture, long-lasting, heavy-duty, tires. And they license a recapping process. A great many long-distance truckers buy them. I've heard they last half-again as long as other tires and recaps. Of course they're more expensive than the others, but the economies to the truckers must be well worth it."

"Did Bacon get his share of the assets when the assets were sold to Rubber Master?"

"Well, I wouldn't really know that for sure, but Stan pretty quickly started the business he now owns, so I would assume he ended up with his share. But remember: the patent was in Sean's personal name, not in Vulcan's name so Stan got no value for the goose that's been laying the golden eggs."

I closed my notebook, thinking what a hard case Caughlin had been. Fraternity brother, army buddy, prep-school friend, partner ... over time, he had screwed them all. I asked a few more innocuous questions hoping to dampen whatever curiosity or suspicions McCormick might have about my case and then took my leave. As I drove away, I could readily believe that Bacon held a smoldering hatred for Sean Caughlin. I also pondered the fact that Bacon's own company sold tires for general aviation aircraft. All these men had been laced together in a cat's cradle of resentment and inter-dependency. And Bacon was the one poker player who had declined my request for an interview.

My gas gauge read nearly empty and I stopped to tank up. Waiting for the attendant to finish, I used my cell to call Dr. Lewis. His nurse said he was tied up but would return my call as soon as he could. He rang back right after I finished at the gas station. I explained that I had recovered Caughlin's pacemaker and wanted him to look it over. He said even though he was Caughlin's long-time physician, he was not a heart specialist and would not be competent to analyze the pacemaker. He gave me the name and number of the cardiologist who had treated Caughlin, a Dr. Michael Kurlinski. I was able to convince Kurlinski to see me at the end of the afternoon. In the meantime, I headed for the houseboat.

Back in my office, I tried again to get through to McCaffrey. This time, I caught him. He was in his Chicago office at the end of his day. I had not told his wife very much when I spoke with her two days ago, so I introduced myself and explained in very general terms why I was calling. He sounded wary, but said he'd try to help if he could.

"So how did you become friends with Mr. Caughlin?"

"Quite a few years ago, I was in charge of procurement in the Pacific Northwest and Sean was out hustling to sell this new vulcanizing process his company had developed. We got along pretty well and I agreed we'd run some tests on a demo set of his tires. The lab test results looked really good so we bought a couple of sets to put on two of our trucks. Our drivers said the tires behaved completely normally, so we started buying our tires from Rubber Master. Along the way, I sort of got on Sean's list of friends."

"Do you still buy Rubber Master tires?"

"As new tires? Yes. And Rhinos as well for recaps."

"Exclusively?"

He hesitated for a second before answering. "Yeah, pretty much. They are quite incredible so far as wear is concerned. They are very long-lived."

"Does Rubber Master have any competition in that regard?"

"Well, another manufacturer has started to come out with its own version of ultra-durable truck tires ... this other company is marketing its product pretty heavily."

"But your company is sticking with Rubber Master?"

"Yes, I suppose so ... what has this to do with Sean's illness or his death?"

"Illness?"

"Well, his heart condition. We all knew about it."

"Tell me about the poker game. You had to come out from Chicago. Was it important to you to be there?"

"I was already going to be out there on business, so I just extended an extra weekday. I had been talking with Sean after Paul called to invite me and Sean wanted ... I mean he thought if some of us came, we should all show up ... all of us who used to play cards together when I was working out of Portland."

"How much advance notice did you have?"

"Oh, over a month. Paul said he wanted to make reservations and all. Maybe it was even five or six weeks."

"After the game broke up Saturday night, did you ever see Sean Caughlin alive again?"

"No. I was kind of whipped and I left the poker room straight-away after the last hand. I think he was still standing beside the poker table when I left. That was the last time I saw him."

"When you ate dinner Saturday night, were you all at one table?"

"Yes. One long table."

"Do you remember where people sat?"

"Why do you care about things like that? Didn't he die of heart failure?"

"It looks that way, but I want to recreate his last hours if I possibly can."

"Well, Sean was seated across from me. I think Stan was on his left. I'm not sure who was on his right … maybe Stephen … I do remember Stephen was involved in our conversation. Paul was next to me … on my right. On my left … let me think." He paused. "I guess it must've been Marshall Kleidaeker. I remember he almost knocked over his wine."

"Did anyone take any medication with their meal?"

"You mean prescriptions? I don't know. I think maybe I saw Tony swallowing something, but I'm not sure.

"Where was he sitting?"

"Further to my left, I think."

"Was Carl Maitland at the table?"

"Maitland? Oh, Kleidaeker's guy? No. I think he was eating at the same time, but maybe in the larger dining room. We had a little room to ourselves."

"How did you get along with Caughlin on a personal level?"

There was a momentary silence on the line. "All these questions. You think one of us somehow caused his death?"

"That would be very, very unlikely. But this gathering was somewhat unlikely too. I'm just trying to understand how you all related to one another. Whether it was a stressful occasion."

"Sean was okay. He could enjoy a good party. He was a shrewd businessman. He was a valued supplier."

"How about the others? Were they all good buddies with Mr. Caughlin?"

"The others? Well, they all had .... " He stopped. "I don't think that's my place to say. They all went back a ways with Sean, one way or another. It was complicated."

"Had Caughlin ever loaned you money?"

"No. Never."

"Had you ever invested in any of his enterprises?"

"No."

"Did you and your wife ever socialize with Mr. Caughlin? You said he enjoyed good parties."

"Yes, we went out with them a few times when I was based in Portland. And once when he came to Chicago. But those were essentially business entertainments."

I had saved my most loaded question for last. "Did Caughlin ever pressure you to continue your company's de facto exclusive purchasing arrangement with Rubber Master?"

"Sure, in a sense. He was always pushing his product; always mending his fences with us. He gave us 'most-favored' pricing on a quantity-scaled basis."

"What does that mean?"

"Well, like all vendors, he had to be careful of those price discrimination laws ... couldn't give us any special deals, but he essentially guaranteed us that he would never undersell to one of our competitors in comparable volume."

"How about you personally? Did he ever pressure you on a more individual level to stay loyal to his company?"

"What the hell are you getting at, Conwright! I've tried to cooperate with you in this bizarre 'investigation' of yours, but I'm not going to let you insult me like that!"

He hung up. Maybe the question *was* a little insulting or maybe I had just hit a nerve. It was pretty clear to me that there was no warmth in McCaffrey's relationship with Caughlin. I felt there was an undercurrent of resentment or possibly even fear. And yet, he, like the others, had come to the poker game to be 'up close and personal' with the late Sean Caughlin.

⟨=+=⟩

Dr. Kurlinski's office suite was on the top floor of a three-story medical-dental building on tree-lined Flanders Street in northwest Portland. Kurlinski was around five-nine, with a receding hairline, a stocky frame and a ready smile. He ushered me through the reception area, then past a records room and two examining rooms to his private office.

"You said you actually have the pacemaker?"

"Yes. As you may have heard, no autopsy was done, but I was able to get the pacemaker from the mortuary." I made an annotation on the envelope and handed it to him. He opened the flap and spilled the little device into his open palm.

"What do you want me to check?"

"Basically, I just want to be sure the pacemaker wasn't defective. That it is still functioning the way you intended it to."

"Mr. Caughlin had had it long enough I can just about assure you there wasn't any design or manufacturing defect. That type of thing would've been evident long before his death. Before you arrived, I had time to check Mr. Caughlin's records. It shouldn't be hard to tell whether the pacemaker is still capable of operating within the parameters that I set when I implanted it."

He led me into a small laboratory down the hall from his office where he picked up a pacemaker programmer. It was a device about the size of a household iron. He studied the small display panel. "Whoa! This is all wrong! This setting would quite possibly lead to ventricular fibrillation."

"Hold on, Doctor. What's that?"

"Oh. Sorry. Essentially, it's a condition where the heart merely quivers at high speed, but does not pump blood. Mr. Caughlin was what we call pacemaker-dependent. He needed a continuing stimulus triggered by his own heart's rhythm to maintain normal cardiac function. Right now, the pacemaker appears to be in a fixed-rate mode. Over a period of many minutes or several hours, in that mode, the stimulus from the pacemaker could, sooner or later, coincide with the vulnerable instant of his heart's contraction – we call that the T-wave. Then his heart would shift into fibrillation."

"Can the mode be changed from outside the patient's body?"

"Yes. Almost any cardiologist would have a device that could be used to reprogram the pacemaker – without surgery – *if* the patient's situation called for an adjustment of the rhythm."

"Can you open this one up to see how this happened?"

" I'm not competent to take the pacemaker apart. But I suspect if you get a technician to open it up, you'll find the little reed relay inside has closed and, for some reason, stayed closed causing the pacemaker to generate the wrong stimulus."

"So that could have been the cause of death?"

"As I said, in the case of a pacemaker-dependent patient like Mr. Caughlin, if it continued in that mode for more than a couple of hours, it certainly could."

"Can you connect me with a technician who could check the inside?"

"Well, the manufacturer's rep could get it examined for you at the manufacturer's lab, but they might not be comfortable doing it for fear of product liability issues. But I have a better idea. Last year, I was an expert witness in a trial and the plaintiff and defendant agreed to have an independent technician testify on pacemaker mechanics. I can get you his name."

We walked back to his office where he produced a file and found the man's business card stapled to a page of notes. He copied off the name, address and phone number and passed the slip of paper to me.

"Tell me, could the pacemaker have been dropped or mishandled in any way at the mortuary?" he asked.

"No, I questioned the man who removed it very specifically about that. He said he simply dropped it into a pail of soft trash and that was that."

"This is very puzzling. It was set correctly when I implanted it. And Mr. Caughlin's having lived for many months after that and my having checked it several times is proof that it was doing its job. Yet somehow it got in a condition to generate an improper, quite possibly fatal, stimulus. A stimulus that was fixed and not variable as originally programmed."

I nodded to show that I shared his puzzlement. "Thank you for checking this for me, Doctor" I handed him my card. "Please send me a bill. It is possible that I may ask you later for a written opinion of your findings and your analysis of Mr. Caughlin's condition. And you can be sure I'll be getting in touch with this other expert," I glanced at the paper, "this Mr. Weatherly."

I thought about the anomaly of the pacemaker as I drove away. Certainly no one had opened Caughlin's chest to change the device's setting. I was fairly sure that no other cardiologist had altered it using a programmer because Dr. Lewis would have known if Caughlin had switched specialists. Unless Kurlinski had a motive unknown to me and a very evil psyche, it could not have been him. But it *had* been changed somehow and that change could very well have spelled the end for Sean Caughlin.

SEVEN

Saturday morning

My first priority was to contact the technician, Donald Weatherly, to look over the pacemaker. My call found Weatherly in his office even though it was a Saturday. I told him what I needed and he agreed to examine the pacemaker over the weekend and call me as soon as he had anything to report. His office was near Lloyd Center in northeast Portland and twenty minutes later I laid the little device on his desk. I had him sign the envelope to document that the chain of custody had temporarily passed to him.

My next stop was the attorney, Del Crocker's, office. I was having a little run of good fortune because, when I placed a hurried call to him on Friday, he said he had some matters to work on at his office Saturday morning and could see me there. The firm of Allison,

Forbes & Crocker occupied the eighth and ninth floors of the Portland Building in the heart of the downtown fronting on Fifth Avenue. This was the building that had the iconic Portlandia statue in front. Crocker had given me an inside phone number and told me to call him when I got to the building lobby. He cleared me with the lobby guard and he opened the doors to the firm's pecan-paneled reception room – resplendent with leather easy chairs and a huge Kirman oriental carpet -- when I emerged from the elevator. He showed me to his large corner office where I saw a rosewood credenza behind his desk stacked with bulging file folders. He seated himself in a straight chair away from the desk and motioned for me to have a seat across from him on a chocolate-colored suede settee. Crocker was a tall man with graying hair. He looked both formidable and elegant in slacks, a silk polo shirt, and a golf sweater. He offered to bring me a cup of coffee from the employee lounge, but I declined.

"As I told you, I'm a private investigator working for Amanda Nelson, Sean Caughlin's daughter."

"Ah, Yes. I've met her on a couple of occasions."

"She is concerned about the suddenness and the cause of her father's death and has asked me to look into it."

"She suspects foul play?"

"I wouldn't say that exactly, but she will definitely feel better if everything points simply to bad luck with his not-so-strong heart."

"Yes. I knew Sean was having some difficulties with his heart. Had a pacemaker, I believe. So how do you think I could help you?"

"I have reason to believe that Mr. Caughlin had a pre-nuptial agreement with the second Mrs. Caughlin. Is that correct?"

"The existence of such an agreement will become public knowledge at the time of probating Sean's estate, so I'm comfortable in telling you that, yes, they did have a pre-nup."

"Did you prepare it?"

"I certainly listened to Sean's ideas and laid out the general shape of it, yes."

"That sounds like someone else finalized it?"

"Yes. Wes Gullickson, one of my partners who specializes in estate planning, did the detailed drafting."

"Did you also represent Mrs. Caughlin?"

"No. That sometimes happens, but I feel quite strongly that arrangements of that sort just invite trouble … conflict of interest issues … recriminations. I was glad to learn that she had hired her own attorney."

"Is there any way I can get a copy of the agreement or at least read it over?" I asked.

"Is Mrs. Nelson worried about losing out regarding his assets? Is she gearing up for a challenge of some kind?"

"No. I'm sure she's hoping to be treated fairly, but this definitely is not about money. As I said, she very much wants to know whether her father's death was due to natural causes. On the weekend that he died, he was in the close company of several people who may have had long-standing grievances against him. The family physician did a simple examination of the body and stated on the death certificate that it was just a case of heart failure. If, when my work is done, that still appears to be the case, my guess is that my client will be content with whatever she's entitled to under the law."

"I see. And you don't care to ask Mrs. Caughlin to share this information with you?"

"I don't think she is enthusiastic about Mrs. Nelson's idea to have me working on this. And, I gather the two women are not close."

"Tactfully put. Yes, I can imagine the two of them would not get along very well. But, Mr. Conwright, you surely are familiar with the attorney-client privilege. I don't think I can talk to you about what Sean wanted in that document."

"I'm no lawyer, Mr. Crocker, but let me say I'm not asking you to repeat to me motives or characterizations or desires that Mr. Caughlin may have communicated to you before your firm prepared the agreement. I want to see the agreement itself. That doesn't sound to me like it is within the privilege. Besides, I'm guessing it was your client who held the privilege, and he is no longer alive. If there were anything amiss with regard to his death, surely he would welcome my exploring every factor that could possibly be in play."

Crocker looked at me thoughtfully for a good ten seconds before speaking. "You are incorrect about the privilege ending with the death of the holder." Another pause. "I'm not ready to let you see the document either. However, I might be able to answer a few questions about its thrust."

I took that as an invitation to dig further. "Did everything go to Mrs. Caughlin upon his death?"

"There was a 'good faith' waiting period of eight years. Assuming Sean lived past the end of that period– which he just did by a couple of weeks –yes, she will get almost all of his estate beyond several hundred thousand to Mrs. Nelson. If they were to have divorced before the eight years were up or if he died before that time, the widow would have received modest, but adequate, support for her lifetime or until she remarried. After the 'good faith' period, if they were to divorce, she would get half of everything that he had earned or accumulated during their marriage. If they had not divorced, and she survived him after the eight years, she would take everything beyond that set-aside for your client. But there was a kicker. If he made a will and died, the terms of the will would override the pre-nup terms even after the eight years, although Ms. Caughlin would still be guaranteed that original, modest support."

I looked up from taking notes. "Had he made a will?"

"No. Wes and I had urged him several times to have an estate plan and a will or a living trust, but he never got around to it. Our reasons had very little to do with Mrs. Caughlin. The idea was to optimize the tax impact and minimize or eliminate probate complications."

"So he was content with the pre-nuptial arrangement? With his marriage to GeorgeAnn?"

Crocker sat silently for several seconds, then cleared his throat. "I don't know. He never said anything about that to me, but my wife and I sat at their table one night about six months ago at the Waverly Country Club. We both had the impression that things were quite tense between them. And he had made an appointment with me to make a will. We were scheduled to get together the Friday morning following the Sunday that he died."

"Did he give you any advance hints as to what the will should say?"

"If he had, it would probably be within the privilege unless your client, his daughter, and his widow got into litigation over their respective shares of his estate. But, that's somewhat beside the point since he did *not* disclose his intentions when he called to schedule the appointment."

"Did he ever speak of his daughter?"

"Only in casual conversation. I gathered they weren't especially close and he seemed to regret that. Sean was not an emotional person, but I had the sense that he was fond of her."

"Was there any 'front money' to his wife? A 'signing' bonus so to speak?"

He repositioned a paper weight on his desk before answering. "There was an immediate settlement on her. In the middle five figures."

I was not sure why Crocker had softened his position and decided to disclose some of the details of the pre-nup, but at least I now had a little insight into the widow Caughlin's financial situation and I knew that Caughlin had not made a will. I caught Crocker subtly glancing at his watch. I thought I had learned about as much as he was willing to give me, so I said my thanks and left him to his morning's work.

I wanted to ask Stephen Takimoto more questions. He had told me that his office was in the back of his pharmacy on Lovejoy Street in northwest Portland. The street trees stood like soldiers in their brilliant red and yellow coats. I left the Acura in the Good Samaritan Hospital parking garage and hoofed it half a block to his drugstore hoping he would be there. He was. He did not look especially thrilled to see me, but he did not slam the door in my face.

"Sorry to have to take up some more of your time, Mr. Takimoto, but there's another area I wanted to cover that I was unaware of when we spoke earlier. I have learned that the Pharmacy Board received a complaint that your stores were diluting some of the prescription drugs that they prepared."

A flash of anger crossed his face. "I hope you also learned that the complaint turned out to be groundless. In fact, it never even reached the stage of a formal proceeding."

"Yes. I know that. Did you ever find out who made those accusations?"

"Apparently it was a former employee. One, I might add, that I had fired for incompetence. That must have been his idea of revenge ... start a story maligning our professional ethics and then skip town."

"What I meant was: did you learn who passed the story on to the Pharmacy Board?"

He shifted a file folder from one side of his desk to another, then looked up at me. "Yes ... I found out it was Sean."

"How did you feel about that?"

"How do you suppose I felt! Angry. Betrayed. Astounded at his pettiness."

"Pettiness?"

"I told you we both belonged to Waverly Country Club. We used to be partners in all the tournaments. I'm a pretty fair golfer. Sean wasn't quite as good, but we seemed to compliment each other well. But Sean couldn't bear to lose ... at anything. He started cheating. It wasn't all the time of course, but at critical moments when winning or losing was in the balance. He was always the one who kept our scores. The first couple of times, I thought he was just careless or preoccupied. But then I started paying closer attention. And it wasn't just recording scores. A couple of times I caught him improving his lie to give himself a much easier shot. I didn't want to call him out directly … you never could win a pissing match with Sean. But I couldn't be a part of it. So I just told him I didn't want to be his partner any more. I think he very well knew why, but he never asked. He just gave me the fish-eye and said something like 'if that's the way you want it.' I think others at the club were starting to suspect him as well and my changing partners probably verified it in their minds. A few months later, a story was making the rounds that the handicap chairman wrote him a cautioning letter."

"So you think he turned you in to the Pharmacy Board just for spite?"

"That's my theory. Soon after the story broke – and he probably had something to do with that too -- sales at all three of my stores dropped over twenty percent. It stayed that way for nearly four months. Cost me tens of thousands of dollars. The media finally did some real short follow-ups saying there turned out to be no evidence to support the charge, but by then the damage was done. He was a mean, vindictive son-of-a-bitch!"

"You didn't mention any part of that when we first talked."

"Why should I have? You didn't ask about it. You were nosing around about how he died, who liked him and who didn't. I was mad and disgusted with him at the time, but – in a way – that was Sean. Despite what he did to me, I didn't wish him dead! I saw no reason to tell you something that might make you think I did."

"Okay. You said before that something McCaffrey said made you think Caughlin was pressuring him to continue purchasing exclusively from Rubber Master. Do you have any idea how Caughlin could bring that kind of pressure?"

"No. Maybe McCaffrey owed him big-time for something in their past. Or maybe he had something on McCaffrey. But, whatever it was, neither of them ever revealed it to me."

Leaving the drugstore, I thought that all of these men had reasons to hate the late Sean Caughlin and none of them had told me much about the others at the poker game. Could they somehow have *all* conspired to kill him? Could they have individually offered me small tid-bits of innocuous information while sharing a bond of silence about their darkest act?

⇒╬⇐

It was time to talk with GeorgeAnn Caughlin, but that was something I thought I should run by my client first. I called Amanda and told her that I really needed to talk to the widow to get a complete picture of the relationships among the men at the poker weekend.

"She might refuse to see you," Amanda said. "And even if she will talk, I imagine she will be hostile, especially toward me for starting this investigation. But, what the hell. Our interactions have always been kind

of strained and, now that my father's dead, I don't expect I'll see much of her anyway. Go ahead."

"Thanks. I have learned that your father never
made a will. It seems there is a pre-nuptial agreement
and that she will keep almost everything."

"That little vixen! I knew she would be provided for,
but I'm a little surprised my father was that generous."

"You think their marriage was on the rocks?"

"Not really. I hate to say this, but I think my father
enjoyed having her as a 'possession' and I doubt he was
thinking of a divorce."

"Well, when you feel up to it, you should call
Mr. Crocker and ask him where you stand in terms of
the estate."

I ended the call and punched in the number for
the Caughlin residence. GeorgeAnn herself answered
and, though a little condescending about it, surprised me by agreeing that I could come right over.
The Caughlins owned a penthouse condominium
atop a fifteen-story building, The Elizabeth, on Ninth
Avenue in the north end of Portland's vibrant and up-
scale Pearl district. A lobby attendant called to verify
that I was expected and turned a key to enable the
elevator to reach the penthouse. I faced a broad teak
door flanked by potted palms in the top-floor lobby.
I saw a closed-circuit security camera above the door
as I pressed the doorbell. I heard the muted sound of
a three-bell chime and GeorgeAnn Caughlin opened
the door. She was indeed a fine looking woman. Dark

blond hair feathered to the base of her neck framed dark-brown eyes, a perfect nose and full lips. She was wearing tailored pearl-gray slacks and a white sweater under a toreador jacket. The look was smart and not too showy, yet did little to conceal the contours of a great body.

I probably spent a few seconds too long taking this visual inventory because her opening words were, "Well don't just stand there, Mr. Conwright. Come in."

She walked me down a hallway to a living room with large picture windows opening onto a simple, but elegant, Japanese roof garden and a dynamite view of downtown Portland. She indicated I should sit in a burgundy cigar chair and she settled into a chrome-and-black-leather campaign chair with an oversize coffee table between us.

"So you're Amanda's detective," she said. "I think this project is a waste of her money, but, of course, I'll be interested to know if you *do* find anything amiss with regard to Sean's death."

"I certainly have not turned up anything definitive so far. As I'm sure you understand, the circumstances of his death were a bit unusual. It may well turn out to have been just a natural death at an odd time in an odd setting, but I'm not there yet. In any case, I appreciate your willingness to speak with me."

"I trust you're being discreet. This is not an easy time for me and the last thing I want is for you to sensationalize Sean's death. But if you think I can be of help, I'll try."

I nodded my understanding and appreciation. "Let me begin by asking you about the men at the poker game. Did you know them all?"

"I've never seen a list of who was there."

I read her the names from my notebook.

"I know Marshall and Paul and Stephen and … did you say Ted McCaffrey? Yes, I know Ted also. I've never met Tony Garrison, but I seem to remember Sean mentioning his name. I know who Stanley Bacon is. He used to be a partner of my husband's years before we were married."

"And Carl Maitland?"

"No. He was one of the card players?"

"He wasn't playing cards, but he was there with the others. He works for Kleidaeker."

"Oh, yes. Sean said something once about Marshall hiring a bodyguard."

"Can you think of any of those men who would harbor bad feelings about Mr. Caughlin? Bad enough to want to see him dead?"

"I never got involved in Sean's business dealings and all of those men at the poker table, other than Stephen, were basically business friends, so I wouldn't really know about that."

"Well, how about any of them that might have had grudges?"

"Look. I know Sean was pretty hard-nosed and I can see where he might have made some people angry over the years. From the way Sean spoke about Bacon, I gathered that there were hard feelings when their partnership broke up. He never told me the details, but it's hard for me to believe that someone would want to kill an ex-partner over that."

"And Mr. Caughlin never received any threats from Bacon or any of the others?"

"Not that I know of. I think Sean would've told me about something like that."

"Anyone else with a grudge?"

"I don't think so. We used to see the Eldridges socially and, for some reason, that stopped a couple of years ago. I don't know what was going on, but it was not between Julie and me, whatever it was."

"Do any of the men have violent tempers or seem obsessive or mentally disturbed?"

"Well, Paul Eldridge has a temper … I don't know about violent, but he has a short fuse sometimes. And Sean said something once about Garrison having a little sadistic streak back in their army days, but none of the ones I know seem unbalanced to me."

"Did your husband say anything to you about the poker weekend?"

"Just general stuff. Since it was a men-only type thing, I said I thought I'd go to Victoria with some girlfriends and he said that was a good idea. He told me where they were going to be … just that sort of thing."

"Did he seem to be looking forward to it? Did he seem in any way stressed about going?"

"I think he was a little surprised when he first got a call about it. He wasn't a man to get openly excited about much of anything one way or the other. I do remember that he thought about it for several days before he accepted. But I wouldn't say he was stressed about it. Sean would never do anything he didn't feel like doing."

"How about medications? Was he taking any drugs, on or off prescription?"

"That's an insulting question, Mr. Conwright, but the answer is 'no, he wasn't'."

"Sorry. How was his heart doing? Any recent problems?"

"Well, as Amanda surely knows, he *did* have a heart condition. And I understand you are going to talk to his doctor – or maybe you already have. Sean had to watch his diet to some extent and he had to be careful about strenuous activity. I guess you just have to roll the dice when you are his age, but other than seeming a little tired the week before, nothing I would call a 'problem'."

"No complaints of an irregular heartbeat or heartburn in the days before the game?"

"No. Well, wait a minute! A few days before, I think it was Wednesday evening, he went to bed a little early and said he was having indigestion. He kind of put his hand just below his heart as he said it. But he never called the doctor or made an appointment. And he seemed perfectly normal the next morning."

"Did he mention how he had felt the next morning?"

"No, it never came up."

"Were either of you alarmed the night before?"

"Well, of course when he said that, I kind looked at him to try to see if he was having any real difficulty. But he just waved me off and said it was just his stomach, so I relaxed."

"Okay. Did you two have a pre-nuptial agreement?"

"Yes. Sean was a wealthy man and ours was not his first marriage."

"May I see it?"

"I'm not sure that's any of your business, Mr. Conwright, especially as you're working for Amanda. She may be planning to contest the estate for all I know. I can't remember all the details myself and, in any event, it's in a safe deposit box. I'm sure I'll have to discuss it with my lawyer before long."

"Well, can you at least tell me if the agreement covers the situation of Mr. Caughlin predeceasing you?"

"You mean if he died before me? Yes, I believe it does. I was considerably younger than Sean. Surely, it would be normal to include such a provision."

She rose and I knew my interview with the widow was about to end. I thanked her for talking with me, gave her my card in case she thought of anything more, and pulled on my jacket. We were almost to the door when she touched my arm.

"Hold on. I just *did* think of something. When I picked up Sean's Cadillac, I decided I had no need for an extra car. I thought I might as well sell it. I cleaned out the trunk and the glove box the next day. I found a folder marked 'Bacon' in the glove box. There was a photo and a compact disc inside. The disc turned out to be a digital version of the same picture. The photo showed a person, a man, walking away from a small airplane and looked like it was taken at night."

"By 'small', do you mean a model airplane?"

"No, no. A real plane, but a private plane … you know: one engine."

"Had you ever seen the plane or the man or the folder before?" I asked.

"No, never. You could only barely see the person's face. But you asked me about Bacon having a grudge and now I'm remembering something Sean said to me a couple of weeks ago. Bacon's name had come up in casual conversation and, at the end, Sean said something like 'Bacon was always a sore loser, but now I have something that will quiet him down'."

"Did you know what he was referring to from the context of your casual conversation?"

"No. He just kind of threw it in at the end."

"So he didn't explain what he meant by it? Or make any reference to a photo?"

"No. Sean was that way. He would just spout off about something that was on his mind, but he would almost never explain it. Once in a while, I'd be curious enough to ask, but then he'd say something like 'oh, it's just a business thing' or 'never mind, I was just babbling'."

"Do you know who took the picture?"

"I have no idea. I was curious enough to check our digital camera and if the camera *was* used, the picture wasn't still in the camera's memory."

"Would you let me have the folder?"

"I guess I can. It all means nothing to me."

She left me at the door while she fetched the folder. I gave the picture a quick look, thanked her again and pushed the button for the elevator.

I drove away wondering if Sean Caughlin had included blackmail in his arsenal of dirty tricks. He could not have needed the money, but perhaps he needed leverage over Bacon. But why? Was Bacon threatening to renew his claim that Caughlin had stolen his rubber discovery? I would have to parse every detail of the photo when I got back to the houseboat.

EIGHT

Saturday evening

Angie had to fill in on the six o'clock news desk and would not be coming over, so I was planning to eat alone. It crossed my mind to call Justine's hotel. Partly, I felt sympathy for her because she felt lonely and because Seattle was not working out as a fresh start. I bore her no ill wishes and wanted to offer a little support. To be honest, there was also probably a little lingering desire on my part to see if the old vibes were still there. I wrestled with it over a microwaved lasagna dinner and almost picked up the phone a couple of times. Each time, I thought of my feelings toward Angie and how right our relationship seemed. Each time, I decided that spending part of an evening with my ex-wife whether at her hotel or out on the town was too risky an idea. Risky to whom I asked myself.

Possibly to all of us, I concluded. If Justine were suddenly seductive, things might snowball. I might end up being unfair to Justine and to Angie. And I'd have a hell of a lot of explaining to do even if it turned out to be just a platonic get-together. In the end, I poured myself a small glass of Bushmills and watched twenty minutes of Sports Center to catch up on the college football games.

I turned the television off when they moved on to a segment about the next day's pro games. I took the CD of the photo and the picture itself to my desk. I slid the disk into the slot in my computer and began manipulating the photo. Looking at the printed picture, I could tell there was a number on the tail of the plane, but it was too small and too dim to read it. I used the imaging software to increase contrast and enlarge the area of the tail. That let me read the identification number painted on the tail: CP 2843. I could tell from the picture that there was a building in the background with some kind of a sign on the outside. I swung the magnification crosshairs over to the image of the building on my computer monitor. The sign read "Pilot's Choice." I had never bothered to check the address of Bacon's store, but it made sense that it would be next to an airfield. Next, I focused on the person walking from the plane. He – it looked tall and stout enough to be a man -- was dressed completely in dark clothing and appeared to be carrying a dark rectangular object in his hand, possibly a book. His arm was extended as if to offer the object to someone approaching, but beyond the camera's view. Manipulating the image of the face did not help. The camera angle was from the far side of the plane and the man was walking away from the plane in the general direction of the Pilot's Choice building. This afforded only a partial view of his profile. I could make out a prominent jaw and heavy brow and possibly a receding hairline.

The picture was obviously taken at night and the depth-of-focus suggested it was taken with a telephoto lens. No people were posing for the picture. These facts meant to me that it was a surveillance photo taken without the subject's knowledge. There was a digitally imprinted date in the lower right indicating the photo was taken one month ago. So what did it all mean? Had Caughlin or one of his minions discovered some clandestine operation at the airstrip? What was out there: a chop shop for stolen aircraft? A drop-off point for drug smugglers? I could not be sure that the photo was what Caughlin had been alluding to in his cryptic remark to his wife, but it seemed likely. He had written Bacon's name on the file folder and it was Bacon's store in the background. I would have to check county records in the morning to see if Bacon also owned the airstrip. In the meantime, I wanted a look at the airstrip even though it was after dark.

It took me a good forty minutes driving southeast to reach the little airstrip half-way between Oregon City and Molalla. It was dark as pitch and the gate across the airstrip's access road was locked. I drove on past the gate until I found a pull-over spot on the dirt shoulder about a quarter of a mile away. A barbed-wire fence apparently surrounded the airstrip property. The strip itself was buffered from the road by a good-sized patch of land that looked as though it was being used as a Christmas-tree farm. I had walked several hundred feet when I found a place where the middle strand of wire was broken. I was about to squirm through that gap when I saw a man approaching on the road. He would know I was a stranger, so I decided to be friendly and try to come up with a cover story for skulking around in the dark of night. As they came closer, I saw he was an older man accompanied by a Golden Retriever.

"Hi. Last outing of the day for Fido?"

He stopped and relit the pipe in his mouth before responding. "Yes. Old Copper here likes his evening walk. And a mile or so in the fresh air lets me sleep better so it's a good time for both of us. What brings you out?"

"Doing a survey. Seems there's been some complaints about plane noise at night and I've been sent to observe some of the rural airports after dark."

"This one's supposed to be closed at night."

"Supposed to be?"

"Well, I live on a couple of acres not far from here and I can't remember it ever being open at night, until recently."

"Oh?"

"I live alone, see? Copper and I go out for a walk every night unless it's really stormy. About two months ago, we were taking our walk kind of late and I see blue lights out on the strip and damned if a plane doesn't come in for a landing."

I wanted to stick with my cover, so I asked, "Was it noisy?"

"Not especially. I mean you could tell it was a plane coming in low, but it didn't bother me and I probably live closer than anybody."

"So somebody was just arriving late, perhaps? Or maybe the airport is staying open longer hours?"

"Didn't seem that way. The plane was only there about five minutes ... not over ten certainly. Then it took off again and the lights went out."

"Well perhaps it was some kind of an emergency. Has it ever happened again?"

"Matter of fact, yes. About a month ago. We were out again, maybe even a little later that night and the same thing happened."

"Could you tell if it was the same plane?"

"No. I was too far away to see anything like that. Sounded the same, though."

"I see. Do you remember the date?"

"No. Well ... maybe I do. I like to look at the night sky on our walks. I know most of the constellations and the planets and, you know, once in a while you see a shooting star. Well, anyway, that works best when the moon isn't out. I remember that night the stars were bright and it was because there was a brand new moon. Kind of the same deal as tonight ... another new moon night."

"Thank you, sir. You've been helpful. It sounds like you and your neighbors haven't really been bothered, especially if it normally isn't operating at night. I'll make a note of your comments about the noise not being a problem. You can give me your name if you wish, but you don't have to."

"That's okay. It's Mel. Melvin Osterman."

He waved goodbye with his pipe and ambled away with the dog happily trotting in front. As soon as he was out of sight in the gloom, I went through the fence. I made my way by dead reckoning through the young Christmas trees until I could make out an open area and the loom of a building at the near end. My brother-in-law, Vince Langlow, had given me a pair of night-vision binoculars for Christmas. I had saved him from a homicidal kidnapper the year before and Vince was forever showing his gratitude, nice guy that he is. I had brought the binoculars with me and I hunkered down behind the last row of trees and scanned the area. There was nothing to be seen and, after ten or so minutes, I was almost ready to head back to the car when I saw headlights turning off the road at the gate to the airstrip. The car paused, presumably for the driver to unlock the gate, and then drove up to the building. Presently, I saw a man wearing a watch cap go into a small hangar and come back out pushing what looked like a very large reel or spool on wheels. It appeared to be hard work, and he started paying out some cable as he pushed the device along the side of the runway. When the spool was empty, he returned to the hangar and came out with a second spool and repeated the process down the opposite side of the runway.

It was then that I remembered there was a pattern in the old man's story. The two times he had sighted a plane, there was the new moon and tonight was the same. I had already figured out that the man with the spool was probably stringing temporary lights. Something was going down and, like it or not, I had a front row seat.

It was growing colder than a well-digger's ass and I was wishing I had worn my down ski parka instead of a denim jacket. Before I could feel too sorry for myself, the runway popped into full outline with blue lights every seventy-five feet or so. Four minutes after that, I heard the sound of a light-aircraft engine. Less than a minute went by and suddenly I saw the bright landing lights of a small plane hurtling toward the strip. It bounced lightly once, then steadied on its nose wheel and rolled toward me. The low-winged, single-engined plane slowed to a crawl near the end of the asphalt and pivoted into a ninety-degree turn. I lowered the binoculars at the last minute and dropped prone on the ground as the plane swung in front of me and taxied on toward the hangar-office-store complex. The pilot closed in on a gas pump, then braked to a stop and cut his engine. The same person who had laid out the blue lights began to fuel the plane. I trained the binoculars on the pilot. He was carrying a black object and walking to the side of the store. The security lights on the front and back of the building did not shine on the window-less side wall. I activated the night-vision feature and focused on the shadowy area the pilot had entered. I saw the pilot hand the object to a tall man I had not previously noticed. The two men talked for a few min-utes and, at the end of their conversation, the other man handed the pilot a packet the size of a large bar of soap. I could see no details, but I guessed the packet had to be cash. The pilot climbed back into the cockpit the moment the man in the watch cap finished refuel-ing the plane. The blue lights flashed on and I realized that they had been turned off as soon as the plane had landed. The engine turned over and caught and the plane taxied to the runway. For a moment, the plane was still illuminated by the security light on the store. I raised my binoculars and read the number on the tail: CP 2843. I had brought along a digital camera with a telephoto lens attachment. I started snapping pictures of the plane and I got a couple of the guy who seemed to be manning the airstrip as he left the hangar. Seconds later, the plane lifted off into the darkness and the run-way lights were again doused.

Then I had a choice to make. Should I confirm that Bacon was the person operating the lights and the fuel pump or should I try to follow the person who picked up the object delivered by the pilot? I watched the man with the package head for a Jeep Cherokee in the parking lot and chose him. Leaving the area, I had to hope that the picture would be clear enough to identify Bacon ... or not. Crouching low, I cut through the tree farm on a heading to reach my car directly. Tender young branches slapped my face and scented the air as I raced by. Having angled away from the gap in the wire, I picked up a couple of good scratches sliding under the barbed-wire fence. My sense of direction had been pretty good and I regained the road only forty feet from my car. I took an extra few seconds to hide my wallet, the camera, and the binoculars in my spare tire well. Then I used a small rock to smash the light over my rear license plate. I did not know how this was going to end up, but I did not want to appear to be on a stake-out or to be identifiable if anything went wrong. I left my headlights off as I charged down the road after the Cherokee.

It took all of my concentration to speed along on the unfamiliar road without lights. I broke an instant sweat when I almost lost it careening through a curve. I finally saw tail lights ahead when I cleared a rise about two miles down the road. I eased back on the accelerator and held position a quarter of a mile or more behind the target. The car was headed back toward Portland and I considered phoning my friend Paul DeNoli, a homicide detective with the Portland

Police Bureau. But even if Paul were willing to call in the Clackamas County Sheriff's Office in the middle of the night, I realized there would not be probable cause to stop and search the Cherokee or its driver. So I had seen a plane land on a field not normally used at night. And I had seen the pilot hand something to a man who had then driven away in a Jeep. So what? It certainly was strange, even a little suspicious, but nothing I had witnessed could be described as a crime. I bagged the idea of calling Paul and slowed my Acura a little as I sensed the dashed divider line arcing into a tight right turn.

I got around the turn and immediately saw the Cherokee stopped and straightening out perpendicular to the road right ahead of me. I slammed on the brakes and came to a stop twenty-five feet from the wagon. The tall guy wearing all-black clothing jumped out of the Cherokee and came toward my car holding a gun. His face was faintly familiar. For a second or two, I spun my mental wheels trying to place him, but his identity became a minor detail given the pointed gun. I was about to peel out in reverse when I heard a car coming up fast behind me. The driver skidded to a stop two feet from my rear bumper and turned on his headlights. I realized I had fallen for my own trick. The pick-up man had a partner who stayed behind as a lights-off sweeper. It was he who followed me without my making him and probably called ahead to set up the trap. I wondered if they had seen my car at the pull-out or had somehow spotted me around the airstrip or had simply picked me up on the road. A short, stocky man, also in black, left the second car and came up to join the first man.

The tall one yelled at me through the window, "Why were you following me, fuckhead?"

I knew I had to do some World-Poker-Tour-class bluffing to get out of this. With a little road rage thrown in for good measure, I yelled back, "I wasn't following you, you crazy bastard! But you damn near caused a collision by blocking the road!"

"So you always drive with your lights off, wise guy?"

"I must have a short in the electrical system. They just went out a few miles back."

He wasn't buying it. "Enough of this bullshit!" He yanked on my door handle which I had damn-well made sure was locked. "Stop the engine and get out of the car! We're going to have a little chat."

I saw by the headlights of the car behind me that there was just enough shoulder to the left of the Cherokee to make it past if I was lucky. I leaned over slightly to make it appear that I was unlatching my seat belt. He stepped back a step or two and I spun the steering wheel, took my foot off the brake, and punched the accelerator. My car missed the car in front by inches, but I was heading for the roadside ditch. I pulled the wheel back to the right and gritted my teeth. The wheels spun in the softer dirt and the car began to fishtail. Then the computerized traction control kicked in and I powered off the shoulder and lurched back onto the pavement. I heard shouting behind me and fully expected to hear bullets smashing into the car or the tires. There were no shots and I risked turning on my lights as I streaked down the road at close to eighty.

I expected them to come after me and when I saw a country-road intersection coming up ahead, I turned off my lights and slewed around to the right onto the other road. Half a mile down that road, I saw a barn looming up on the right-hand side. I turned in. I saw a two-horse trailer parked around the corner of the barn. I pulled my car right up to the trailer hitch and got out. The barn's large sliding door was padlocked, but I found a small unlocked door at the rear of the barn and ran inside. I threw the beam of my mini-Maglight back and forth to size up the inside layout. I saw some pieces of farm equipment, but no animals. There were two horse stalls on the far wall and each had a manger for feed with some left-over hay. I ran into one of the stalls and climbed into the manger. I pulled the loose hay over me and lay still. The dust made me sneeze. There was the sound of cars passing on the road. The sound faded into silence, but a few minutes later the sound returned and two cars pulled into the barn area. Then I heard the hushed voices of the two men who had stopped me. I thought it hopeful that they had not shot at me when I tore out of their blockade. They probably did not need a murder or attempted murder investigation poking into their smuggling operation, but they obviously wanted to learn who I was and how much of a threat I presented. I chambered a round in my Beretta and held it ready under the hay. If they discovered me, I still had a decent chance to fight my way out of it.

"Look, by the trailer! That looks like his car!" I heard the taller man say.

A minute went by when I could hear the sound of their voices, but they were too far away to make out the words. They came closer to the barn again. A voice I had not heard before, probably the guy in the back-up car, said, "The fucker can't be far away. Let's see if there's a way to get into the barn. He might be hiding his sorry ass in there."

They tried, futilely, to get in through the main barn door. Then the taller one said, "I see a door at the other end. Try that."

I had to sneeze again. I pinched my nose and suppressed it. Before there was any sound of that door opening, a new, third voice shouted, "Stop right there! Turn around and walk over to the Cherokee with your hands above your head. Face the car and spread!"

I heard some fast shuffling steps and then the unmistakable sound of someone firing a silenced pistol.

"Ah –h – h …Ohhhh!"

"Now drop that gun!"

"Okay! Okay! I'm hit!"

Then I heard the voice of the taller guy: "Where the shit did *he* come from!"

"It was a mistake for your buddy to reach for his gun. We were giving you a chance to be frisked without any shooting. But if you're dumb enough to think I'd come at you alone, you had to learn your lesson the hard way."

Then I heard a second new voice. "I have his gun. I hit him in the shoulder." Then, "Get up and join your friend on the car!"

"Who the fuck are you guys?"

"That's not important." That sounded like the first of the newcomers. The two men spoke English as though it was their native tongue, but with an accent I could not quite place. "We want that little package you have. Give us that and you can get your partner to a doctor. Don't make us have to persuade you."

The tall man spoke up. "What package? We don't have any package."

There was the sound of someone being pistol-whipped. I could hear it all the way inside the barn.

"A – a- ah. Don't hit me again. I told you ..."

"We don't have all night. And my friend has a hot temper. If you want to be cute about it, that's just the beginning. He likes to shoot kneecaps."

Then the shorter man cut in, "Okay! Okay! I'm bleeding a fucking river! It's inside the arm rest in the back seat!"

"I'll check it out."

I heard a car door opening and then, a few seconds later, slamming shut. "I found it! A hard shell glasses case … even has a pair of glasses in it. I'll cover them, you check to see if we got the real package."

There was a pause and then, "Oh, yeah! They're behind the lining. A nice little delivery!"

"Good. You guys are fast learners. Now go tell your masters this door is closed. They try to reopen it, and we take the gloves off. Capice?"

"Yeah, we got it. We're just hired hands, we just do …"

"Shut up and get out of here."

"Can you drive by yourself?" asked the taller man.

"I think so. Anyway I'll have to. We can't leave a car here."

I heard two car doors slam shut and what I figured was the Jeep Cherokee and the other car starting. Tires threw gravel as the cars tore down the driveway to the county road. I had no idea who my rescuers were or if they even knew about me. Whoever they were, they were armed and dangerous. I reckoned I would stay where I was and see what happened next.

"I'm glad you went around the other way, Willy."

"Yah. In case they were carrying, I figured it'd be best to cover them. Why the hell did they come in here? Could they be running their operation out of this farm?"

"We can't be sure of that. I've entered the position of this place on our GPS just in case. But they were out of their cars and hadn't unloaded the package. I thought I saw a third car on the road. Maybe they thought they were being followed and this barnyard was just the first place they could duck into to shake a tail."

The other man laughed, "Yah, they had the right idea, but the wrong car!"

"I don't know whose property we're on, but we got what we came for. Let's get going."

Those two must have left their car out on the main road because minutes went by before I heard the faint sound of a car starting and driving away. I lay there under the fodder for another ten minutes just to be sure one of them had not stayed behind to see if anyone came out of the barn. I finally decided it was time to get up and get the hell out of there.

As I drove away, I thought about all that had happened. There was clearly a smuggling operation of some kind at the little airstrip by Bacon's store. I had found a picture of Bacon on the Portland Yacht Club's web site. It was hard to be sure looking through the binoculars, but I thought the man who placed the lights and fueled the plane looked like Bacon . If my photos turned out, I could compare the faces. At this point, it certainly looked as though he was involved. I did not know what was being smuggled, but it was something small enough to be hidden inside the lining of a small case of some sort. I tried to think what would be valuable enough to be worth the trouble and risk and yet small enough to be packed in the case. Precious collectable stamps? Jewels? And who had hijacked the package and why? A rival gang? I knew they couldn't be customs agents. I was sorry that I had not gotten the license number for the Cherokee, but it was sideways to me when I got close and when I blasted out of there, I had my full attention on driving with no time to check plates. Then I started to worry that the shorter thug who pulled in behind me got *my* plate number. But between the broken light and his haste in jumping out of his car, I figured that he had not thought to do that. They might have looked at the plate when they saw my car beside the barn, but things were moving pretty fast then too, and they were concentrating on finding me close by. With luck, I would remain unidentified. I was very careful that I was not followed by cars with or without lights as I drove home. It had been a long night and I had not seen a single shooting star.

NINE

Sunday early morning

It was three-twenty A.M. when I reached my house-boat. I showered and put some hydrogen peroxide on the scratches I got from the barbed wire. As my adrenalin high wore off, I desperately wanted to hit the sack. But I knew I had to call Paul DeNoli. Before, I had only observed some suspicious goings-on, but now I had been threatened by a man with a gun and I had overheard a shooting.

Paul and I go back a good ways. When I was still a reporter, he was a police officer aspiring to be a detective. A liquor-store robbery gone awry had led to a shoot-out with the police. The robbers were trigger-happy on methamphetamine. Paul had shot and killed one of the robbers. What Paul could not have known in the heat of the gun battle, was that the man he shot had emptied his magazine, thrown down his gun, and was trying to make a break for it. The shooting quickly became political and Paul's career was in jeopardy. As I started doing stories about the incident, I was able to turn up a reliable eye-witness who supported Paul's version of events. He testified that Paul had every reason to believe that the man was still armed and dangerous and was still participating in the battle. That witness turned the tide at the lethal-shooting hearing. Paul was absolved and went on to make detective and I had a fine wrap-up article for my series on meth crimes. Ever since, Paul and I have been friends and he has been an invaluable contact for me inside the law enforcement community.

I knew the chase and the shooting occurred outside of the jurisdiction of the Portland Police, but, if Caughlin's death turned out to be a homicide, Paul and his colleagues would be involved sooner or later. I also thought, given the photograph, that the night's happenings could be linked to Caughlin's demise. I punched in DeNoli's number and shortly heard a groggy voice as he picked up the phone.

"This better be good, Rick. It's three-thirty in the morning!"

"Remember last year you chewed my ass for not keeping you informed about developments in the Langlow case? Well, things have gone down tonight that you may want to know about. They're going to be under the jurisdiction of the County Sheriff and the feds, but they may tie in to a local homicide."

"Okay. You have my attention. What happened?"

"I was staking out a small airstrip out in the county as part of a case I'm working on about an untimely death. While I was out there, I stumbled onto a smuggling operation using a light plane. I tailed the local crew that was on the receiving end, but they made me and chased me into a barnyard. I had enough time to hide before they arrived, but then a second pair of men arrived and forced the first guys to turn over the smuggled goods. In the course of …"

"Wait a minute! What were they smuggling?" DeNoli demanded.

"I couldn't see, but it was something small enough to be in a little packet. In any case, one of the smugglers must have tried to draw his gun and one of the interlopers shot him."

"Jeez, Rick! You should've stayed home and watched a movie on HBO! So it sounds like Customs needs to know, maybe the FBI too. And the shooting would be for the Sheriff. Could you identify any of them?"

"Maybe one of the smugglers. And I have photos of the person running the airport. But I was hiding inside a barn when the two hijackers arrived."

"So you didn't actually see the guys who ended up with the smuggled goods?"

"That's right. I heard everything, but didn't get eyes on those two. The smuggler who was shot didn't sound like he was fatally injured, but he was bleeding. There might be some blood at the scene."

"Do you know who owned the barn?"

"No. The private road continued past the barn and there may have been a farmhouse somewhere in the distance, but it was too dark to see."

"And the airport?"

"It's possibly owned by a man named Stanley Bacon. I'm going to check on that today after I get some sleep. There are some temporary blue landing lights on long power cords that are stored in the airstrip's little hangar. They used those to guide the plane in, but I suppose the owner will say it's not illegal to own the lights and they have them in case of emergencies."

"Alright. Give me the locations of the airstrip and the barn. I'll pass them on and you can get some sleep. If the FBI takes an interest, they'll probably want to talk to you later. And I want to know about this case you're working on that involves a possible homicide. I'll get in touch with you on Monday about that."

"Oh, yeah, I just remembered something else, Paul. The plane that landed, refueled, and then took off as soon as it unloaded that little package? The number on its tail was CP 2843."

"Nice! If Customs is going to look at this, they'll be glad to have a fix on the plane. Now, those locations?"

I gave Paul the locations he needed and staggered into bed.

It was mid-morning. I was in the dining area stoking down a breakfast of scrambled eggs, sausage, English muffins, and coffee when an FBI agent knocked on my door. He showed me his credentials and said his name was Masters. I offered him a cup of coffee and told in great detail what I had seen and heard the night before. I trimmed a bit off the start of the story by simply saying that in the course of investigating a different matter, I had come across the photograph of the plane in a folder with Bacon's name on the outside. When I finished, we sat together at my computer and I went to the County Assessor's website. We confirmed that Stanley Bacon was, in fact, the owner of the airstrip as well as the hangar and the building with the office and the store.

As soon as we had settled the ownership question, we uploaded the digital photo I had taken the night before onto my computer. We compared the yacht club photo with the picture of the man coming out of the hangar. We could not be absolutely certain, given the marginal lighting, but we were both convinced that the man at the airstrip was Bacon.

I had the feeling that Agent Masters already had some background on the way the goods were delivered and what type of goods they were. I asked if he knew what was going on, but he blew me off by saying only that he and the people at Customs were constantly tracking down things of this nature. He said he would need a copy of my photo and I made a disk for him. He added that he would almost certainly need to speak with me again and left me a business card with a phone number, but no name. He printed "Masters" on the card and was on his way. I guessed that was his "work name", but probably not his real name.

There was one thing I had neglected to ask the staff at Hamilton's and the next thing on my list was to go back there. I wanted to talk to the person who was on the reception desk the Saturday night that Caughlin died. My luck held, and he was still on shift when I arrived a little before noon.

"So you worked straight through from last night?"

"Well, today is a little unusual. I'm filling in the four hours until noon for my friend, Larry. Normally, I work eight in the evening 'til eight in the morning."

"And that's what you were doing a week ago?"

"Yes. Even then, it's a long shift, but there isn't much to do at night so it's not that hard."

"Okay. My question is: Mr. Caughlin was in room C-6. Did he or anyone else ever ask for a second key-card for that room?"

"Well, yes, as a matter of fact, someone did."

"And it wasn't Mr. Caughlin?"

"No. I remember Mr. Caughlin. He was kind of bossy. Like he was used to throwing his weight around and getting his way."

"So who got the second card?"

"I gave the second card to another man on Saturday night. I normally would never give a keycard to someone who wasn't the occupant of the room, but I knew this man was one of their party. He told me Caughlin had apparently locked himself out … left his keycard in his room … and now he was pretty drunk and the rest of them were trying to get him into bed. So I figured it was all right to give him a duplicate card."

"Do you remember what time that was?"

"I think it was around quarter to ten. We had a guest who'd called earlier to say they'd be arriving late and I'd just finished getting them checked in around nine-thirty when this man came in wanting the duplicate card."

"You said you knew he was with the party. Did he give you a name?"

"No. I don't think so."

I pulled out the photo of Bacon I had printed off the yacht club website and showed it to the young man. "Could it have been this man?"

"Yeah. That's him."

I walked out of the reception area and sat in my car while I called Tony Garrison on my cell phone. "Mr. Garrison, Rick Conwright here. I just heard a detail about that poker game Saturday night that hasn't come up before. I was hoping you could verify it for me."

"Something about me?"

"No, no. About Mr. Caughlin. I heard he got so drunk that a little before ten several of you had to get him back to his room."

"That's bullshit. Sean had had a drink, maybe two, but he wasn't even close to being drunk! In fact, all through the evening he was remembering what cards people had folded, telling us the odds of pocket queens winning before the flop ... stuff like that. He was sharp as a tack and in full control. Who told you *that*!"

"It doesn't matter. The staff was probably mixing him up with some other guest. How about Caughlin locking himself out of his room? Needing help getting back in?"

"No! Well, when we finally quit for the night, I left the poker room before he did, so I suppose it might've happened then and I wouldn't have known."

"Did any of you leave the game at any point in the evening?"

"Sure, to go to the can. But the poker room had its own bathroom so nobody left our area. Oh, wait a minute. I think Stan left for fifteen minutes or so. He said he had a pretty good headache and was going to go back to his room to take some Excedrin and lie down for a few moments."

"Did he come back?"

"Yeah. I remember thinking he didn't look so hot, but he got back in the game."

"Do you remember what time this was?"

"Not really. Somewhere between nine-thirty and ten-thirty. It was still fairly early."

"Okay. Sorry to have bothered you at home, but thanks for straightening that out for me."

I left Hamilton's and drove straight to Bacon's home as soon as I finished the call. He lived in Raleigh Hills, an unincorporated community just west of the Portland city limits. I saw he had a rambling ranch-style house. It was a little dated, but nicely maintained and fronted by a carefully landscaped yard. I rang the doorbell hoping I had arrived before the federal agents. A balding man just under six feet and wearing glasses opened the door.

"Yes?"

I introduced myself as a private investigator and said I wanted to ask him some questions about Sean Caughlin's death.

"Are you the PI who called me a few days ago? I *told* you I had no interest in talking with you!"

"I think you should, Mr. Bacon. We could begin by your telling me about the plane that you refueled last night."

"I have no idea what you're talking about, Conwright."

"Can it, Bacon! I know all about the special lights and the quick turnaround of your friend in the plane. And Caughlin knew about your little operation, too. So tell me how you managed to keep him quiet."

I noticed a tic starting under Bacon's left eye. He looked quickly over his shoulder and then stepped onto the front porch with me, closing the door behind him. He glared and asked in a low, but demanding, voice, "What right do you have to come to my house and make these crazy accusations? I wasn't at the airstrip last night. It isn't even open at night!"

"That's kind of the whole point, isn't it? Closed to the public after dark, but very available for your plane to make a discreet landing on nights when there's no moon."

"It's not my …" he began, then stopped himself. The tic resumed in double time.

"Not your plane? Whether you owned it or not, you are in on the deal. So Caughlin was blackmailing you and you had to stop it. You trick the reception desk at Hamilton's into giving you the key card to Caughlin's room. You wait until everyone, including Caughlin, is asleep. Then you enter his room. And I'm thinking you smothered him in his bed."

Bacon looked up and down the street as if he feared the entire neighborhood was out on the curb overhearing our conversation. "No! That's not what happened. All right, Sean told me he had evidence, a damaging photo, about my business. I didn't know what it was, but business has been slow lately and I'm having some serious cash-flow issues. Whatever he thought he had, I couldn't afford any bad publicity. I asked him what was in the picture. He said he'd show it too me on Sunday after the poker game ended and we'd have a 'little talk'. I panicked. Sean has screwed me over before and I wasn't going to let him do it again, whatever the reason! Yes, I got a card to his room. I made an excuse to leave the game around ten and I searched his room. But I found nothing! No photo, nothing. I had to hurry, but I checked everywhere in the room that I could think of. I even checked between the mattresses on his bed. But that was it. That was all I did. When I got back to the game, Sean was there. In fact, he had just won a pot."

"What did you do with the keycard?"

"There's an ornamental fountain between the building we were in and the next building. It has some shrubs around it. I just chucked the card into the shrubs before I went back to the card game."

"And you never did see the photo and he never told you what it was a picture of?"

More of the tic as he paused before answering. "No. Just that it was 'compromising' or 'damaging'. I don't remember exactly which word he used."

"Was he demanding money?"

"No. I said he had screwed me. Some years ago, he cheated me out of some very valuable intellectual property: a patent for a tire vulcanizing process. It has made him rich. He covered his tracks pretty well and I never thought I had quite enough hard proof to challenge the patent. But, because I've had this dry spell in my own business, I've again been demanding some kind of a cash settlement from him. At first, he told me to fuck off, but I kept after him. I told him I was going to get an attorney and fight it out once and for all. Sean didn't need money, but he wanted me to drop the idea of law suits and settlements. *That's* what it was about."

I left Bacon's house, thinking he had come up with a story that was consistent with what he thought I already knew: a story that carefully made no admissions whatsoever about nocturnal smuggling operations or committing murder. His version of what happened at Hamilton's was a story that I did not believe, but could not disprove. I was willing to bet that Caughlin *had* told Bacon that the photo showed the smuggler's plane at his airstrip and *had* threatened him with exposure of his criminal activities if he did not drop his patent claims. It was true, according to GeorgeAnn, that the photo and the disk had been in Caughlin's car, not in his room. But Caughlin and Bacon had stayed behind, talking heatedly as the others were leaving the game room. It was then, I figured, that Caughlin delivered his ultimatum and that Bacon knew he had to carry out his plan to kill Caughlin. As I saw it, when he entered Caughlin's room, it was much later and it was not to look for a photo, but to commit murder.

TEN

Sunday afternoon

It was almost two o'clock and I was heading back to Hamilton's. I wanted to look for that keycard Bacon claimed he had pitched into the bushes by the fountain. I had crossed the Willamette River on the Ross Island Bridge when my cell phone beeped. I picked it up and heard Weatherly's voice.

"Can you come over? I've finished studying that pacemaker and think we should talk. I'll be here for another half-hour or we could get together tomorrow if that suits you better."

"No. Now's fine. I'm in my car. It shouldn't take me long to get there."

I turned off of Powell and headed north on Twelfth Street to Weatherly's place. When I arrived, he showed me to a windowless, utilitarian office where he handed me his two page written report. Before I had time to read it, he gestured for me to follow him into his small workshop. I saw several oscilloscopes and articulated magnifiers hovering like praying mantises over work-benches strewn with components of electronic gadgets. He walked over to one of the benches and picked up the little pacemaker. He wasted no time on small talk.

"This little bugger has been set to fixed-rate mode," he began. "From what Dr. Kurlinski told me, that would be the wrong functionality for his patient. He said it might well have been fatal if it had remained in that setting for several hours."

"You said, 'has been set'. Who could do that?"

"Well, a cardiologist or a person like me. But you understand it's an *implanted* device. It's inside the patient's chest. If doctors need to change the setting, they normally do a non-invasive reprogramming, but that would, obviously, require the cooperation of the patient. My understanding is that neither of the patient's doctors undertook such a change. That makes sense since it would have been inappropriate and harmful."

"Then the product must have been defective?"

"No. I'd be very hesitant to say that. First of all, the quality control and quality history on this model are superb. Second, the devices are thoroughly checked out again before they are implanted. Third, if there were a defect, it would almost certainly have come into play long before now."

"Could it just have worn out?"

"Well, it's true that they don't last forever, but this one is by no means near the end of its useful life. Even the battery is usually good for between six and fifteen years and the doctor can tell when it is getting too low."

"There has to be *some* explanation. What's left?"

"I was thinking the same thing. One thing I could see was that the little reed switch had closed, which is what changed it to fixed-rate mode. That switch is operated magnetically. It is *still* closed – latched shut, if you will. That is definitely unusual. To me, that means that it has somehow been subjected to quite a strong magnetic field for an extended period of time. That's certainly not anticipated in the design for normal operation."

"How could that have happened?"

"If the patient had undergone magnetic-resonance imaging, that might do it, but competent radiology technicians and his own cardiologist would not allow a patient with a pacemaker to undergo an MRI. Had he been near any large electromagnetic scientific equipment? A cyclotron for example? "

"I can't see that. At this stage of his life, he was a businessman, and he never was a physicist."

Weatherly scratched his beard absently and readjusted the glasses on the bridge of his nose as he considered other possibilities. "I've heard of one case where a man was working at the base of a commercial broadcasting antenna and nearly died when his pacemaker stopped functioning. Did your guy hang out around big transmitters or antennas?"

"No. He was in and out of chemistry labs and manufacturing spaces, but not near any antennas."

"That's all I can think of," said Weatherly. "I think you now know what happened to the device, but where and how it happened ... I guess that's your line of work."

I wrote him a check for his services and started off for Hamilton's wondering how in the hell Sean Caughlin got himself into a powerful magnetic field.

I called DeNoli as soon as I left Weatherly's office. If Caughlin had been murdered as I now suspected, the keycard could be important evidence against Bacon. I wanted someone from the Police Bureau with me if I was able to find it. DeNoli agreed to meet me at the resort. The Seattle Seahawks were playing the Forty-Niners and I caught a little of the fourth quarter as I drove east on Halsey. The Hawks kicked a field goal that put them into the lead as I cruised through the gate at Hamilton's. I stayed in the Acura until I saw DeNoli's car coming through the gate a few minutes later. He parked and walked over to my car where I briefed him on the Caughlin case and told him what Bacon had told me.

"Rick, you got a kind of a screwy get-together with a bunch of guys who didn't like the deceased. I grant you, most of them had motives and this guy, Bacon, had opportunity. Maybe the others did too, if there was a time at the game when someone could've slipped some slow-acting poison in his drink."

"And one of the players, Takimoto, who is a pharmacist, would know all about poisons and he actually did pour the last round of drinks that night," I interjected.

"But as for means, you're just guessing! Suffocation? Poison? There was no autopsy and the deceased's own doctor thinks 'natural causes'. And then you've got this weird thing with the pacemaker. I can't see us getting into it, at least not at this stage. And this guy Bacon … you didn't rough him up did you, to get him to talk?"

I knew where Paul was coming from. When I was first starting as a PI, I had tracked down a man who had left his wife and stopped paying support for their child. Just hours before I located him, I learned that this dirtbag had also been sexually abusing his thirteen year-old stepdaughter. When I confronted him, he rushed me. That was all I needed. I beat him up pretty good before I served him with the court order to show cause. DeNoli's supervisor heard about the incident and has considered me a loose cannon ever since.

"No. I never laid a hand on him."

"Glad to hear it! Well, now that you got me out here, I'm ready to go hunting for the keycard with you."

"I'm thinking I should probably tell the front desk what we're doing. I'll just say you're helping me look for something outdoors that might be important to my investigation. Kind of keep it more relaxed. You won't even have to say you're with **PPB** unless they give us a hard time."

"Okay by me," DeNoli said.

"Before I go to the office, tell me if the Sheriff's people found any useful evidence at the airport or the barn."

"They told me they saw your tire tracks on the shoulder and got tread imprints at the barn, one which is compatible with original-equipment tires on Jeep Cherokees. They also saw some places on the packed earth near the barn that could be bloodstains. They took some samples, but they didn't sound too confident the lab could process them. They said they would be checking with hospital emergency rooms to see if anyone was treated for a gunshot wound last night."

"Anything from Customs or the FBI?"

"Not so far, but they don't usually share much. Have they talked to you?"

"Yeah. This morning an Agent Masters questioned me at my place."

"The fibbies are going to be pissed that you confronted Bacon."

"I suppose so, especially since I'm quite sure that I got to him before they did. He didn't want to see me, so I had to say that I and others knew what went on at the airstrip to get some leverage. I made it specific enough to get his attention, but vague enough that he wouldn't know that the feds might be closing in and that he couldn't be sure that I personally witnessed anything."

The man at the reception desk seemed to buy my story that I wanted to look for something that got lost over by the fountain. He had an earbud in his right ear and I guessed he was listening to the Seahawk game and could not be bothered to question our purpose. The bushes and shrubs surrounding the fountain were carefully trimmed, but densely spaced. We spent fifteen minutes on our hands and knees before Paul spotted something inside a camellia bush.

"This might be it," he said.

He reached into the interior of the bush and pulled out a key card, holding it by the edges. We looked it over. It had the Hamilton's logo on it, but there was no way to tell which room it would have unlocked. We went back to the front desk and I showed it to Earbud.

"We found this. We'd like to know which room it is keyed for. Can you tell us that?"

"Well, yeah ... but who are *you*?"

"I'm a private investigator. I've been talking with your manager and several of the staff about the circumstances relating to a death here last week. There is no reason to believe that Hamilton's is in any way responsible, and I've appreciated everyone's cooperation."

That seemed to satisfy him. "Oh, yeah. I heard that some guest had a heart attack."

"Yes, that's the one. So can you tell us the room?" I handed him the card and asked him to handle it only by the edges.

He slid the card into a reader with a keyboard and looked up. "It says C-6"

"I see. Another one of the reception staff told me you had state-of-the-art software for security. Would your machine be able to tell when the card had been used?"

"Yeah. Pretty slick, huh? Was that the dead man's room?"

"Yes."

"Okay then. I guess he won't care if I tell you," he said with a wink. He keyboarded a command into the device and looked at the readout. "It was used only once. At nine-fifty PM a week ago Saturday."

"I'll need the card back. Please handle it the same way."

He looked like he might refuse on the grounds it was Hamilton's property, but finally shrugged and handed it back. "How come you found it at the fountain?"

"Oh, someone said the man had stumbled around there and they thought they saw something fly out of his hand. We went looking and that's what we found."

I figured that was close enough to the truth and was all he really needed to know. DeNoli and I walked back to my car.

"So your number-one suspect was telling you the truth," DeNoli said.

"Yeah. Looks that way, doesn't it? But there may've been some way he could have deactivated the door lock or taped over the latch and come back later. I don't know how he worked that out, but he's still at the top of my list. He already felt screwed by Caughlin, he was implicated in criminal activity, and Caughlin was blackmailing him. Can you keep the card for me? And have it checked for prints?"

"Yeah, I can do that. I'll let you know if they lift anything. In the meantime, I'm going home to enjoy what's left of my weekend."

Angie had invited me over to dinner and I called her to see what time I should arrive and to find out how last night's evening news went. We agreed on five-thirty and she said the newscast went smoothly. I knew she had joined a tennis club and that she played in a women's tennis league. Angie said they had a match starting in a few minutes, but that she would be back at her apartment before I arrived. She had been on the varsity tennis team at Whitman College and still played a mean game. I almost lost interest in working on the Caughlin case as I thought of the evening ahead, but the sun had come out and it looked like a good afternoon for a drive in the country.

It would take me nearly an hour to get to the Pleasant Acres horse farm on Parrett Mountain just south of the suburb of Sherwood. I wanted to get a little more background on Kleidaeker's bodyguard, Carl

Maitland. Kleidaeker told me he was not concerned that Maitland had previously been fired for hitting on the farm-owner's daughter. Perhaps it had not bothered Kleidaeker, but that little character flaw made me think it might be worth a trip to the farm. I turned south on Ladd's Hill Road and climbed above the modern housing tracts that frame Sherwood. The terrain became a mixture of pocket evergreen forests and open meadows as the densely spaced homes were left behind. I crested a ridge and started to see the white-railed fences that characterized up-scale horse country. Three-quarters of a mile further and I saw a sign with an outline of a horse marking the entrance road to Pleasant Acres.

I pulled to a stop where that road ended in a stable-workshop-home complex. I saw a horse corral to the right and a riding lawnmower parked beside the fence. The sight of the lawnmower brought me back to the night almost a year ago when I rescued Vince Langlow from the clutches of a demented kidnapper. Before I extracted Vince from a torture chamber hidden in the countryside, the madman had tried to turn me into mincemeat using a riding lawnmower. It was a case that got a lot of publicity and probably doubled my business, but I have flinched at the sight of riding lawnmowers ever since.

A man in his early fifties wearing rubber boots, rumpled black pants, and a brown pullover came out of the stable. I introduced myself and confirmed that he owned the place. He said his name was Charles Mulaney. I told him I was running some employment background checks and had seen that Carl Maitland had worked at Pleasant Acres.

Mulaney frowned for an instant before he replied. "Yes. He worked here. He was capable in many ways. Didn't have much experience with horses, but he learned quickly and he was very handy with mechanical stuff. I had to let him go, however."

"Why was that, sir?"

"We have a seventeen-year-old daughter. Maitland has a sort of rugged handsomeness. Our daughter wanted hi-fi speakers wired into the ceiling of her bedroom. She knew Maitland had installed a heater in the stable and she asked him if he would wire the speakers. I was quite busy that week as we had a mare that had just foaled, so I didn't think much about it. Well, in short order, he was trying to seduce her. It didn't go far enough that anything happened, but her head was turned. I realize teenagers today are not all that naïve about sex, and perhaps she just saw it as an adventurous flirtation, but my God! He was more than twice her age and was my employee in a position of trust to boot! No matter how useful he was around here, I wouldn't have it!"

"I see. Was he honest in terms of cash and equipment and horseflesh?"

"Yes. He presented no problems in those areas, especially since my wife and I alone control the cash."

"How about his employment history before he came here? Did you check on that?"

"I have a friend who's a deputy sheriff and I ask him to run criminal record checks on all my would-be employees. Maitland's check came out clean. Maitland said he had previously worked as part of the technical staff for touring rock concerts. I called the promoter and he confirmed Maitland had worked for him with no problems ... did a good job with all their sound equipment. And Maitland told me that, before that, he and a partner had owned a charter boat down in the Caribbean – Antigua, I think he said."

"Do you have other employees who would have known him?"

"Yes. Sam, our trainer, has been with us for almost ten years. He would surely remember Maitland."

"Would you mind if I spoke with Sam?"

"No, I guess not. I think I just saw him bring Brandy back into the stable. I've got to run into town, but you can ask him about Maitland."

Mulaney climbed into a Ford pickup with dual rear wheels and I headed for the stable. I heard a low voice coming from one of the stalls. Then I saw the trainer's back and realized he was sweet-talking a beautiful brown horse as he inspected its front leg.

"Hi. I was just speaking with your boss. He said I might ask you a few questions, if you have a minute."

The man turned around and I was looking at a slender man with graying, close-cut hair and a trim mustache. He wore cowboy boots, faded jeans, and a denim shirt. Right out of Hollywood casting, I thought. He eyed me warily and said, "I guess that'd be alright. What do you want?"

"I'm doing a routine background check on Carl Maitland. I know he used to work here. Were you his supervisor?"

"No. Charles was his boss. Of course, Maitland didn't know much about horses at first, so I told him how to do things without spooking the animals."

"Can you tell me anything about him? Good character? Hard worker? Honest?"

"Not sure I'd say he was a *hard* worker, but he was an efficient one. He seemed to catch on pretty quick and he got things done. Never stole anything that I knew about."

"Even tempered?"

"Yeah, seemed calm enough."

"And his character?"

"He wore his hair a little too long to suit me, but I guess I'm a little old fashioned about some things."

"Anything else?"

"You know about Charles's daughter?"

"Yes. He told me why he let him go."

"He liked his nookie. He was banging one of our customers."

"How did that come about?

"She was a pretty woman. Drove a nice black Jaguar, too. Wore a wedding ring though. She came looking to buy a horse. I was gone that first day, so Carl showed her the horse. Came back at least a couple of more times and had a vet check the horse before she finally closed the deal. She talked with Carl more than with me. About a week after that, Charles was out of town and I had been away all morning getting some veterinary supplies. I had told Carl I would probably stop for lunch and then get a haircut and run by the feed store. Well, I didn't know it when I left, but I must've been coming down with the flu, because I got into town and felt like hell. I came back early and saw that black Jag parked down that little road that goes to the pump house. That woman had already had some guy come get the horse, so I was curious why she was back. I walked over to the pump house. Before I even got to the door, I could hear them. You know what I mean? Couldn't hardly mistake what was going on with all that moanin' and talkin'."

"Did you ever see either of them?"

"Hell no! I'm no peeping Tom! But I recognized voices ... Carl's definitely and I'm pretty sure the other voice was hers. And her car ..."

"I understand. Thanks for the information."

I considered what I had learned at Pleasant Acres as I drove back to Portland. It turned out that Maitland was something of an ass man, and didn't win any gold stars for moral behavior. But I still could not see him changing from bodyguard to killer on Kleidaeker's behalf. It looked like a dead end, but, in the detective racket, three quarters of what you do is to chase down dead-ends. I was reentering Portland north of Milwaukie when my phone chirped. It was Pete McCormick, the retired supervisor at Vulcan Rubber.

"Mr. Conwright, you left me your card and said to call if I remembered anything else that might involve Sean Caughlin or Stan Bacon."

"Yes. Thanks for calling. Did something come to mind?"

"I suppose it's unimportant, but I did get the idea you thought there might be foul play connected to Sean's death. Anyway, last night I remembered a funny thing that Sean said to me one day. Vulcan had been doing some testing of tread designs for Pacific Freightways and another company was trying to take that testing business away. We'd been dealing with a guy named McCaffrey who did Pacific's procurement. One day I said something about the competition getting tougher even for little testing jobs, like the one for Pacific. Sean looked at me and said, 'don't worry, I've got McCaffrey's balls in a vice.' I didn't quite dare ask what he meant, but I guess I looked dubious so he said 'old Ted married the CEO's daughter so he's on a fast track at Pacific. Pretty perfect, huh? Rich wife, guaranteed career. But Teddy has a little problem. It seems he's AC-DC.' I guess I looked kind of stupid at that and Sean says, 'he likes boys, Pete. He likes boys! Only when he's out of Chicago, I suppose, but I happen to know he has a pal here in Portland'."

"Did it ever come up again?"

"No, never did. It was kind of unusual for him to share stuff like that with me, but I think he'd had a couple of drinks at a business lunch that day … maybe loosened his tongue a little."

"Did you ever see or hear that he and McCaffrey ever discussed that 'problem' as Caughlin called it?"

"No. I just ran the shop. I knew who McCaffrey was, but I didn't do deals or drum up business. But, I know that the new company Sean started, Rubber Master, sells a lot of tires and I've heard that one of its biggest customers is Pacific Freightways."

"Thanks, Mr. McCormick. I really appreciate your calling me back."

I was cutting it close, but I thought I would only be a few minutes late arriving at Angie's place. As I drove, I pondered the fact that I had turned up another victim of Caughlin's heavy-handed tactics: another man who would have been happy to see Sean Caughlin dead.

ELEVEN

Monday morning

Angie had served mouth-watering crab-and-shrimp in alfredo sauce over fettuccine with a Waldorf salad. I had brought a bottle of King Estates Pinot Gris and a bottle of Willamette Vineyards Riesling and, before the evening was over, we had finished them both. We cleaned up the kitchen and then adjourned to her bed to watch a DVD of "Into the Void". The mountaineering movie was gripping to say the least, but, when it finished, our thoughts turned to a more romantic agenda. As our kisses became more urgent, Angie clicked off the television and I felt the heat of her body pressing against mine.

It was the next day and before we had finished our mid-Monday-morning breakfast, my cell beeped. It was Paul DeNoli. "I caught our criminalist as he was coming into the office and talked him into checking that keycard for prints first thing. He just called to tell me that it was wiped clean."

"Wiped?"

"Yeah. He said a plastic card like that would be a natural place for at least a partial. But he found nothing at all, so he concluded the user either wore gloves or wiped it off after he was through."

"Thanks for having him check. Bacon already admits that he obtained the card and used it, but I guess that shows he was anxious that it not be connected to him."

"True," said DeNoli, "but the timing suggests he didn't kill this Caughlin guy. Maybe he was just feeling guilty about entering the room to search it."

"Yeah, maybe so. But since he didn't take or disturb anything, he could've just returned the card to reception and played out his cover story."

"But what if he didn't want to show his face again and turn it into a memorable incident with the risk of having the desk check with Caughlin and expose his deception?"

"I guess that's a possibility. Anyway, thanks, Paul. Keep that card though. I still have doubts about this guy."

Angie brought me a fresh cup of coffee and I finished the last of my Eggs Benedict. It was our favorite breakfast and she had whipped it together by the time I emerged from the shower. I wanted to call Amanda Nelson to report on what I had learned over the weekend. Amanda picked up the phone on the third ring and I started to fill her in. I did not want to explicitly say that her father had been blackmailing at least two of the men at the poker game, so I sugar-coated it a little. I phrased it in terms of his learning things about Bacon's and McCaffrey's activities that they could not afford to have divulged.

"And they knew he had this information?" she asked.

I wanted to hedge a little, so I said, "I'm pretty sure they were aware that he knew something."

"Was it something Bacon and McCaffrey were involved in together?"

"No. I don't see that."

She may have suspected that her father had been the one that had informed each of them and that he had been leveraging the information for his own advantage, but she did not pursue it further.

"Have you been able to talk with GeorgeAnn?"

"Yes. She agreed to see me that same morning."

"That's lucky. She usually goes riding on the weekends. Was she helpful?"

"Yes. She thought I was wasting my time, but she was cooperative. She knew most of the men, but obviously didn't know anything specific about the weekend. She said your father had an upset stomach a couple of days before the weekend, but seemed fine the following morning. She also gave me something that ended up getting me an interview with Bacon. I learned some interesting stuff, but that's a whole 'nother story. And, so far, it doesn't tie Bacon directly in to your father's death."

"So you are thinking that it wasn't just his heart?"

"That's the most important thing I have to report. I was able to get ahold of your father's pacemaker. It turns out mortuaries routinely remove such things before a cremation. I had a couple of experts look it over. It looks very much as though it was sending incorrect signals to your father's heart. Signals that could well have been fatal."

"Oh, my God! So it was defec --"

"No, they don't think it was defective. There is reason to believe that your father was exposed to some kind of a strong magnetic field and that field changed the operation of the pacemaker."

"What does that mean? How could that have happened?"

"At this point, I don't know. But it certainly changes his death from being due to altogether natural causes. I suppose coming into contact with that magnetic field *could* have been accidental, but I'll be giving this new development a lot of thought."

"I don't know what to say. I just had a feeling something wasn't right about his death. Don't worry about the time you're spending. I still want to get to the bottom of this and I'm glad you're going to follow up on this magnetic business."

Something had been bothering me as our conversation proceeded, but I could not bring it to mind. I had finished my reporting and was about to end the call, when it hit me.

"Amanda, did you say something about GeorgeAnn *riding*?"

"Yes. She often spends time with her horses on one of the weekend days. My father wasn't interested in horses, so that was something she did on her own."

"How many horses does she have?"

"I think she has two now. She got a second one about a year ago. Why?"

"Oh, in my business, it's always helpful to know details about people's interests and hobbies. Tell me, what kind of cars did your father and GeorgeAnn have?"

"Father drove a Cadillac and GeorgeAnn's was a Jaguar."

"What colors were they?"

"The Cadillac was burgundy and the Jag was black. What's that ....?"

My brain was working overtime, but I did not want to explain my questions to Amanda. I simply told her I had some more calls to make and said a hurried 'good-bye'.

Angie had heard my end of the conversation and raised a questioning eyebrow.

"You have a gleam in your eye!" she said with a grin. "Are you on to something? This magnetizing business?"

"No, I'm still in the dark about that. It's something else. A brand new angle. I've got to make another call and then I'll know if it's just my overactive imagination or a real possibility."

I used Angie's phone book to look up the number and called Charles Mulaney at Pleasant Acres. His wife answered, but said he was in the corral and she would get him.

"Mr. Conwright?"

"Yes, Mr. Mulaney. Something else has come up that I wanted to check with you. Sam was telling me about a horse you sold some months ago to a woman who drove a black Jaguar. Does that ring a bell?"

"Yes, I think it does. She was out here several times before she made up her mind. She got a wonderful gelding. He had great confirmation."

"Could you tell me her name?"

"Ah, well, it would be a little unusual, but I suppose I could."

"I'm not interested in the horse's lineage or the price or anything confidential like that. All I need is the name of the horse and the woman's name."

"Give me a moment to look at our records." I waited for a minute or two and then he came back on the line. "Caughlin was the name. The name on the check was Sean Caughlin …. probably her husband. I remember now. She signed some of the breeding papers and her name is GeorgeAnn … all together like one word, but the A is a capital A. Kind of fancy, if you ask me. The horse is a beautiful Morgan. His name is Skylar."

"Thanks so much," I said hoping to end the call right there.

"What's the sale of that horse got to do with your employment check?"

"Well, it's important to my due diligence. I think that's all I'd better say. But please don't worry. Nothing about it reflects on Pleasant Acres."

Mulaney sounded puzzled and a little frustrated, but let me go without further questions. I closed my phone and chewed on the fact that yet another person had lied to me. GeorgeAnn Caughlin not only knew Maitland, she was – or had been – having an affair with him. Suddenly, I saw how the dots could be connected in an entirely new way: a way that might make a trip to Victoria nothing more than a cleverly planned alibi.

I wondered if it was the embarrassment of having to admit being unfaithful to her husband that had caused GeorgeAnn to lie to me. But she could have said she remembered Maitland from buying the horse and let it go at that. If it had not been for the talkative trainer, Sam, I would never have known about the tryst in the pump house. Or was it much deeper than mere embarrassment? Had it been a love-triangle where the wife and her lover did away with the husband leaving a rich widow? Even if she did not love Maitland, could GeorgeAnn have used his lust or greed to manipulate him into killing her husband? I could even imagine a scenario where Maitland acted alone out of jealousy or out of hope of wooing and winning the rich widow, but that seemed less likely. In any case, I thought it would be useful to find out if she had continued cheating on her husband with Maitland.

I remembered that Del Crocker, the attorney, had said that Sean Caughlin had made an appointment to discuss a will. A will that could have radically reduced the amount GeorgeAnn would receive when Sean died. Depending on the viewpoint, Sean's untimely death might have been seen as very timely indeed.

Angie had an early afternoon hair appointment and I had to get back to the houseboat. We agreed to call each other the next day and I headed home. I stepped through my front door and was dumbfounded to see Justine sitting on the couch reading a magazine.

"I thought you'd gone back to Seattle! How did you get in?"

My ex-wife looked at me coyly and said, "You haven't changed the hiding place for the key, Rick. I thought you would be home, but you weren't ….." She kind of let that hang in the air, then continued, "It was cold outside and I knew you wouldn't mind if I waited in here."

I was not liking this on several levels. I did not like the idea of anyone, even Justine, coming in uninvited, especially as I had all my confidential files just down the hall. Most of all, I did not feel comfortable with her reinserting herself into my life with the assumption that she had a special call on me starting with my spare key and going on from there. I tried to indicate my dissatisfaction as gently as I could.

"Well, you know I have my office here now … my investigation records and all that. It's really not too cool to have a guest arrive when I'm not home."

She flipped her hand in a tiny gesture as if to suggest that was a mere technicality. "After we had lunch, I was so hoping you'd call me, Rick. You implied you were getting involved with someone, but that's just because you've been lonely. We could make it work again, Rick! I told you I made a mistake … but I know I belong here. You remember when we were first married? That was so good … "

This was not the Justine I remembered with affection. This pushy, needy woman was almost a stranger. And a stranger that was making me uneasy. "Look, Justine. Like I said before, I'm truly sorry things haven't worked out as you'd hoped in Seattle. You grew up in Cincinnati and always liked that town. Your sister is there. Perhaps you should go back where you have old friends. I've kind of turned the page in my own life. What we had … well, that's the past. And I think it's best left that way."

She stood up with flushed cheeks and tears welling in her eyes, then gave a tiny nod and picked up her purse. She crossed quickly to the door. There, she turned back to face me. "You can't know what it cost me to come here … to say how I felt. I can see I shouldn't have. I'm sorry."

Justine's eyes were on the floor as she spoke, but I saw expressions of hurt, anger, and resignation flash on her face. Then she straightened and looked me in the eye. She gave a small sigh and blew me a kiss. She left without a further word.

I felt crummy about cooling her down like that, but I was a little relieved at the same time. I played back our conversation at Nordstrom's in my mind and concluded I had not given her any unfair encouragement. I sat there for a good twenty minutes trying to think if there was a way of helping her through this without sending her the wrong signal. I decided to wait a few days in hope that Justine would pull herself together. If she paid me another visit, I would call her sister to see if she could offer Justine some support.

I am by no means a high-fidelity connoisseur, but I know enough about loud-speakers to know that they contain permanent magnets. If Carl Maitland had been talented at working with sound systems, he would know all about the magnets inside the huge speakers needed for the outdoor concerts attended by thousands. It was time that I educated myself about magnetic fields. The first thing I did was to Google "pacemakers" and "magnetic fields". I was led to web sites that discussed electromagnetic interference risks in physics labs and promoted devices to warn pacemaker users of electromagnetic fields. I found confirmation of Weatherly's theory that a strong field could dangerously disrupt the operation of a pacemaker. I was surprised to learn that even cellular phones could occasionally present minor problems. I also saw anti-theft devices in retail stores and loudspeaker magnets listed as possible sources of hazardous interference.

I looked in the Yellow Pages for companies that specialized in sound systems. I chose an outfit in northeast Portland called Sound Systems, Inc. and punched in their number. I explained that I was not a customer, but needed to talk to someone who was knowledgeable about speakers and the magnets inside them. The switchboard operator referred me to a Rueben Lefkowicz whom she characterized as "our mad genius engineer". I told Lefkowicz I needed tutoring in magnetism and offered to take him to a late lunch in exchange for bending his ear. He laughed and said that he had already devoured his brown-bag lunch, but that I could come by anyway and he would be glad to talk to me.

Twenty minutes later, I was shaking the hand of a medium-height man in his late thirties with sandy-reddish hair. He wore a tee-shirt with "Hood to Coast" printed on the chest. He looked wiry and fit enough to convince me that he had earned it. He soon admitted to being a member of one of the twelve-person relay teams of recreational runners that enter the annual hundred-and-twenty mile race from Mt. Hood to the Pacific Ocean. He walked me back to a workroom in the rear of the store and motioned to a folding chair.

I told him I appreciated his willingness to help me and explained, in reasonably specific terms, what I needed to know.

"So this pacemaker could be vulnerable to fields as low as five gauss?"

"That's what I read on some web sites I looked at," I said.

"And you want to know whether someone could devise something to generate a magnetic field of at least that strength?"

"Yes. That's basically it."

"Okay. The permanent magnets in some of these large woofers would be strong enough to do that, especially if they were aligned properly. You could take one of the big speakers, like they use for outdoor concerts, and remove the permanent magnets. Then you'd have to heat them … say, bake them in an oven at … oh, around two-hundred degrees or so. That would allow you to separate the plies of metal. Then, you'd have to reassemble at least five of those plies and link them to a mild-steel rod. With an assembly of that sort, I'm pretty confident you could project a focused magnetic field to produce that interference at a distance of four, maybe five feet."

"What size of a rod?"

"Inch or inch-and-a-half diameter."

"Would you need a big power source?"

"No. The system would be passive. No electricity needed."

"How close to a person's body would the magnets have to be?"

"Hmm. Well, ideally, I suppose they would have to be suspended close above the person's chest."

"But surely the person would be aware of that, wouldn't they? I mean unless the person were asleep or anesthetized in a special room that had such equipment poised above his or her body."

"I *did* say 'ideally'. There might be other ways, but the magnets would have to be carefully placed."

"Would the field be strong enough to penetrate a floor or a ceiling?"

Lefkowicz considered my question for a few seconds and said, "It could probably penetrate alright, but, like I said, the effect would fall off sharply beyond four or five feet from the tip of the rod. The strength of the field decreases as the cube of the distance from the tip of the rod. There's something else too. The target's pacemaker would not be as strongly affected if it was at the null of the field."

"What do you mean by that?"

"You'd want the lines of magnetic force to be as perpendicular as possible to the axis of the reed relay. You couldn't be absolutely sure of the orientation of the relay, but the easiest way to optimize that and avoid the null would be to offset the rod somewhat, both vertically and horizontally, from the axis of the victim's prone body."

"How heavy would this thing have to be? How big?"

"Well, it would likely be about the size of an old-style computer monitor. Probably a little thinner, but about that height and width. It could weigh around twenty, twenty-two pounds."

"Would it have to be custom made?"

"Yeah. More or less like I said. There might be something like it available in laboratory equipment catalogues, but, even if there were, it would have to be reconfigured for what you're talking about. And given the illegal purpose you're hypothesizing, I'm betting your culprit would not want to make a specialized purchase that could be traced. I'd say almost certainly it would be hand-made."

I asked Lefkowicz to draw me a sketch with some simple specifications to help me visualize the set-up he had described. He also made copies of brochures from manufacturers of high-powered speakers.

"I have one more question," I said as he handed me the sketch and the brochure pages. "Has your shop sold any single large woofers in the last two months to anyone? Somebody who wasn't a regular customer or was not recognizable as being in the entertainment business?"

Lefkowicz said he would check and asked me to follow him to the customer service area in the front of the building. He stood at the keyboard of a PC and ran a sort by product type. That turned up ten sales, but all were for pairs of speakers and all were to entities that were known to Lefkowicz as music groups or entertainment venues. He finished scrolling down the list, looked at me, and said, "These all look like normal sales to me and there were no sales of singles. Of course, if money were no problem, and your guy really wanted to cover his tracks, he might have ordered more than one."

"Thanks for checking. If I can get a picture, I might come back later to show it to your colleagues, but that's plenty good enough for now."

I could tell that Reuben Lefkowicz was very smart in his field and relished challenges. He was also an outgoing guy who was happy to explain things at length to a science dummy like me. He refused to consider my offer to pay him for his time. I left, telling him that I might be back for a further discussion as I got deeper into this new angle. And that next time I would, for sure, buy lunch.

TWELVE

I called Detective Paul DeNoli as I drove away from Sound Systems and asked him to get me a photo of Carl Maitland. I knew Paul could get the picture and have it digitally transmitted from DMV's Licensing Division whereas I would almost certainly get turned down if I made the request. I did not worry about that end run on my behalf getting Paul in trouble. I was guessing it would be handled as an informal request leaving no paper trail.

In the lobby of the Justice Center, I went through a phone book and wrote down the addresses of all the hi-fi equipment stores and of companies like Sound Systems. By the time Paul called me on my cell to say he had the photo, I had identified seventeen places in the greater Portland area. I went up to the thirteenth floor and gave Paul a summary of what I had learned from Reuben Lefkowicz and what I had found out about the widow Caughlin and Carl Maitland.

"I can see why your nose is twitching, Rick. You've uncovered things that *do* cast suspicion. But your theory is still just that … a theory. You've got connections and lies and an idea as to how it could have happened. But 'could have' is not probable cause that it '*did*' happen that way."

"I understand. You're not in the game yet. But I think you *could* be any time now. I've got a lot of leg work to do, and I'm going to canvass all the places Maitland could have bought a big speaker. If that turns out to be a non-starter, I'll have to take a harder look at Mrs. Caughlin."

I asked Paul to make me three color copies of the picture. With those in hand, I thanked him and headed for my next stop. I was going only half a mile away to my friend, Julio's, place. Julio's quite a guy: an energetic young businessman, a trusted friend, and definitely one of the good guys. I first met him in my days as a working journalist. I was researching a series of stories about young Latino hoods and their chances of rising above a life of crime and violence. Julio Mendez had done time in juvie for petty theft and helping steal a car. He was still in high school and doing relatively well when he was arrested. The ugly future he glimpsed from inside the correctional facility gave him the guts to break away from his delinquent friends. He stayed out of trouble after he got out and earned an Associate of Arts degree from Chemeketa Community College. Then, Julio started his messenger/delivery business. At first, he had only four teenagers riding bicycles. From the start, he hired tough young men and women. But, before he would hire them, he had to be convinced that they had the desire to make a lawful living and move beyond their troubled backgrounds. As it has turned out, all of his employees have justified his faith in them.

His little company grew and developed loyal customers. By the time I did the story, he had fourteen employees and used three Volkswagen vans and two motorcycles in addition to the bikes. And, he had started a foundation to award college scholarships to deserving young adults, especially those who had overcome an earlier juvenile record. His dedication and social vision were so inspiring that I featured his business and his foundation in one of the articles in that series.

Julio and I became friends and, once I started my detective agency, I had actually employed his people a few times. He always insisted – and I readily agreed – that they were not to be directly exposed to danger and that I would never ask them to do anything that might be construed to be illegal. His young men and women knew the city and the suburbs very well and were already street-wise, so they were naturals to help me. I use them for surveillance, the occasional tailing assignment, and sometimes they do factual research. I am still a one-man operation, so being able to temporarily scale up my forces with reliable helpers from Julio's ranks is a great advantage. I only bring them on when Julio can spare them and I pay half-again as much as Julio can pay. They seem to like the work and, I suspect, even take a little pride in helping out a professional investigator who is not a cop. When they have worked with me on a job, I make a point of mentioning that and telling the client about Julio's foundation. This usually leads to a nice donation from the client.

Julio was talking on the phone when I got to the small building near 17th and Morrison with his living quarters on the second floor and his office, storage area, and bike garage on the street level. He waived me through the door. I plopped myself into a chair and waited. When Julio finished his phone conversation, he spun his chair away from his venerable roll-top desk. He grinned and looked me over, his dark eyes sparkling with warmth and good nature.

"Yo, Rick! What's up?"

"Hey, Amigo! I got a project that some of your troops might be able to help me with."

"No more maniacs roasting victims like wienies on a spit, I hope!"

"No. Nothing like the Langlow case! I'm thinking this may involve a homicide, but right now all I need is for your people to make inquiries at a bunch of hi-fi stores to see if a certain guy purchased a certain type of equipment."

"That doesn't sound too hard."

"No. It should be pretty straight forward."

"How many stores? How many of my people?"

"There're seventeen stores. I'll take a few myself. For the rest, it would probably take two of your guys a good half-day each."

Julio turned back to his computer and worked his database for a few seconds. He finished at the keyboard, swung around and said, "We're looking pretty light tomorrow so that should be okay. I can see if Juanita and Tony are interested. If they don't want to, I'll ask Mike and Lorenzo. Tell me exactly how you want them to handle it."

I gave him two of the photos and explained how I thought they should proceed. "They should start with a general question about sales of large woofers in the last eight or nine weeks, especially if someone bought only one. If that leads to a positive response, then have them ask for the purchaser's name. If they get that, or even if they don't, have them flash the photo to see if any of the salespersons recognize the face. The name I'm interested in is Carl Maitland, but they shouldn't reveal or confirm that unless they get a hit on a sale and can't get cooperation any other way. You know the drill: we try to get information, not give it out. If they have to, they can say they are working for me, but I'd rather they would just say they are working for a private investigator and that their inquiries have nothing to do with a consumer claim of any kind."

"Sounds cool to me. What's your case about?"

"I'm working for the daughter of a person who died under somewhat unusual circumstances. She wants to know if there was foul play. The deceased had a pacemaker and, lately, I've learned that there's a way to screw up a pacemaker using powerful magnets, like the kind used in big woofers. I'm interested in this guy, Maitland. He probably has the know-how to work with the magnets and he had opportunity and possibly a motive. The easiest way for him to have gotten the magnets would be to buy a large speaker. All that's for you to know, but not your people. It's better for them that they don't know the details and, besides, we don't want them defaming this guy if it turns out I'm wrong."

"Got it! What's your timeline?"

"The sooner, the better, Julio. You said they might be able to do it tomorrow and that would be great. How are things going with you?"

"Real good, amigo. My nephew made the honor roll at his middle school and I have a new employee that I have high hopes for. On top of that, we got a fairly large new client last week. How are things with Angie?"

"We're getting along great. You remember last summer at our barbeque? When she was hoping to get on the evening news?"

"Yeah. And I've seen her doing the show this fall!"

"Right. She usually anchors the eleven o'clock news and she's quite often on the broadcast desk for the early evening news. I think she's doing really well."

I gave Julio a copy of my list of stores and told him I would take three in the Portland area and would check the stores in Salem and Eugene. Once that was settled, Julio produced a couple of bottles of Fat Tire from his little office frig and we talked some about a Miles Davis album we both admired. We had switched to a controversial proposal before the City Commissioners to rename a street when Julio's phone rang. He suddenly had to deal with a minor accident involving one of his bicycle messengers. I waved goodbye and headed for the first of the three stores on my local list.

I managed to get to the third store just before it closed. The last store had sold a single speaker to replace one of a pair that had shorted out, but they knew the customer and it was not Maitland. The first and second stores had been the same: no hits. It was dark by the time I was driving back to the houseboat.

I parked the Acura in our parking area and walked to the marina gate and punched in the code for entry. My houseboat was the next-to-the-last one on the north end of the berthing float. The float has overhead lights every seventy-five feet but, in between, the shadows were deep. I strode down the increasingly decrepit gangway to my boat and remembered that I still had not acted upon my resolve to replace it with a newer, sturdier one. I had picked up a New York steak on the way home and my thoughts were already on grilling the steak when I stepped aboard. My neighbors to starboard had winterized their houseboat and left for Arizona two days earlier, so there were no lights on that side. The husband and wife on my port side both worked and often ate dinner downtown. Tonight, their boat was also dark. I had a close call last year when a guy out to do me bodily harm had been lurking on my boat when I got home after a long day. I now have a security system on board that will sound a siren if triggered, but most systems can be circumvented if the intruder is a real pro. I have resorted to an old trick as a back-up. I attached a few inches of monofilament line to the door frame about a foot off the deck. When I leave, I pinch a dab of putty on the other end of the line and press it against the door itself. If someone were to work the lock and open the door, the puttied end would readily pull off the door and leave the monofilament hanging down. I was thinking about my steak and almost missed it. I knelt down to be sure. The puttied end of the monofilament was hanging straight down like a miniature plumb-bob. Someone must have climbed the fence or arrived by boat and then picked my lock to get inside.

I stood up as silently as possible and considered my options. The thieves were most likely long gone if the place had been burglarized. It was a different story if someone were still inside. I wondered if Mutt and Jeff from the Saturday night chase were back in play. I do not carry my gun on days I am just making inquiries or checking facts so my Beretta was inside, hidden under a baking pan in a kitchen cupboard. I had some backpacking equipment stored in a small gear locker on the forward deck. I eased the locker open and retrieved a can of bear spray. I let two or three minutes pass as I listened intently for any sound from within. I heard nothing, so I tried the doorknob. The door was locked. I turned my key and slowly pushed the door open and left it open. I darted inside and crouched beside the door, leaving the lights off. I waited again and there was more silence. I crept into the kitchen holding the canister of bear spray. I had the bear spray in my left hand and the package of steak in my right. I eased my right hand around the corner and felt for the hallway light switch. I used the steak to push up the switch. He stood at the other end of the hallway leading to the bedroom at the aft end of the boat. He was dressed in black again and held a silenced Glock in his hand.

A bullet flew past my shoulder and blasted through the bulkhead behind me. I knew I had only a split second to save my life and hurled the steak at his face. He staggered back a step, cursed and held his other hand over his bloody nose. I flicked off the light and sprinted for the door. I made it outside as his next shot hit the door jamb. There was a crashing sound from inside and I heard him curse again. I was, by then, across the creaking gangway. The long reach of the access float back to the gate would leave me too exposed if I ran. There was a three-foot high metal housing close beside my gangway that contained a fire hose. I crouched behind it holding the bear spray at the ready.

The same tall man who had tried to block the road with his car and had followed me to the barnyard came pounding out the door and across the gangway. Once on the float, he turned toward the gate, then stopped abruptly, obviously puzzled not to see me running ahead. I rose from behind the fire-hose housing and triggered the spray. It hit him full in the face as he turned around. With a howl of pain, he threw both hands to his eyes and dropped the Glock. He quickly realized his mistake and tore his hands from his face trying to locate the gun. I switched the spray to my left hand and snatched the gun off the decking of the float with my right.

"Keep your hands up! Then turn around and walk slowly ahead of me.," I yelled.

"You fucker! I can't see!"

He was cringing and twisting and howling, but not turning around. I hoped I could march him down closer to an occupied houseboat and yell for the resident to call the police while I held the tall intruder at gunpoint.

"Listen shithead! I told you to turn around and start walking! Now *do it*!"

He kept rubbing his eyes and groaning, but he slowly turned. He began to lurch ahead and looked at me over his shoulder with one open eye. "You're dead meat, Conwright! I'm going to personally see to that."

"You've already tried, buster, and it didn't work! You're headed for a nice long stay at that State-run hotel down in Salem. Now keep walking!"

We got almost to the gate and I started yelling for someone to call the police. An older man walked toward the gate from the parking-lot side, oblivious to my yelling. I recognized him as soon as he entered the spill of the lights mounted beside the gate.

"John! Keep away. Don't come in! I've got a man at gunpoint here!"

That was the instant when the tall thug made a run for it. He was through the gate in a flash and had grabbed old John before I could stop him. With one arm around John's chest, he pulled him to a car and forced him inside. I would not have shot him once he left my boat and could no longer threaten me and I certainly was not going to try to shoot him while he held John as a human shield. But once they were inside the car, I went for the tires. I got off three shots as the car burned rubber leaving the lot. I missed with all three.

Several people were now on the float coming to see what the yelling was all about. I knew most of them and told them to stay away from my boat because it had become a crime scene. I ran to my own car and started after John and his captor. I did not know old John all that well and I could have let the police take over. But, unbidden, a vision from twenty-two years ago flashed into my brain.

We were just kids ... fifteen-year-old boys with too much bravado and too little sense. My father and his new wife had taken me with them on a vacation to southern California and allowed me to invite my best buddy, Chris, to come along. Chris and I were swimming at Huntington Beach. My step-mother had rented a beach chair and was watching us from afar. My father had gone to a tourist agency to get us all tickets to the Universal Studio tour. Chris and I were both fairly good swimmers, but neither of us had ever body-surfed before.

The breakers were forming as they passed over a sand bar about a hundred yards off shore. People would swim out to the bar where they could just barely touch bottom and then ride the waves to shore. What we had not realized was that there was a slight undertow that could carry weak swimmers back out to the sand bar and possibly beyond if they missed getting a ride on an incoming wave. That happened to us twice in a row. When our third attempt to catch a wave failed, we were getting a little panicky. Chris was exhausted and I was not much better.

On the fourth try, we caught the surge of a wave and started swimming for shore. I had almost made it to the beach when I heard Chris yelling for help. I looked over my shoulder and saw his arm waving wildly a good forty yards behind me. I was so frightened and tired that I continued stroking for shore. Seconds later, my feet touched bottom and I staggered ashore to collapse on the sand. I quickly stood up and looked for Chris. He was nowhere to be seen. My step-mother was running down the sand toward me and I watched as two lifeguards plunged into the surf.

My best boyhood friend, Chris, drowned that day. I was told by many others, including my second cousin who was a psychologist, that there was nothing I could have done in my exhausted state. Perhaps so, but I have lived with the shame and horror of that day for many years. In going after old John, I was not trying to be a hero. I was digging down to find my own courage; in a sense, to head back toward Chris in the surf at Huntington Beach.

I used my cell to call the police as I drove. I told them a man had tried to kill me, gave the marina's address and said my houseboat was in slip number fourteen. I said I had disarmed the man, but he had driven away with a hostage. I described his car as a late-model Chevy that was either dark green or black and said I was giving chase. About a mile down the road, I saw John in my headlights crawling on the shoulder.

"What did he do to you, John?" I asked as I helped him into my car.

He had abrasions all over his face and hands and a big rip in his pants at the knee.

"He told me to open the door. I was scared, but I did it. Then he slowed down a little and shoved me out."

"Do you think you have any broken bones?"

"Maybe. My right leg hurts like hell and I can't put much weight on it. When I landed on the pavement, I got the wind knocked out of me and now I'm sore all over. Jesus, I'm shaking like a leaf!"

"That might be shock. You're going to be alright, but I'm taking you to the emergency room so they can look you over and check that leg."

I got back on my cell and told the police dispatcher that the perp had thrown the hostage out of the car and I was taking him to the Providence Hospital in Milwaukie. I was hoping the police would intercept the car, but I knew the tall guy in black would reach the Sellwood district in a manner of minutes and then could lose himself in the maze of city streets. I said I would be back at the houseboat to meet with the officers as soon as I could. The dispatcher said they would also send an officer to meet us at the hospital. An emergency-room doctor x-rayed John and confirmed a simple fracture of his fibula. A nurse wrapped him in a warm blanket while the officer quickly interviewed him. When the interview was finished, the nurse pushed John's gurney into another room where they would set the bone and apply a cast. I assured him that I or his good friend Wes would return to bring him home when they released him. I drove back to our marina where I saw two police cars and an unmarked sedan drawn up beside the gate. There were now a couple of dozen people on the float milling around the taped-off area and buzzing with speculation over what had happened at slip fourteen. I saw a detective I knew waving at me from the gangway to my boat.

I walked through the group of neighbors, saying I was unharmed. I told them I had accosted a burglar. I thought it best to characterize it that way so that I would not become a pariah because of my profession. They seemed content with that explanation for the time being. The detective, Mark Davis, ducked under the crime-scene tape and greeted me.

"Hello, Conwright. Glad to see you're okay! I understand this was an ADW. We'll need to take your statement."

"Of course. And I'm mighty glad it was *just* an assault with a deadly weapon and not a homicide. I kind of doubt this was a professional hit man, but there's no question that he was out to kill me. He knew how to get in and disarm my security system and he had a silencer, so, whoever he was, he was no two-bit hood!"

"Do you know what was behind it?"

"Yeah, I'm pretty sure I do." I proceeded to tell him about the smuggling at the airport, the FBI's involvement, and that my assailant was one of the men who took delivery of the contraband, whatever it was. And I gave him a short version of how they tried to trap me after I tailed them.

"And you say his partner was shot at that barn by parties unknown?"

"That's right. I only saw this guy's face for a few seconds out on that county road, but I did hear his voice both times. I'm sure it was he at the barn and again, here tonight. The feds can fill you in on that end of it, if they're so inclined … which they may not be."

"So this guy took shots at you?"

"He sure as hell did! Twice, both times he fired from inside my houseboat. Whether your guys can find the slugs or not, I don't know. One hit the forward bulkhead, the other hit the door jamb. Outside, I hit him with bear spray and I ended up with his Glock. When he took a hostage into his car, I tried to shoot out the tires, but I missed. So he's fired it twice and I've fired it three times."

"Let me have it," Davis said, "and we'll see if we can lift his prints off the magazine or the barrel. We'll run a ballistics test too."

I handed him the gun and then we walked inside where I showed him the relative positions of the intruder and myself during the confrontation. A criminalist with a camera followed us and took photos from various angles. She dusted the door latch and the security console for fingerprints even though I told her I thought the man was wearing gloves. I described the man as six-three, one hundred eighty-five pounds, with black hair on his head but no facial hair. We found two empty cartridges in the hallway and saw that my coffee table had been tipped on its side. I told Davis that must have been what the guy tripped over when I heard the crash. My office obviously had been searched, but was not totally trashed.

Eventually, Davis and the criminalists left and I had the place to myself. After I had finished looking at the photo GeorgeAnn had given me and ones I had taken at the airstrip, I had looked for someplace to hide the CD, my digital photo card, and the prints. I remembered a Stan Getz disk that had been scratched and was not usable. I had chucked the Getz CD, placed the photo CD, the card, and the folded prints of the photos in the Getz case, and shelved it with my music albums. Now, I reached for the album cover and opened it. Every thing was still there. If the smuggler had been searching for it before I arrived, he had not found it.

I knew that the Portland police would contact the FBI, but I wanted to call Agent Masters myself. I had to leave a message with the night dispatcher but, in less than five minutes, Masters called me back. I told him what had happened and gave him Mark Davis' name and number.

"I remember you told me that your office was also on your houseboat," he said. "Was your place searched?"

"Yes, but it looked like he only had time to search in my office."

"Would they've known that you had photos?"

"I don't see how. I'm pretty sure they suspected me of staking out the airport, but they would only be guessing about pictures."

"Well, either way – with photos or without – they see you as some kind of an eye-witness to the operation at the airstrip. Rightly or wrongly, you are perceived as a real threat. We have been closing in on a ring that smuggles blood diamonds into the United States. We know the diamonds move from Sierra Leone to Jamaica to western Canada and then somehow get across our border to Seattle, Portland, and Spokane. This is the first time we've known that they use a light plane and land at that little airstrip you were watching."

"So my case has dropped me into the middle of an international smuggling operation. Wonderful!"

"Seems that way. And now you have a target painted on your back! I'm going to arrange protection for you. We'll have to have a boat watching for a water approach as well as people on the land side. I'll coordinate with the Portland Police Bureau for round-the-clock coverage at least for a few days. Are you going to stay on the boat?"

I thought for a second. I was not about to move to Angie's or my sister's with a price on my head, but I also was not too thrilled to stay on the boat. "I will for the rest of tonight. I'm going down-valley tomorrow and I'll book into a motel when I get back. After that, I'll check in with you and play it day-by-day. Tomorrow, I'll set up some light timers so it will look like I'm home in the evenings. Maybe that bait will get you a fish."

"Sounds sensible. We'll have someone in place within the next hour. Stay in touch. And keep that business about the diamonds to yourself! I figured you were entitled to know why you were a target, but, until we can crack this ring, that's strictly confidential."

I poured some Bushmills and sank onto the couch. When I finished the drink, I turned on all the outside lights and flopped, fully clothed, on my bed. I caught a few hours of fitful sleep punctuated by dreams where a tall man pointed a metal rod and enveloped me in a magnetic field.

THIRTEEN

Tuesday morning

The first thing I did the next day was to carefully inspect my security system. I found the place on an outside wall where my cable line had been cut and, on the boat's flat roof, I saw that the wire to the siren had also been snipped. I called Comcast and the security company to have repairs made that morning. Before they left the evening before, the criminalists had dug a slug out of my door jamb. I called the handyman that people at our marina use and made arrangements for him to replace that part of the door frame ASAP. Then I hit the road.

My talking to employees in sound system outlets in Salem led to nothing. I kept driving south on I-5. Another hour, and I arrived in Eugene. This college town straddles the Willamette River and spreads from low hills in the south to flat, valley land in the north.

The campus of the University of Oregon with its grace-ful red-brick buildings and stately old firs lies just east of downtown. I had four sound companies and one up-scale hi-fidelity store on my list for that city. I struck out at my first stop and moved on to Smart 's Communication Services. A smiling woman wearing a green smock met me at the customer counter. I said I was a PI trying to locate a particular person and that the only real lead I had involved his buying a large woofer within the last few months.

"What's this person done to ...."

I could not blame her for being curious, but I was not going to go into any detail, so I cut her off. "I'm re-ally not at liberty to say why I need to locate him, but I can assure you that it's important ... a serious matter. I'm especially interested in someone who may've pur-chased just one large speaker."

"There *was* such a person about three weeks ago!"

"Can you tell me his name?"

She looked doubtful for a moment, then smiled and said, "I guess I could. Let me check." She opened a file drawer and fingered through invoices. "Here it is. A JBL and a very large one at that. There's one even larger that they use in giant auditoriums, but this one is plenty big. In fact, it's the biggest one we carry in inventory. I think he said it was for an outdoor event of some kind."

She studied the invoice a moment longer. "Oh, I remember something else now. I made the sale and

he paid cash. His paying cash was a little unusual because that speaker wasn't cheap. We're always on the
alert for new customers, so I asked him his name and
he just said it was 'Jack'. So that's all I wrote on the
invoice. I asked if he didn't want to register for war-
ranty purposes and he said he never bothered with
that. I thought that was a little strange for someone
connected with big outdoor productions, but I didn't
say anything more".

I pulled Maitland's picture from its envelope
and laid it on the counter. "Would this happen to be
'Jack'?"

"Why, yes. I think it is!" She picked up the photo
and studied it; then gave a vigorous nod. "Definitely.
That's him."

I asked her for a copy of the invoice and wrote
down her name and phone number. Hunger made
me stop for a to-go burrito at the Fifth Street Public
Market on the way out of town. I ate as I drove. It was
delicious and I needed all five of the napkins they
gave me. I pushed the speed limit all the way back to
Portland. I called Julio to tell him I had my speaker-
buyer and he could call off the troops if they had
not finished already.

Back in the city, I went directly to Hamilton's. I
would not say the manager was glad to see me, but
at least she no longer required an explanation of
my purpose. I asked if there was the modern-day

equivalent of a bellman to help guests get their luggage to their rooms.

"Yes. Definitely. We don't offer that service after eight in the evening, but we always have someone to help from ten to eight."

"I'd like to talk to the person who had that duty a week ago Friday."

"That would've been Bob. He's on today, but he's in the break room at the moment. I'll get him out here."

Bob turned out to be a phlegmatic young man who looked to be barely into his twenties. The manager introduced us and Bob and I sat down in the comfortable lobby chairs.

"Thanks for helping me here, Bob," I began. "I'm interested in the time when guests in that group of eight were checking into Building C on the Friday before last. Do you remember that afternoon?"

"Yeah. That was the weekend that guy died in one of the C rooms."

"Right. Were you carrying luggage to the C rooms that day?"

"Yes, for most of the guests. A few of them just had little totes or duffels, but I probably helped all the others."

"Do you remember helping the fellow in C-five?"

"Well all the rooms are the same, you know? I'm not sure I could remember them by room number."

I produced the photo of Maitland. "How about this man?"

"Oh yeah! How'd I forget about him! He had several suitcases. He arrived in a big car with another man and I think he was handling the stuff for both of them. I was right there with my trolley after they finished checking in and I started to lift the first piece of luggage out of the trunk of their car. I remember it was fairly heavy, but the guy in your picture stopped me. He wasn't exactly crabby, but he made it real clear that he would handle their luggage himself. So I suppose I lost a tip, but I wasn't about to argue."

"Do you remember what that heavy piece looked like?"

"Umm. Sort of. It had stiff sides and reinforced corners. Kind of like a case for a musical instrument, but a little too boxy for an instrument."

I thanked the kid, wrote his name in my notebook, and gave him a fiver. I figured it would make up for his lost tip. My next priority was a place to lay my head. I checked into a Holiday Inn not far from Lloyd Center and the Rose Garden where the Trailblazers play their home games. My cell phone beeped before I had even brought my overnight bag in from the car. It was Agent Masters.

"Did anyone fall into your trap at my place today?" I asked.

"No. All was quiet out there, but we *have* had a serious development. Stanley Bacon has been murdered. His body was found in a roadside ditch a few miles from his airstrip."

"Oh, shit! You think it was the diamond smugglers that did him?"

"That's our working theory at this point. His car was still at the airstrip so we think they abducted him from there. He was shot at close range. We can't completely rule out the mysterious third parties you heard out at the barn, but our best guess is that those two were working for the diamond cartel. We know the cartel has people out all over the world tracking down and intercepting blood diamonds before they reach the market. Cartel officials deny it, of course, but we know they don't think Interpol and national customs are doing a good enough job. There is reason to believe that they've hired their own operatives to confiscate the diamonds wherever and however they can. If we're right about that, those two would have no interest in Bacon. That means the smugglers know that airstrip is no longer usable and they killed him to cover their tracks."

"That's lousy! If I hadn't used the airfield thing to get him to talk, Bacon might still be alive. He wasn't all that likable a guy, but he'd had a tough break in the business world. On top of that, he told me he was having a short-term cash-flow problem. I don't see him as an insider with the blood-diamond gang. I'm guessing he just gave them a landing spot once every month or so in exchange for a hunk of cash. He must have known they were smuggling something, but I'll bet he didn't even know for sure what the cargo was. If I hadn't pressed him by telling him the game was up at the airstrip, they might not have panicked."

"We're not happy about you talking to him before we did, but don't feel too bad about his death. He very likely gave them your name after you questioned him. If he did, he damn near got you killed!"

"True, although the smugglers could've seen my license plate or my vehicle registration that night at the barn and gotten my name that way."

"Maybe. Anyway, the reason I called was to warn you again. These guys are playing for keeps. Be careful!"

He ended the call and I sat there doing a slow burn. Whoever was organizing the smuggling, had given orders to kill me. And they *had* killed Bacon. It was time to mount a counterattack! I decided to take tomorrow off from the Caughlin case and focus on "Mutt and Jeff", my only leads to the smuggling gang. I called Angie from my room. She agreed to meet me for dinner between the six o'clock news and her late-evening newscast. I told her I had an idea of how she might be able to pick up the slack in the Caughlin investigation.

We met at the Laurelwood Meat Market on East Burnside. The place has fabulous steaks and you usually have to stand in line to get a table. I managed to get a seat at the bar that spanned the far end of the room. I had been sitting there only a few minutes when Angie came through the door. With her pretty face and nearly perfect figure, she often turns heads when she enters a pub or a restaurant and tonight was no exception. She gave me a kiss and the guy next to me at the bar was glad to move over a chair to let her fit in.

Angie declined a drink since she had the late-evening newscast coming up. After a few minutes, our server said he had a place for us. I carried my old fashioned and followed Angie to the table. I chose a New York steak and Angie went for a Porterhouse. Toward the end of our meal, our conversation turned to my case. I told her about the new information that tied GeorgeAnn and Carl Maitland together and about the killing of Caughlin's former partner. Then I told her what had happened to me the night before.

"Oh, God, Rick! Why didn't you call me last night? It really scares me that these men are after you! Come stay at my place. Get away from your houseboat for a while!"

"No, Angie, I'm not going to risk them finding out about us and learning where you live. I'm in a motel for tonight and, after that, I'll have police protection at the marina for a while."

"Can't you just leave town for a week or so? Take a vacation until they catch these people?"

"I can't do that. I need to keep working on Amanda Nelson's case. You know how that works: if too much time passes, witnesses' memories start to fade, and the killers can contrive explanations for their actions or, worse yet, leave town. I *am* going to ease off the case tomorrow though, because I have an idea that may help the cops catch those bastards that are after me."

"I can understand that, but I'm going to be worried about you all the time."

"We'll have to be careful about getting together until this all shakes out, but I'll call you every day. I can take care of myself. And you have your broadcasts to do."

"What's your next move on the case?"

"If I'm right that the bodyguard is the killer and they're in this together, what was his motive? I figure it had to be lust, love, or money. There's not much I can learn about the first two but, if someone could work on his bank accounts, the deposits might show that he was a killer-for-hire. From there, I'm hoping I can 'follow the money' back to the person who ordered the killing. And that may well be the widow."

"Banking information is not easy to come by. Any ideas on where you're going to begin?"

"Yeah. Tomorrow morning, I'll call a banker who has been willing to help me in the past. If he'll cooperate, that might take care of Portland or, at least, will give me a starting point. My second idea is this: didn't you tell me once that a journalism-school friend of yours went to work in Antigua?"

"Yes. Beth was from there and she went back home to a good job on the paper in St. John's."

"Okay, here's where you come in. I've found out that the bodyguard used to live there and that he and another man owned a sailboat they chartered out. See if your friend, Beth, can learn if the bodyguard has an offshore account in Antigua. If we need to hire someone to dig at that end, my client will cover the expense."

"Or my station might."

"No. Not yet. I need to keep control over what we learn for now. And my client would have to approve releasing some of the non-public details. But you know you'll get the first shot to run with it once my job is done."

"Alright," Angie said. "I'll set my alarm and call my friend early tomorrow. And, I've already started doing some deep background research on the deceased and his former partner." She looked at her watch. "I need to get back to the studio, so let's skip dessert. What a perfect evening! Got to see my man, had a lovely dinner, and got a lead to possibly pry open a great story. But, Lord, I wish someone hadn't tried to shoot you!"

⊱──⊰

I called Richard Bonaface's number after I had seen Angie to her car around the corner from the restaurant. His wife said he was at the club. I had a favor to ask and decided it was best to ask him in person. The Hunt Club was a strip joint out on eighty-second. 'Richie B', as he was known, owned the club and was a small-time player in the Portland underworld. I would not exactly call Richie a friend, but we had gone through some heavy stuff together in the Langlow matter. In the final analysis, he and his contacts had been instrumental in my solving the case. I had concluded that, despite his rough edges and his sometimes questionable activities, Richie was a decent enough guy when the chips were down.

Even on a Tuesday night, there were a lot of cars in the club's parking lot. I walked in and waved at a huge man standing off to one side of the greeter's stand. "Hey, Crusher! How goes?"

I suppose Crusher might, once in a blue moon, check someone's ID, but I knew he was really Bonaface's "muscle". He subtly screened people as they arrived, served as a bouncer when needed, and did whatever "errands" Richie needed doing. Crusher had turned out to be a welcome ally in the final hours of the Langlow case and we enjoyed some level of mutual respect as a result. I walked over and quietly told him I needed to talk with Richie. He nodded – with his oddly high-pitched voice, he did not waste much breath on speaking – and walked down the hall toward Bonaface's office. He returned a minute later and, with a jerk of his thumb, gestured me to go ahead. Inside his office, Bonaface leaned back in his desk chair and eyed me.

"Conwright. Haven't seen you in a while. You bringing trouble to my doorstep?"

"I'm going to try hard not to, Richie. But there *is* something you could do to help me. Here's the deal. There're some out-of-town folks, maybe even out-of-country folks, who are apparently bringing blood diamonds into the States. I was staking out a location on an entirely unrelated case of my own and stumbled onto one of their deliveries. Later that same night, some rivals showed up and relieved the pickup men of the diamonds. In the course of that little business, one of the pickup guys got shot. Along the way, they made me. And a local guy whom they had bribed to get his cooperation may have identified me by name. In any case, they found out where I live and tried to kill me last night. The feds seem to be hot on their trail and to cover their tracks, they *did* kill the man they had bribed."

"Shit, Conwright! I've heard talk here and there about blood diamonds in Portland, but I want no part of that! I may see some hot items from time to time, but diamonds are way over my head. And, like you said, the feds will be all over it, too."

"If you can help me, I'll keep you completely out of it. I need to nail the out-of-town guys before they try for me again. The guy who got shot that night was bleeding pretty good and I'm sure he needed a doctor. On the other hand, he's not likely to show up in a hospital emergency room, right?"

"Right. They got to report gunshot wounds."

"So I'm thinking, somewhere in this town, people must know of a medical guy that isn't too particular who his patients are or what the law says about reports."

"And you want me to finger this doc, if there *is* such a doc?"

"Look, all I want to do is stake out his place. I figure the guy who was shot will have to come back any day now to get dressings changed or stitches removed. I want the guy who was shot, not the doctor. I hope to catch him leaving the doctor's place. That way, I won't have to implicate the doc."

"But, if you catch the guy, he may snitch out the doctor. Or the cops will work backwards to dig him up. I dunno, Conwright. I'm sorry they're trying to pop you, but …."

"Listen to me, Richie! If it doesn't work, nothing at all happens and I'll have to try something else. If it does work, no one will ever know how I figured out where to look. This guy's partner is the one who tried to off me last night! The cops and the feds may not wrap it up soon enough and I've got to do something to protect myself from these diamond guys!"

He lit a cigarette and took a deep draw. Even though I quit smoking a couple of years ago, there are times when I still crave one. I doubted Bonaface would offer me a smoke and I summoned enough self-control not to ask. Bonaface sat drumming his fingers on his desk and I stood there to wait him out.

He finally said, "This blood diamond thing is terrible stuff. Cutting off arms and killing children and shit like that. And then there's your ass in a sling." He took another puff, squinted up at me, and continued. "There could be more than one of these docs around the city, but there is only one I know about. The dumb shit couldn't stop trying to diddle his lady patients. Some of them complained and the medical board jerked his ticket. Now he runs a vitamin shop out east on Stark. I think he works out of the back of the shop after hours. His name's Downey. I think the shop's name is 'Nutrition Plus' or something like that. Now get outa my face."

Bonaface is not the kind of person you shake hands with, at least not when he is in his lair at The Hunt Club. I simply said, "Thanks, Richie. I owe you."

I checked the phone book at a gas station to get the address for the vitamin shop. Mutt and Jeff had seen my car twice and I could not afford to have them spot it on my stake-out. There was a car rental agency at the airport that I knew would still be open at that time of night. I made a fast trip to the airport, left my car in the garage and headed back to Stark street in a rented Ford.

I found the shop on Stark close to one-hundred-nineteenth in the last few blocks before east Portland turns into the suburban community of Gresham. I drove around the block and found an alley that ran parallel to Stark behind the mix of a few modest homes and many one-story buildings. The lights were out in Downey's store front, but I could see that an interior light was on in the rear of the building. I stopped my car a little over a hundred feet from the rear entrance to the shop and parked on the edge of the alley. Two other cars had parked that way behind homes, and I hoped my car would fit in and not draw any special attention. I had my gun on the seat and the night-vision binoculars on my lap. I got DeNoli on my cell.

"Paul, it's Rick. I suppose Davis has told you by now about the attack at my place last night?"

"Yeah, he has. Protocol says I'm not supposed to work any case where a personal friend is the vic, but Davis is keeping me posted on everything."

"That's great. Listen. I got a lead on a place where the partner of the guy who was at my place – the guy I told you got shot out at that barnyard – might've gone for medical attention. It didn't sound like a fatal wound, but he almost certainly had to be patached up even if the bullet passed on through. That means tonight or tomorrow night or the next, he may need to have some follow-up care. I'm staking out a place where he's likely to have been helped right now. It's near Stark and East hundred and nineteenth. If he shows up, I'm going to tail him when he leaves. I'll call Davis with our route and that's when I'm hoping you guys will send in the cavalry and nab him. Once you have him, I'm hoping he'll give you his partner. If he isn't in good enough shape to drive, his partner might even be driving for him and you'll get them both. However you get the partner, with him in custody, I think I'll be in the clear."

"That's a great plan if you've staked out the right place. How'd you get a lead like that?"

"I have my sources, Paul. Are you guys on board on this?"

"Hell, yes. I'll call Mark right away and get him to have officers ready to act if you call. What will be our basis for stopping the car? We don't have a warrant out."

"If the tall guy shows up with the wounded guy, you've got attempted murder with me as the victim and the witness. If it's just the wounded guy, you'll have to go with something more creative … maybe something like conspiracy to threaten deadly force? I'm the vic again and the witness from that county road incident. Or you could try conspiracy to violate federal customs law. The linkage there is pretty weak because the only one I saw through my binoculars at the airstrip was the tall guy. Maybe the fibbies can help you on that if you want them in on it."

"Okay. We'll think of something. Good luck and watch your back!"

"Thanks for the support, Paul. I sure as hell will be careful, but – if they show up – they won't be expecting me to be there so I should have that advantage. If nothing happens, I'll call you tomorrow. I probably can't do the stakeout every night, so we may have to cook up a 'plan B'."

I hunkered down in the seat and took a test look through the binoculars. The trick on night-time stakeouts, as always, is to stay alert and not fall asleep. I started going over the Caughlin case in my mind. After nearly an hour, I thought of something I should have checked on when I was at Hamilton's and kicked myself for not seeing it more clearly at the time. I put it on my mental list of things to do on Wednesday. I knew that if this turned out to be an all-nighter, I would not be worth a damn in the morning. I would have to catch some sleep at home after the sun came up and hit it hard in the afternoon. My next-day planning was cut short by lights in the alley. I slumped down below window level and waited for the car to pass. A Jeep Cherokee rolled by and came to a stop behind the vitamin shop. Two men got out and knocked on the rear door. I got the glasses on them just as the door opened. I had no trouble recognizing my old friends, Mutt and Jeff.

I held a penlight under the dashboard and checked my watch. It was almost eleven-forty-five. I had already put detective Mark Davis' number on my speed-dial list and I laid the phone on the seat beside me. I was getting uneasy because it seemed they were inside too long. Finally, after a good twenty minutes, they came out. I stayed low until they were driving down the alley. I watched them turn right at the end of the alley and head back toward Stark. I drove with my lights off and stopped at the end of the alley to see which way they turned on Stark. They turned left to go west toward Portland. I cruised slowly down to the intersection to let them get far enough ahead that I would not be too conspicuous behind them.

I turned my headlights on and went straight across Stark and north for a block, then turned left, gunned it down a block and took another left. That put me heading back to Stark. They were a good block-and-a-half ahead by the time I got to the intersection. I turned right onto Stark and reached for my cell phone. I hit my speed-dial button and Davis picked up.

"Mark, it's Rick Conwright. Did DeNoli reach you?"

"Yes. I know what you're doing."

"Good. They *both* showed up. Now they're heading west on Stark, doing about thirty. We've just crossed two-oh-five. I'm about two blocks behind them in a blue Ford Taurus."

"Nice going! You really pulled a rabbit out of the hat this time! Did you definitely make the guy who was on your boat?"

"Yes. Through my binoculars. There was an indoor light shining out the door so I didn't need the night-vision feature. I got a few seconds of full-face view and I'm sure it is him."

"Roger that. What are they driving?"

"It looked like the same dark, late-model Jeep Cherokee to me."

"Okay. We have our people already in that area. We'll have two cars closing in and two up front. We may play with a stoplight to keep it red and get everybody at a standstill if we can stage it right. We'll let you know as soon as we have a visual; then you hang back. We don't want you too close if it gets nasty."

"Works for me. I'll stay with them until I get your call."

A minute went by before their call came in. I turned off on a side street just as a black-and-white and an unmarked sedan passed by, speeding west. I swung my car around and crept back to the intersection with Stark. I got out and looked down the street. After a moment, the street four blocks ahead ignited in a display of blinking blue and red lights. Five minutes after that, my phone beeped again. It was Mark Davis.

"We have them. Now we need you to come down here and identify these mugs."

I told him I was on my way. I pulled in behind one of the police cruisers and got out. They had the tall man cuffed and they had cuffed the short guy's left hand behind his back to a ring on a vinyl-covered chain that was secured around his waist. His right arm was held against his chest in a sling. Davis brought me to the two men.

"Do you recognize either of these persons?" he asked.

"I do. The tall one is the man who was inside my houseboat trying to ambush me. He shot at me twice."

The man shot me a smoldering look. "That's crazy! I don't even know who this guy is!"

"How about this other man?" Davis asked me.

"He was the man who came up behind me on the road out by the airstrip. He and this guy ..." I pointed at the tall man, "were working together. I had followed the tall man from the airstrip when they both stopped me. The tall man pulled a gun and told me to get out of my car."

Davis turned to one of the officers. "Take them downtown. Book the tall one on attempted homicide and the shorter one on conspiracy to intimidate and attempted kidnapping. I'll contact the D.A."

The cruisers with the prisoners inside left the area and Davis walked over to me.

"That's a good night's work, Rick! I'm keeping DeNoli clued in about what's happening. He said if we caught them, he'd call this fibbie, Agent Masters." He scratched under his arm. "I hate these flack vests, but you never know how these things are going to go down. We got lucky tonight. They stopped on the red and we slowed down the light long enough for the two cruisers waiting on the side street to come out and make a nice little blockade. By then, we also had two cars right behind them. That seemed to kind of take the fight out of them. They got out of the car quite meekly. The tall guy was carrying, too."

"They'll probably lawyer-up fast, but I hope you get a no-bail ruling pending trial. I don't want any more visits from that pair."

"An Assistant D.A. will probably be contacting you ... possibly even tonight. And you can bet we'll argue for no-bail. Given the ADW aspect, that should be a slam dunk."

I called Angie as I drove back to the motel. She was still awake, having just got home from the broadcast studio. I told her what had happened, leaving out any reference to Richie B. I also told her the feds were still working on the smuggling case, so she could not break the story. I assured her that no one was going to leak anything to her competitors and that, when the feds *did* wrap up their case, she would have a head start on the story. She kept asking me if I was okay. I told her I was fine and reminded her that the two biggest threats to my well-being were now in custody.

I took the rental back to the airport and got into my own car. I was dead-tired by the time I reached the motel. It did not seem worth it to repack, check out, and go back to the boat when a decent bed was only a few feet away. I was going to sleep well tonight and, in the morning, Angie and I were going to start sniffing along the money trail.

FOURTEEN

Wednesday morning

I was back on my houseboat by ten o'clock to change clothes and to check on the handyman's work on the door jamb. I called Bill Ellison at Great Western Bank. Almost two years ago, I helped the bank catch an embezzler. Ellison was Vice President for Operations and we had worked well together. Last year, I had prevailed upon him to give me access to some information as I worked on a case that did not involve his bank. I had earned his trust and I felt I could ask another favor of him. He agreed to see me and I arrived at the bank's headquarters on Everett Street in northwest Portland half-an-hour later.

We talked about Oregon Duck football for a few minutes and then I asked for his help.

"I'm on a case now that involves a mysterious death. A death that's looking more and more like a homicide.

I need to know if two individuals have bank accounts somewhere in Portland and, if so, whether there have been any large withdrawals or deposits in the past three months. Is there any way you can find that out for me, on a totally discreet basis?"

He frowned and asked, "Can't the police get a subpoena?"

"We aren't that far along in developing proof yet. I've turned up a lot of circumstantial evidence that makes me want to find out about these accounts, but the account holders are not police suspects at this point."

"I see why you're doing this on your own, then. I trust your discretion, Rick, but that's a delicate area. I'll do this much: I'll find out if there are accounts in these persons' names in the Portland area. But I doubt I can help you with the transactional stuff. Can I call you with whatever I can find?"

"That would be great, Mr. Ellison. Here's my card. The best way to reach me is on my cell. Whatever you can learn will be much appreciated and your bank will never be mentioned."

I wrote the names 'Carl Maitland' and 'GeorgeAnn Caughlin' on a slip of paper and handed it to Ellison.

I realized yesterday that when I was looking over the layout at Hamilton's, I had asked about Caughlin's room and had concentrated on looking for signs that someone had forced an entry to that room. I remembered Lefkowicz speculating that the magnets might have been hung from the ceiling. That seemed unlikely, given the limited access that Maitland would have had to the rooms. I had only made a cursory inspection of Maitland's room to gain a sense of the layout. Now, I wanted to look at the shared heating ducts and the wall between Maitland's and Caughlin's rooms. And there was that statement of the maid's about a smell like model airplane dope: a statement that I had never been able to fit into the puzzle.

The manager at Hamiliton's seemed to be nearing the end of her patience with me, but grudgingly allowed me to look at rooms C-5 and C-6 since the guests had already left. I studied the ceiling and wall and carpeting in what had been Caughlin's room. Everything I saw looked perfectly normal. I asked about the crawl space under the units and was told it had only one access: a hatch in the entertainment suite that was padlocked. The manager and I went to the suite and found the padlock intact. Then, with the manager still following me, we entered Maitland's room. Again, the ceiling and carpet appeared undisturbed. The wall looked the same, but I asked the manager if I could move the bed to look behind the headboard. With an audible sigh, she consented.

We worked together to roll the bed forward. I leaned into the space nearest the wall and saw nothing. Well, almost nothing. Just as I was ready to shove the bed back against the wall, I thought I saw a slightly different coloration on the wall. I tugged the bed further away from the wall and squatted beside the area

I had seen. I aimed my mini-Maglight at the wall. I saw a faint circle on the wall and the paint around it was a little brighter. I looked more closely. The circle was about an inch-and-a-half in diameter: exactly what Lefkowicz had hypothesized as the diameter of the rod needed to focus the magnetic field! Suddenly, I knew what the maid had smelled that morning. Maitland had cut a hole in the wall to minimize the damping of the magnetic field. After he finished with the magnet, he had tried to hide the hole by replacing the circle of drywall he had cut out, mudding in the gap caused by the saw blade, and repainting it with quick-drying paint to match the wall color. It was the drying paint that Rosa Valasquez had smelled that morning.

The manager was shocked to see that the wall had been opened. We went back to Caughlin's room and moved that bed away from the wall. The wall was unmarked. That made sense. Maitland could have cut the hole on his side before Caughlin arrived, but there was no way that Maitland could have gotten inside Caughlin's room to open that side of the wall. The noise of a portable jigsaw probably would not have been heard by anyone else and the hole made it possible to shove the rod up against the sheetrock on Caughlin's side. That improved the chances of the magnetic field focusing on Caughlin's chest as he slept in his bed. I left the manager in a very nervous frame of mind. I told her not to mention what we had discovered to anyone else. I said it would be a police decision as to what could be disclosed and that she should keep our discovery to herself. I also told her not to let anyone occupy the room until the police could take photographs and obtain paint samples.

DeNoli was out in the field when I called. I told him that Maitland *had* bought a very large speaker and that I found a carefully positioned hole in the wall between the room he had been in and Caughlin's room. I also sketched how I had learned of the widow's affair with Maitland and how she had lied to me about knowing him.

"Rick, I hear you. You've turned up some more fairly powerful circumstantial evidence. But if we arrest him, a grand jury wouldn't indict on what we have. I can already hear his lawyer's argument: 'So he bought a big speaker. So what? He used to be in the entertainment industry. He was thinking of becoming an independent promoter.' And the hole in the wall? We can't prove it was he who drilled the hole. He'll claim it was there before he got there and he never even saw it!"

"What about the smell of the fresh paint?" I asked.

"That tightens it down a little, but still not enough."

"So I have to push him into doing something that links him unequivocally to Caughlin's death. That's what you're saying?"

"Basically, yes. I'm getting more and more convinced that your explanation of the death is on the money, but the Lieutenant still doesn't think we have enough to open an investigation."

"Okay, I'll keep chasing down leads. Will you at least send some criminalists to examine that wall in room C-5 before the resort puts someone else in the room?"

"Yeah. I'll authorize that, so long as the resort consents."

"I'm pretty sure they will. I intimated to the manager that it could be a crime scene, so they should cooperate."

"Good. Keep at it, Rick, and good luck!"

"Right! But if this thing breaks open, Paul, it may break fast. Your guys have to be ready."

"You remember our talk last year? You keep me in the picture for every move, Rick! You do that, and we'll watch your back."

DeNoli had given me his five-dollar lecture for going it alone in the Langlow case. I had felt that I could move faster than the police and had the best odds of rescuing my brother-in-law alive. It worked, but it was a damn close thing and my independent action did not endear me to the folks in law enforcement, especially to Paul's boss.

I met Angie at noon at the Ringside restaurant off Glisan. Despite its pugilistic name, it is next to the Glendoveer golf course in east Portland. We chose a table apart from the few golfers who were eating. I gave her a detailed description of the arrests the night before and then asked her if she had made her early morning call.

"I did. I got through to Beth at her paper, The Antigua Observer," she answered. "Beth thought Maitland's name

216

sounded familiar and said she would call me back with whatever background she could dig up. About an hour ago, she called back. It turns out Maitland and another man owned a forty-foot sloop. They chartered it out: sometimes they went along as skipper and cook; sometimes they let the charterer do the crewing. The reason his name was familiar to her was that the sailboat was found adrift at sea, unmanned, and a charred hulk … a total loss. That led to an investigation, of course. They were never able to prove anything, but the authorities suspected the boat had been used for transporting drugs. They found the floating wreck near Puerto Rico. The prevailing theory was that rival drug runners hi-jacked the drugs, killed the couriers, and set fire to the boat to send a message to the competition."

"Heavy! Were Maitland and his partner implicated?"

"The boat was chartered without crew, so they couldn't be linked to the fire or the drugs. There was nothing more in the papers about them, but Beth said the talk on the street was that although they weren't in on the drug deal, the hire for the boat was about double the norm. And the partners collected on the insurance. I guess it was helpful that the hulk had been adrift long enough that arson could not be proven one way or the other."

"What about a bank account?"

"Beth said that was beyond what she could find out. She gave me the name of a private investigator, Tommy Baruda. He's a guy who supposedly has 'connections' everywhere down there. She thought he might be able to ferret it out for us."

"That's great. I'll discuss it with Amanda Nelson and see if she's willing to hire him."

A steady drizzle had begun and the golfers had disappeared by the time we finished our hamburgers. Angie said she would come to the houseboat after her late-evening newscast. She jogged to her car with a cardboard menu over her head as a makeshift umbrella. I called Amanda and arranged a meeting. I did not want to explain my suspicions about her step-mother over the phone. I also thought I might need to be there in person to convince her that it was worth hiring the Antiguan PI.

Amanda and her husband live in a one-story rambler with siding stained a natural wood color. They are on Westwood Drive, a street that is even higher than Terwilliger, the road that winds through the forested southwest hills to reach the vast campus of the Oregon Health Sciences University. Amanda showed me into a smaller room across the hall from her living room. We sat at opposite ends of a hunter-green leather couch facing a television set framed by bookshelves.

"Amanda, I've turned up more information about magnetism and pacemakers. I now *do* believe your father was murdered and I think I know how it was done. That faulty calibration of his pacemaker that I told you about? I think that was done deliberately by exposing him to a strong magnetic field."

"My God! Do you mean that happened at the resort?"

"Yes. Marshall Kleidaeker's bodyguard, Carl Maitland, was the one who made all the arrangements at Hamilton's and he must have made sure his room was right next to your father's. I know he bought a very large loudspeaker. I believe he stripped the magnets out of the speaker and built a device to focus the field. We found a hole in the wall in his room: a hole that was positioned right next to the head of your father's bed in the next room. I think during the night, as your father slept, Maitland deployed the magnets and disrupted your Dad's heart rhythm."

"But why?" she implored as her eyes teared over. "I don't think my father even *knew* this man! And this Marshall? You said he's an odd duck, but why would he have wanted to kill Sean?"

"Amanda, I'm not at all sure that Marshall was involved in this. I think ..."

"Well *why* then? Is this bodyguard a homicidal maniac!" she interrupted.

"No, he's not a crazy: amoral surely and maybe a sociopath, but not crazy. Amanda, he and GeorgeAnn have a past. I don't know whether it's ongoing, but I have evidence that they were having an affair."

Amanda stood up and gave me an anguished look. "Oh, No. Poor father! This is getting even uglier! You think she put this Maitland up to it?"

"Remember the prenuptial agreement? If your father died without making a will that changed things,

GeorgeAnn would do very, very well financially. Your dad had made an appointment with Del Crocker for the very purpose of making a will. That appointment was scheduled for the Friday after his death. Paul Eldridge started promoting the poker weekend two months ago. There was an eight-year good-faith period under GeorgeAnn's pre-nup and it ran out two weeks ago. There was time for her to enlist Maitland's help, and he had the technical knowledge to make it look like a natural death."

"The perfect crime! And he did it so that he and GeorgeAnn could go away somewhere and live off my father's money?"

"I don't know that. Their relationship may have ended by now. She may have simply paid him. She had some up-front money from the pre-nup that she could've used. I've hesitated to even mention my suspicions about her. All I really know right now is that she lied to me about not knowing Maitland. But, if she wasn't behind it, I, like you, find it much harder to understand why Maitland would do it."

"And she gives herself a nice alibi by going to Victoria with her girlfriends!" Amanda's eyes filled with tears as she continued. "I asked you to dig into this. I hoped you could tell me whether or not my father really died of natural causes. Now this is sounding so horrible, I almost wish I hadn't started you investigating! Have you talked to the police?"

"Yes and no. I've shared some of these facts with a friend who is a homicide detective with the Portland police. He understands we have a lot of circumstantial evidence, but I have to agree with him that, right now, we have nothing compelling … nothing conclusive. Until we do, I don't think the police will act."

Amanda snuffled her tears away and took a deep breath. "Mr. Conwright, I know that we have to be sure but, if you can find that kind of proof, I want to see those two on death row!"

I nodded my understanding. "The next thing I want to do is to look for money transferred from your step-mother to Maitland. If I can find evidence of that, it will tie her in much more closely. That's not going to be easy. The federal government, with access to the banking system, can do things like that, but we'll be much more limited in our approach. One thing I'd like to try is to see if Maitland has any offshore accounts. Specifically, I'd like to make inquiries in Antigua. He used to live there and he had a charter-boat business there. It will be expensive if I have to go down there myself and I would have no connections there … I wouldn't know the ropes. But I have identified a private investigator in St. John's, the capital city. Even without my going, it could get expensive … probably several thousand. Will you approve hiring him?"

"Yes I will. And I'll pay for you to get there too, if need be! Bruce and I try to live within our income and even save a little, but father had given me money over the years. This is a perfectly good way to spend some of it! And send me a bill for your services to date. I suspect I've used up that retainer by now."

"Yeah, we're a little past that. I'll e-mail you an invoice if that's okay."

"Sure. An e-mail will be fine."

I tried to determine the time difference between Portland and St. John's as I drove back to the houseboat. I concluded it was already mid-evening in Antigua. It was not too late to call the PI Angie's friend, Beth, had recommended. Back on board, I saw that I had two calls on the message machine. Given the time difference, I called Baruda before listening to the two messages. I ended up with an Antiguan answering service. I left my number, said it was about a new job and urged him to call back, collect. Five minutes later, my phone chirped. It was Tommy Baruda. I told him I had been referred by Angie's friend, Beth Carrothers.

"Ah, yes. Beth with the paper," he said with a slight Caribbean lilt to his voice.

"Here's what I need," I began. "I want to find out if a former resident down there has a bank account in Antigua. His name is Carl Maitland. If he does, …"

"The man whose boat burned a few years ago?"

"I believe that's the man, yes. Anyway, if he does have an account, I want to know if there have been any large deposits to that account in the last two or three months. The amounts and exact dates would be very helpful. And, most important, -- if there were such deposits – where they came from ... who was the source."

"Ah, bank information. You perhaps know that banking is very secret in Antigua? They say we are the Switzerland of the Caribbean."

"Yes, I have heard that. But I've also heard *you* have remarkable skills and resources ... that your contacts are excellent."

"Ha! In our profession, I suppose that's a good reputation to have, eh? But getting this type of information, it could take a lot of effort, if you understand me. It may be costly to undertake this investigation."

"Give me your best estimate, Mr. Baruda. Perhaps a high-low range?"

"Two thousand dollars, minimum. Possibly as much as six thousand."

"That will be acceptable, but check back with me if and when your 'billing meter' hits five thousand. And I need this information quickly. Can you have it by the end of this week?"

"I cannot guarantee that, or even that I can get it at all, but I will try."

I gave him my fax number and e-mail address and asked him to give me a progress report by Friday night or Saturday morning. He gave me his own bank information and I promised to wire him a two-thousand-dollar retainer in the morning.

I reported the arrangements with Baruda to Amanda and then returned to the two phone messages. One was from the police detective, Mark Davis.

"Rick, this is Mark Davis. We booked those two hoods. Their names purport to be Samuel Hostings ... he's the short one, and Terrance Radich, the tall guy. We didn't get much from them last night. They've never seen you before, there's been a mistake, bla, bla, bla. Then the FBI came in and took over the questioning ... kicked us out. They went most of the night and they were back at it this morning, although the two guys were lawyered-up by then. It sounds like the short guy with the sling may be ready to give them something on the smuggling business, but he's obviously scared shitless about talking. That gun you took away from Radich? Of course it had your prints, but nothing else on the gun. Like you told us, the guy wore gloves on your boat. But our criminalists checked the magazine and, guess what? He forgot to wear gloves when he last loaded it. The prints were Radich's. Oh, yeah. Thanks for your help last night!"

The last message was from Agent Masters, asking me to call him ASAP. I punched in his number. The switchboard kept me waiting a good minute before he came on the line.

"Mr. Conwright, I need to schedule your deposition about how you got there and what you saw at the airport, the chase down the county road, and your conversation with the late Mr. Bacon."

That was Masters: all warm and fuzzy. He was barking out commands without so much as a "howzit goin' Mr. Just-been-shot-at?"

"Well, when do you have in mind?"

"Tomorrow morning. At the Federal Building. I'll give you the room number."

"Suppose tomorrow morning isn't convenient?"

"Listen, Conwright. We're considering putting you in the witness protection program, but doing this deposition instead is what would be most *convenient* for you."

That, I knew, was a load of crap. The information I had would certainly be helpful to their case, but was not critical. They weren't about to go the expense and trouble of a WitPro program with me. Masters was just using it to try to bully me into his timeline. Of course, there was no way I would agree to going into that program anyway. I had a life and a business to run. I had Angie. On the other hand, I knew what kind of a deposition he had in mind. It would be a deposition to preserve testimony. If you read between the lines, that meant they wanted to create a formal record of what I could say before the bad guys killed me or scared me out of the country.

"Yeah, okay. Tomorrow morning. I might as well get it over with."

I was already trying to figure out how I could testify under oath without disclosing that the photo that led me to the airstrip had come from Amanda's late father.

"How about Bacon's killer?" I asked. "You think it was one of those two they picked up last night?"

"We like either or both them for it. Bacon was shot twice. We're hunting for the slugs. Your friend Davis has turned over the Glock to us. If we find a slug and get a ballistics match, Radich is toast. And he might be more inclined to tell us about the smuggling syndicate if there's a death penalty hanging over his head."

That sounded like a win-win for me and the feds. I pushed Masters a little further. "Did those two guys give you any information about where the plane came from?"

There was a pause and, to my surprise, he answered the question, sort of.

"I can't go into details, of course. But some data we've picked up – not from those two – suggest eastern British Columbia, maybe around Nelson. And that matches up pretty well with some indications the Mounties have. And that kind of information stays with you."

The messages taken care of, I put my feet up on my desk and considered how to put pressure on Maitland and where, if anywhere, I could find conclusive proof that he was the killer.

FIFTEEN

Thursday morning in Antigua

Tommy Baruda shifted his considerable bulk in the hammock and sipped his second cup of morning coffee. He looked out from the veranda of his second-story living quarters to the street below as it came to life with the morning traffic. He had been pondering a strategy to get the information the American desired. There were only two banking chains in Antigua and he knew most of the officers in both of them. With a sigh of resolution, he drained his coffee mug and heaved himself out of the hammock. He retired to his bedroom where he added a bright yellow tie to go with a white shirt and a powder-blue tropical suit. On a day when it was important to blend in, he would have worn a colorful, open-necked shirt and slacks. But today, talking to bankers, he chose the suit. He moved down the exterior stairs with surprising grace and unlocked the door of his street-level office. Five years ago, Baruda had collected a very sizable fee for locating and bringing back the drug-ravaged son of a wealthy Antiguan family. He had used the cash to purchase the small building that became his home and housed his detective agency.

Baruda opened the safe inside his office and removed a packet of large-denomination bills. He tucked the Eastern Caribbean Dollar currency in an inner pocket, and collected his cell phone and his notebook.

The main office of the Commonwealth Bank was at the intersection of Cross and High Streets. He waved and greeted people as he walked the few blocks to the bank. Many persons in Antigua knew Tommy Baruda. His father had owned a popular fish restaurant in English Harbour and Baruda had worked there as a teenager and a young man. There was a ready smile on his round face and his gleaming teeth set off his dark countenance. He had always been a curious, observant person and these qualities led him easily enough to his chosen profession. His amiable nature caused people to talk freely, but he was no innocent. Having grown up amongst wealthy visiting yachters, venal financial operators, and desperately poor natives, Tommy was a student of human nature. At thirty-six, he had already encountered the corrupt or secretive aspects of some Antiguan businesses..

Baruda entered the bank's small, but traditional, public lobby. The modest scale of the space belied the astonishing amount of funds that flowed into and out of the bank. Baruda approached a customer-assistance desk and asked to speak with a vice president named Boflower. A thin man with angular features and a mustache greeted him minutes later and they entered a small conference room.

"Tommy!" Boflower greeted him. "What can I do for you?"

Baruda had formulated a two-part plan. He would get the less-sensitive information, the facts he needed to get started, at a high management level. Then, he could work on a relatively low-level employee for the more delicate facts.

"Jorge, I was wondering whether a certain person might be banking somewhere in Antigua. The name is Maitland, Carl Maitland. Is that something you could help me with?"

Boflower's gaze narrowed. There was an indiscretion in Boflower's past … a mere passing peccadillo. Baruda was aware of it, but he had always kept silent. Bank boards of directors could blind themselves to some dubious transactions, yet be highly critical of personal behaviors. Boflower owed the man. He made a few keystrokes on his computer and glanced at his monitor.

"Well, ah, Tommy many of our clients choose to bank in Antigua just so details like that remain confidential. Maitland, eh? I've seen that name somewhere … the newspapers perhaps. By the way, have you been to our branch in Falmouth recently? The refurbishing came out very nicely: all new carpeting, new lighting ... very nice indeed. You ought to drop in and see it."

"I understand completely, Jorge. I'm sorry to have put you on the spot. I would've done the same thing in your shoes."

Flashing his trademark smile, Baruda waved good-bye to the slender banker. He also smiled inwardly as he thought his assignment for Conwright had begun successfully. He now knew that Maitland did have an Antiguan account and that it was at the Falmouth branch of the Commonwealth Bank.

It was no more than five miles from St. John's to Falmouth on the south coast. Baruda considered what he knew about the manager of the Falmouth branch as he drove. The man was not a righteous person, but – unfortunately for Baruda's task –he *was* likely to be righteous about bank secrecy. The branch did its share of the offshore banking trade. It also did a great deal of business with the affluent visitors whose sailboats crowded the harbor. Baruda guessed that the manager would not be one to jeopardize that trade by disclosing account information. Baruda had been light-heartedly flirting with one of the tellers for years. And he knew her mother had been diagnosed with lung cancer. He chose her as his point of attack. He stalled at the table in the center of the lobby until she was free.

"Maureen!" he exclaimed, resting his elbows on the counter giving her hand a squeeze. "How's your mother doing? She dealing with it okay?"

"Hi, Tommy. It's been rough. They caught it early, but she's going to need a lot of treatment. How goes it with you?"

"Lovely, sweetheart! Lovely. Right now, though, I need your help." He lowered his voice and leaned closer. "Do you think you could tell me whether there've been any big deposits in the account of a Carl Maitland in, say, the last three months?"

"Oh, Tommy. You know I'm not supposed …"

"Couldn't you just check on whether there were such deposits? If you see any, we can talk some more."

The woman cast an eye toward the next teller's cage before answering. "I go on coffee break in ten minutes. The coffee here is terrible. I usually get my coffee from the vendor down the block."

Baruda had an account of his own at the Commonwealth Bank and he signed a withdrawal slip. The woman counted out his two hundred ECDs and Baruda left as another customer approached the window.

They walked slowly away from the coffee stand, cups in hand. "There was a big deposit, Tommy. But that's all I can say. You know I could lose my job. I can't afford that with my mother and all …"

"Maureen, my client is very anxious to get specifics on this. And he's a very humane individual. I know he would want to contribute to your mother's health costs. Say, two thousand American?"

Her eyes opened wider and her trembling hand sent miniature ripples across the surface of her coffee. They had come to a sidewalk bench and she sat down heavily. Baruda lowered himself beside her and seconds passed before she turned to face him.

"God, Tommy, she *does* need the help! I have very little savings and she'll have to go to Caracas for some of the treatment."

"That's tough. I'll see if there might be a little more than two thousand. I better have both the amount and the date of that deposit. When do you get off? I can come by your house."

"I work a split shift on Thursdays. I take a long lunch starting at eleven-thirty and then return at two-fifteen. I'll be home by a quarter to twelve."

Baruda parked further down the street and walked back to the small rental house where Maureen lived with her mother. Geraniums in window boxes and the sky-blue paint favored by many Antiguans gave the house a cheerful look from the street. Maureen answered on his second knock. Her mother was apparently asleep in a back bedroom when Baruda entered. He counted out twenty-four hundred US dollars-worth of ECD bills and handed them to Maureen. She gave him a slip of paper with a number and the date.

"Do you know how the deposit came in?"

"That was peculiar. It wasn't a bank transfer. It was a cash deposit!"

"Who was the depositor?"

"As it happened, I handled the deposit. It was a man. I think I've seen him around town, but he doesn't bank with us. I don't know his name. We don't make them sign anything … I guess that's Antiguan banking. And he didn't ask for a receipt."

Baruda thanked her. He could hear her mother coughing as he let himself out the door. Baruda was hungry and the promise of lunch propelled him to English Harbour. He sat on the broad deck at the Southern Cross and asked for a double order of fried calamari and a Red Stripe. His eyes fixed for some seconds on the spot near the quay where his father's restaurant used to be. When his father sold the property, the new owners promptly razed the modest building. A four-story hotel now stood on the site. Baruda remembered his father's devotion to the business and his own pleasure at working with his father in the family enterprise. Well, he thought, times change.

A young woman wearing a revealing scoop-neck top and clinging capris brought his beer. He mulled over the fact of the cash deposit as he waited for the rest of his order. Whoever was paying Maitland was being careful to cover his tracks. Had they merely used a local courier or had Maitland actually been paid by an Antiguan resident? He took a pull on his beer and his gaze wandered over the crowded marina before him and to the dozens of sailboats tethered to buoys in the harbor beyond. Baruda toyed with the idea that the money had been brought in on one of the sailboats. He slapped his meaty hand on the table as the answer flashed in his brain. Maitland had a partner when he was in the chartering business. It took several moments for Baruda to recall the partner's name. It was Jerry Portino. He thought Portino still lived somewhere in Antigua. He remembered Portino as a bit of an enigma. The man seemed to live by his wits and unquestionably had been involved in a few shady deals. Portino had never been convicted of anything to Baruda's knowledge, but no doubt he had plenty of income that was never reported to the tax authorities. On the other hand, it was known around the island that the man ran some kind of a charity that helped support the children of single mothers in need. The story was that Portino himself had been a street kid and that that experience had directed his sympathies to other unfortunates. The calamari arrived and Baruda ordered another beer. To test his idea, he needed a photo of Portino. He was obliged to Beth, the reporter at the Antigua Observer, for the referral. He would call her after his meal to thank her and to ask if she could provide the photo.

Beth Carrothers had agreed to make a copy if she could find a picture of Portino in the paper's photo archive. Baruda went straight to the newspaper office upon his return to St. John. Beth produced the picture, but she smelled a possible story and questioned him about the sudden interest in Maitland and Portino. Baruda gave her a broad smile and said it was some kind of due diligence for a stateside business deal. Picture in hand, he raced back to Falmouth. He caught Maureen's eye from across the lobby and made charade-like motions of drinking coffee and pointed to his watch. She drew a puzzled look from the customer at her window by holding up both hands with fingers spread. Baruda was working on an iced coffee when he saw her hurrying toward him.

"What is it?" she asked anxiously.

"I just want you to look at a picture of someone and tell me if he's the man who made that deposit." He had been carrying the photo inside a folded newspaper. He pulled it out and handed it to her.

"Yes. That does look like him. Who is he?"

"Never mind," Baruda said. "You're better off not knowing. Now I need one more thing. There's another account I'm interested in. The name is Jerry or Jerome Portino. After you're back at work, I'll drift into the lobby. I won't come to your window. If Portino has an account at any Commonwealth branch, staple something together and hold it high enough that I can see you doing it. If he does *not* have an account with you, just stretch with your arms over your head."

She laughed. "You men will do anything to stare at a woman's chest!" She continued more soberly, "Alright, I'll do this one more thing for you but, please, don't push me, Tommy!"

Baruda entered the bank lobby twenty minutes later. Maureen had finished helping a customer and noticed him pretending to read brochures about the bank's services. She caught his eye and then, with a yawn, she stretched luxuriantly. The large PI ambled out of the bank and into the bright afternoon sunlight. His campaign had taken two steps forward by identifying Portino as the depositor. Then the campaign took a step backward as he now had to pry some more sensitive information from a different bank. Maureen's message, complete with interesting body language, meant that Portino must have an account at the other bank on the island, The Caribbe Bank. Baruda felt he had no particular leverage at Caribbe Bank. No one there owed him any favors and he had not been flirting with any of their female employees. He had started the three-block walk to the Falmouth branch of the bank, but he stopped halfway there and returned to his car.

The drive to Jolly Harbour took Baruda inland and north to the center of the island, then over a low pass in the highlands as he angled back toward the ocean. The last leg was along the southwest coast and its sandy beaches frosted with the white, crashing curls of breakers. The woman he was going to see, Joyce Hollister, was an expatriate American. Rumor had it that she had graduated from M.I.T. with a degree in Computer Science. Tommy knew she had been a top IT systems analyst for a large financial firm where her penchant for hacking into supposedly secure databases had led to her departure. The stories had it that she had never misused any funds or otherwise advantaged herself, but that she could seldom resist the challenge of trying to break into protected sites. She moved to Antigua and became a "consultant". When Baruda had first met her, she was advising a large corporation on improving its firewalls, intrusion detectors, and authentication tokens. He had the impression that the majority of her business was working for the "good guys", but that, if the assignment was intellectually tempting enough, she might broaden that definition a little.

Hollister owned a white stucco house with clean tropical lines nestled on a hill above the harbor. Baruda had called ahead to set up the late-afternoon meeting. Hollister was a little over five-foot-six and wore her blond hair in a ponytail. Baruda judged her to be in her late thirties. He considered her attractive even though she was not a stunning beauty. She met him at her door, looking casual, but professional, in pale-yellow linen slacks and a white satin blouse.

"Hello, Tommy," she said as she led him to a seat in her living room. "It's been a while. So you have a little security problem? Or is it a little security problem you hope to avoid?"

"Yeah, I guess it's the latter. I have reason to believe that a guy here in Antigua is channeling money to someone my client is interested in. I need to know who's upstream in that channel. I'm pretty confident that this local guy has an account at The Carribe Bank."

"I see. That probably means a ledger in his account file and a separate file if wire transfers are involved. It certainly won't be easy, especially with these Antiguan banks, but it can be done. But if it's about organized-crime money, I'm not interested. I usually don't leave any footprints, but that's not a risk I care to take."

"No, there're no hard guys involved in this account. If money *is* being channeled it's not money that's being laundered. It may be a payoff for some nasty work, but it's not an organized crime operation."

"Even so, why should I take this on, Tommy?"

"For one thing, my client is a PI working for a young woman whose father was probably murdered. He's trying to follow a money trail ... the payoff for the killing."

"A private investigator, huh? Not a police detective?"

"No. Just a guy like me."

"Okay, so you're on the side of the angels here. What else?"

"Well, they say The Caribe Bank has world-class security and has some big-shot Chief Information Officer they recruited away from Barclays Bank."

Hollister looked at him with the faintest of smiles. "You do know how to entice a gal, don't you, Tommy!"

"I just thought you could kind of help us here, Joyce" he said softly as his fingers repositioned a Dive magazine on her coffee table.

Hollister looked away for a few seconds before she responded. "Okay. I just finished a job. I was going to kick back for a week or so, but I suppose I can help you out. It shouldn't take too long."

"Great! What's it going to cost my client?"

"On a job like this, I'll charge four percent of the amount we're looking for with a thousand-dollar minimum. You'll need someone inside the bank to plant a key logger for me. I'll loan you the logger, but you'll have to bear the cost of the inside person. And you'll have to guarantee the replacement of my logger if it gets confiscated."

"What do you mean an insider? If I had an insider, I wouldn't need you."

"I don't mean a manager or professional staffer. Just someone who could attach this little dongle-like thing to the cable from a keyboard to a PC. Somebody like a janitor who works at night when staff has gone home. Teach him how and it should take him no more than thirty seconds. The next night he does the same thing in reverse and brings it back to you and you bring it to me."

"So that little device gets me what I need to know?"

"No, no. It just gives me a password to get into their system. Otherwise it would take a supercomputer and several days' time, neither of which you have. Once I get in, I'll use some algorithms I have to crack any encrypted transfer instructions."

"I'll work on finding a janitor. With luck, I'll have the keylogger back to you by Saturday morning," said Baruda.

"What amount am I looking for?"

"I believe this guy passed cash … I think he muled it over from his bank to our target's bank. The deposit into our target's account was about five weeks ago. The amount was …" Baruda checked his notes, "forty thousand in terms of U.S. dollars."

Baruda wrote the amount and the exact date of the deposit on a slip of paper and handed it to her. "The local guy's name is Jerry Portino. I'm guessing that the money coming into Portino's account will be in roughly the same amount and probably came from a bank in the States."

"But you don't know for sure about it coming from the States, do you?"

"You're right. But the odds are high that it did."

"Are you going to tell me why that is?"

"Uh, uh. Need to know and all that good stuff," he answered with a grin.

"Okay. I'll block out time on Saturday. Call me if you're running behind."

Baruda started to rise, then eased back into his seat. "Oh, and Portino has a charity. I think he calls it 'Kids Help' or something close to that. He might have an account under that name also."

She looked at him ruefully. "Hey, friend, do we need a change order here? Are you asking for more work?"

Baruda shrugged and turned the palms of his hands upward.

Hollister gave it a few seconds, then grinned and said, "Okay, okay! I'll look for both accounts."

Hollister gave him the little key-logging device and they shook hands. Baruda stood for a moment admiring the sweep of Jolly Harbour from Hollister's picture windows before taking his leave.

SIXTEEN

Thursday morning

"Do you, Richard Conwright, swear to tell the truth, the whole truth, and nothing ...." So began my deposition on a chilly Portland morning. We were seated around a table in an interior conference room at the Office of the U.S. Attorney in the Mark Hatfield Building. The court reporter turned it over to an Assistant U.S. Attorney when he finished administering the oath. Agent Masters was also at the table, ready to take some notes. The attorney took me through the whole business of my surveillance at the airstrip. She had me authenticate the photo I took and made it an exhibit to my deposition. They even had me describe my encounter with Mel Osterman, the friendly dog-walker who enjoyed looking at the night sky.

The reference to the photo from Sean Caughlin's car was a good deal trickier. I stated that I had come into possession of the picture and its digital version on the CD "in the course of an entirely unrelated matter". I asserted that the source was part of my confidential investigation and declined to go into further detail. The attorney told the reporter we were going "off the record." Then, she patiently, but firmly, told me there was no such legally-recognizable privilege even if the photo's source was my own client. I already knew that, but I still wanted to balk. My goal, for Amanda's sake, was to try to keep her father's rather tawdry behavior out of the public record. The attorney tried coming at the problem from a different direction by asking me if I knew who the photographer was. I had to admit that I did not, and we were back to "so-how-did-you-get-it?" We went back on the record and I finally had to tell them that GeorgeAnn had handed the picture to me after finding it in her late husband's car. I tried to emphasize that the photo had just been an inconsequential artifact, a dead-end tangent, in my investigation concerning an entirely different group of people. I stated that none of them, with the exception of Bacon, appeared to have any connection to the diamonds. I honestly thought that to be true, but I noticed Masters furiously taking notes.

From there, my narrative moved on to the confrontation on the county road, my hiding in the barn, the high-jacking of the diamonds, and the subsequent attempt to kill me. When they wanted to know how I was led to the ex-doctor's office, they were a little more tolerant of my holding back Richie B's name. I figured they would find out about and might question the midnight doc, Downey, to see if he knew anything about the diamonds or the attack on me. But they must have felt that my source, Bonaface, was too far removed to be worth identifying.

The attorney had me hone and polish every detail of all those events until one-thirty in the afternoon. Even to my investigative reporter instincts, her belaboring it seemed like overkill, but there I was.

I wolfed down a hamburger in the federal building's cafeteria after we finished. I had never really been convinced that the smugglers had killed Caughlin. I hoped that Masters and his colleagues would not start interrogating all my suspects and muddying the waters for no good reason. I also thought about GeorgeAnn handing me the photo. At that time, I had not been thinking seriously of her as a suspect. Nevertheless, my questions must have made her nervous. I doubted that she knew all the photo's implications, but she must have given me the picture to suggest a motive for Bacon. I could see it from her viewpoint: if the "natural causes" explanation ever fell apart, it would not hurt to have someone else be a leading suspect.

I had been bothered by the fact that I did not know what had become of the magnetic-field generator after the poker weekend. Maitland could have tried to dispose of it right there at Hamilton's, but that seemed a little risky to me. Since he alone handled the luggage in and out of the car, my guess was that he had taken the device with them when he and his employer left the resort. Kleidaeker's house sat on a good-sized lot with a hedge and a fence offering complete privacy. I thought there was a chance that Maitland had either reassembled the magnets into their more innocuous original form in the large woofer or had hidden them somewhere on the grounds. I wanted to put pressure on Maitland to see if he would take some action that would tighten the noose around his neck.

There was not quite enough proof yet for DeNoli to obtain a search warrant for Kleidaeker's property, but I thought a bluff might work. I could imagine several ways it might play out. I could ask Kleidaeker's permission to search with a gauss meter. I no longer thought of that odd, limping man as a leading suspect, but I could not completely rule out that he was the one who had ordered the killing. Kleidaeker might agree to the search if he were innocent. If Maitland had hidden the magnets on the premises, the search might turn them up right away. If Kleidaeker, innocent or not, refused the search, I could bluff that I would come back the next day with the police and a warrant. That would force Maitland to dispose of the magnets elsewhere before the warrant was served. I could place the house under surveillance and follow Maitland to wherever he ditched the magnets. There were a lot of "ifs" to my strategy, but even if it turned up nothing, it would serve to turn up the heat on Maitland.

I discussed my idea with DeNoli over the phone. He thought it was worth a try, but cautioned me not to expressly say the police were already involved. I asked him who would have a gauss meter and could operate it for me. He said he would call a friend in the local Homeland Security office to see if he knew of anyone. DeNoli called me back forty-five minutes later with the name Dexter Tilson and Tilson's phone number. My next call was to Julio.

"Julio, I need a couple of your people to help with a possible stake-out this evening. The stake-out might morph into tailing someone to see where he disposes of a heavy metal object."

"A heavy metal object like a loud speaker?" Julio asked with a chuckle.

"Yeah, more or less. With care, your people will never be noticed. All they would have to do would be to call me so I can get to the site and then they'd have to stay there until I arrive. There's a possibility that the whole thing will be called off, but I'd like a couple of people to be ready to go at darkness."

"This guy who might dump this object is dangerous? Is he the man in the photo?"

"Yes, he may very well be dangerous. And yes, he's the guy in the photo I gave you. I don't want anyone to allow himself to be seen or to confront him in any way."

"They are all good enough to avoid being made. Will they have to testify about this, if they *do* see him dump something?"

"Yes, probably. But only if it all ends in a trial."

"I don't like the sound of this too much, Rick, especially for my younger ones. We'll help, but I think it will be Ricardo and I."

Ricardo Satello was Julio's oldest employee, both in terms of age and longevity. He had proven his reliability when he helped me in rescuing Vince Langlow last year.

"Thanks, Julio! I'll call you in late afternoon and we'll go over the details. I'll cover it myself from then until darkness."

I called the man with the dingus that measured the strength of a magnetic field, a gauss meter. Tilson and I agreed to meet as soon as I could get to his office. I told him I wanted a fast briefing on how he worked with the instrument and what its limitations were. Then, I called Kleidaeker and prevailed upon him to see me at his home at four-thirty and to make sure that Maitland was present. It was twenty minutes after four when Tilson in his van and I in my Acura arrived at Kleidaeker's house. I told Tilson to leave his instrument in the van for the time being. Maitland answered the door telling us that Kleidaeker was washing up and would be with us shortly. I introduced Tilson as my "assistant". There was no invitation to move to the living room, so we all stood in the foyer until Kleidaeker made an appearance.

"Last time we spoke, I found some of your questions impertinent, Mr. Conwright. Now you've hurried me home from the store on a busy day. I'm trying to cooperate, but this had better be good!"

I had decided on a low-key pitch to Kleidaeker while revealing just enough to hopefully push Maitland's buttons. "There is now reason to believe that your friend, Sean Caughlin, did not die a natural death. In fact we believe that he was exposed to a sizable magnetic field while he slept at Hamilton's. The force of that field effectively destroyed his pacemaker. It looks like a calculated murder."

"My God!" said Kleidaeker. "There were folks that had issues with Sean, but who would …?" he sputtered. "How can you know this?"

I was not going to lay all the evidence on the table in front of them, but I thought a little stretching of the facts was in order. "Polarized sheetrock nails were found in the wall of his room," I said. "Now we are looking for the apparatus that generated that magnetic field. I'm hoping you will consent to a search of your property. Mr. Tilson here has a device that will detect the presence of powerful magnets. He will need to walk through your house and grounds, but his work is non-invasive. You are welcome to accompany us. Nothing will be opened or in any way damaged. Will you please let us do that?"

"You must be nuts! Why would I let two strangers go through my home? Why are you picking on me! You make it sound like I'm a suspect!"

Kleidaeker's tone had gone from righteous incredulity to undisguised fury. I wanted to mollify him, but still send a message to Mailtand.

"We are going to ask everyone to cooperate on this," I said calmly. "You aren't being singled out although Mr. Maitland here *did* have the room immediately next to Mr. Caughlin."

"Sure, and somebody else ... Tony Garrison, I think, was in the room on the other side!"

"Listen, Mr. Kleidaeker, no one has accused you of anything at this point. The search won't cost you any effort and will take relatively little time. If you have nothing to fear, let us do this and we'll move on."

"Listen, Conwright, there's no way I'm letting you go over my home with a fine tooth comb! I had nothing to do with this ... this magnetic-force business and I resent your coming here to invade my privacy!"

I had been watching Maitland out of the corner of my eye as he stood in the background. He had remained impassive except when I tossed out my little embellishment about the polarized nails. At that moment, I thought I saw a quick clench of his jaw.

"Have it your way, Mr. Kleidaeker. Tomorrow, I'll bring the police out here with a search warrant. That will be far more of a high-profile event than just letting us go around your place today."

Kleidaeker flashed a look a Maitland, then growled at me, "You try that and I'll have my attorney waiting for you on my doorstep!" he shouted and pointed to the door.

"Whatever! We'll be back!" I said as Maitland practically shoved us out.

We walked toward our vehicles and I told Tilson that I might yet need his services but, if I did not call him tomorrow, he could send me a bill for his time. I drove slowly down the street looking for a few vantage points for the evening's surveillance. I saw at least two that would work. I could not be sure the magnets were there, but if they were, I had a hunch that our visit would lead to their prompt removal. Tilson's van passed me and we both turned onto Cesar Chavez heading south.

I was still thinking about the missing magnets when I noticed a renovation project on an older building on the corner. There was an industrial-size dumpster in the alley behind the building. A chute came down to the dumpster from a top-story window. That gave me an idea. I could still see Tilson's taillights a block ahead. I gunned it and caught up with him at the next stoplight. The traffic stopped when the signal turned red and I jumped out and ran to his window. He rolled the window down and gave me a surprised look. I asked him to follow me back a few blocks. When we arrived at the renovation site, I explained what I had in mind.

"Maybe I just have a wild hair on this one, but I'd like you to run that gauss meter of yours around this dumpster."

"What for? You think that device could be in *there!*"

"Not necessarily, but think about it. The dumpster is conveniently close to the house back there, it's pretty dark in this alley at night, and the thing's already got some metal junk in it so one more item wouldn't be noticed."

"Yeah, I see where you're going. Okay. Give me a minute to get set up."

He brought the gauss meter from the rear of his van and adjusted some settings. When he was satisfied, he began moving it slowly, close to the outer surface of the dumpster. He made several passes on the near side and then repeated the process across the end.

"I am getting a faint reading," he said with some uncertainty as he started on the far side. "Hold on! Yes, now it's much stronger. There's definitely something magnetic in there!"

He moved the device back and forth and indicated to me that the source seemed to be in the far corner and about three feet down from the top of the sidewall. I found a pair of gloves in the car and pulled them on. I scrambled up and over the side into the dumpster. It was filled to within a foot-and-a-half from the top with shattered sheetrock, broken lengths of lumber, crumpled sheet metal, piping, ... even an old toilet. Tilson clung to the outside and shone a flashlight on the debris. It was not easy to shift things around. There were sharp edges everywhere and my footing was unstable. I concentrated on the general area Tilson had indicated. After digging around for ten minutes and putting a rip in my slacks, I saw a more-or-less cubical chunk of silvery metal. I tugged at it. It was heavy. I braced my feet and tugged again and was able to raise it to the top of the debris. Tilson trained the flashlight on it. What I saw, looked almost exactly like the device Lefkowicz had sketched.

SEVENTEEN

Thursday afternoon

I opened my cell phone and, standing in the junk like a true dumpster diver, called DeNoli. He was still at the Justice Center working on a report, but said he would lay it aside and get to us as quickly as possible. Tilson was a witness to my find, so I asked him to hang around until DeNoli arrived. I climbed out of the dumpster and we walked over to my car. I called Julio and told him that I would not need the stake-out. I offered to pay Ricardo an hour's pay just for being willing to help.

Tilson lit up a cigarette. I must have watched him longingly, because he immediately offered me one. I shook my head and told him I'd made it a whole two years without a smoke and thought I had better keep it that way. He asked me if I had always worked as a private investigator. I said, "no, I had been a newspaper reporter at one time". He snapped his fingers and said he thought my name had seemed familiar and that he now remembered reading many of my articles in The Oregonian. About then, DeNoli's car came into view sparing me from having to explain why I left the paper. I introduced Dexter Tilson and we showed DeNoli the dumpster.

"You actually found the magnet thing, eh? You're on a roll, Rick! Was it in there?"

"Yes, thanks, and yes," I said. "We'd been out to the house where the bodyguard lives and works. The homeowner turned me down on the search … pretty emphatically. I think I told you he was one of the poker players. He's still on my radar. Anyway, we had just left his place when I saw this renovation site and this big, inviting dumpster. I thought what the hell, let's run the gauss meter around this thing. And, bingo! Dex's meter very quickly got a strong signal."

"Was it lying right on top?" DeNoli asked.

"It certainly wasn't! Dex's instrument told me approximately where to look, but I had to dig down a couple of feet. Once I got it up on top of the rest of the crap in there, I left it alone and called you. I wanted to give you as clean a chain of custody as possible."

DeNoli boosted himself to the top of the dumpster wall and used Tilson's flashlight to study what I'd found.

"I've already called for a criminalist. That wasn't too popular at this time of day, but she should be coming any minute. Did you wear gloves when you picked it up?"

"Yes. He probably wore gloves when he used it at Hamilton's and no doubt wiped it clean before he pitched it in there, but you might get lucky."

"Let's hope. After we try to raise some prints, I'm going to hunt for an engineer who can tell me how the damn thing works. And, eventually, the D.A. will need an expert witness."

"I talked to a man who could help you on both counts. His name is Reuben Lefkowicz. He'll talk your ear off, but he really seems to know his stuff." I wrote down his name and phone number on a page from my notebook and handed it to DeNoli.

DeNoli took a short statement from Tilson and told him they would be in contact later if necessary. The criminalist arrived and, after she took a few photos, DeNoli helped her get the magnetic-field generator out of the dumpster and into an evidence box. While they were doing that, I listened to a voice-mail message on my phone. It was Agent Masters asking me to call back.

"This is Rick Conwright. You said to call."

"Yeah. I thought you'd be interested to know that our techies swept that ditch where they found Bacon's body with a metal detector. They turned up a slug and ran it through ballistics. I just heard that it was fired from the same gun that you took away from Radich."

"Excellent! Now you've got even more leverage on him. Thanks for letting me know."

"Just remember that what I told you –"

"—stays with me," I finished for him.

Angie's newscast had already ended by the time I got back to the houseboat. I stood on the aft deck and watched a gravel barge pushed by a tug slide through the ebony water. The tug's engine throbbed and its lights punctuated the darkness. I went back inside and cracked a beer. It had been a good ending to the day: rattling Maitland's cage and finding the fiendish device he had built.

⚔

Thursday late afternoon, Antigua

Tommy Baruda had used the pretext of being a retailer who wanted to outsource the custodial work at his store to ask at the Caribbe Bank whom they used. Having the name of the company, it was not hard for him to spot a man in coveralls showing the cleaning company's logo. The man was about to enter the bank half an hour before it closed. Baruda intercepted him on the sidewalk and struck up a conversation. He offered to buy him a Schnapps at a bar across the street. As they hunched over their tiny table, the man savored his drink, but looked leery of being propositioned. Baruda could sense his unease.

"My friend, I have a favor to ask. A favor for which I will pay you well."

The man looked even more uneasy. "Such as?"

"Your work at the bank takes you into rooms where they have computers on the desks?"

"Yeah. Sure."

"And you're alone in there while you're cleaning the room?"

"Yes. Almost always."

"Then here's what I need." He produced the dongle-like device from his pocket. "See the end with the little pins? All I'm asking you to do is to unplug the line from the computer keyboard to the computer and plug the line into this gadget. Then you plug the little-pins end of this gadget into the computer in the same socket where the line was originally. Just be careful that you have the plug ends positioned correctly so the little pins seat in the socket."

"Oh, man. I could get into big trouble for messing with their computers. I could lose my job!"

"Only if someone saw you. I'll pay you three hundred dollars American. If you study the plug beforehand, it should only take you half a minute to fit that in and get the line reconnected. Then, tomorrow night, all you have to do is reverse the process. Disconnect that gadget and reconnect the line into the computer. Another thirty seconds, at most. Like I said, you just have to be sure both times that the connections are tight and in the right socket."

"Three hundred American, huh? I don't think so. Four hundred, maybe I'll consider it."

"Alright. One hundred now, three hundred when I get the device back."

"So if somebody sees it, I loose the three hundred? No. Two hundred and two hundred."

"Okay. Here's two hundred." He passed him the bills under the table. "There's a doughnut shop half a block down the street. It's open all night. When do you get off work?"

"One o'clock."

"Then we meet at the doughnut shop Saturday morning at one."

⇒⇐

It was three o'clock in the morning when the insistent chirping of my phone awakened me. I groped for it in the dark and succeeded in knocking it off the bedside table. The adrenalin surge that accompanies a middle-of-the-night phone call helped me cut through the fog of sleep. I retrieved the phone and answered. "Yeah. Conwright here."

"Rick, it's Marilyn. Marilyn Watson."

That put me on full alert. Marilyn was Justine's sister. Something had to be wrong for her to call me. "What is it, Marilyn?"

"It's Justine. I just got a call from a Seattle hospital. She's tried to commit suicide!"

"Oh Lord!"

"I want to be there to help her, Rick, but Cincinnati's had a freak snow storm. Our airport is closed and is likely to stay that way for another eighteen hours."

I was hit by a maelstrom of emotions. Justine had been high-strung and sensitive all throughout our marriage. But she had also been loving and kind to everyone. There certainly were times when she seemed to resent my level of commitment to the job. Even so, she had been mostly supportive of me being a reporter, at least until Darmsfeld got under my skin. I had not been able to fully decipher the twists and turns of her emotions as our marriage careened off the tracks. I had gone to some counseling sessions with her and had taken some responsibility myself for working long hours and for my unwillingness to let go of the Darmsfeld story. But I had not been able to purge myself of the compelling need to expose him. Justine eventually became sullen and angry and had sought the divorce, but now seemed to have had a change of heart. Last week, she seemed desperately insecure and unlike the woman I had once courted and married. I had found Angie, found a new career, and I had found a better gyroscope to balance my own drives and ambitions. But Justine was distraught, unable to find her way. The startling news that she had been so defeated, so hopeless that she had attempted to take her own life left me hammered with guilt and concern.

"What can I do?" I asked Marilyn.

"Could you get up to Seattle? Just be with her for a few hours until I can get a flight? I'll drive to Indianapolis and get a plane out of there if need be. Once I get there, I'm going to try to convince her to come back to Cincinnati. But she needs someone with her now!"

I thought about the Caughlin case. I thought about Angie. But, I could not say 'no' to Marilyn. "Alright, I'll try to get a morning flight. Where is she?"

Marilyn told me a work co-worker, who usually gave Justine a ride to their weekly bunco game, had discovered her, unconscious, in her bed. The neighbor had called 9-1-1 and they took Justine to Virginia Mason Hospital. I gave Marilyn my cell phone number and told her to call me as soon as she had booked a flight. I was not going to get back to sleep after a conversation like that, so I got on the internet. There were two seats left on the early morning Seattle flight. I took one of them.

I called Angie from the Seattle-Tacoma International Airport. "Listen, Angie. I'm up in Seattle. My ex has tried to commit suicide."

"Oh, Rick. That's terrible."

"Yeah. Her sister called me in the middle of the night from Cincinnati. The airport there is snowed in and she probably won't get a flight until tonight at best. She asked me to go up here and visit Justine in the hospital. She will come as soon as she can get a flight."

"I see," Angie said solemnly. "There isn't anyone else who could be there?"

"I don't know. Probably not. She's only lived in Seattle a little over a year. Anyway, her sister only knew to call me. I wanted to let you know where I was. I should be back sometime late tonight."

I thought I heard a slight coldness in her response.

"That's considerate of you, Rick. I mean for her. Thanks for telling me."

"Listen, Angie. That's all in the past. But she's been having a tougher time than I had realized. I never would have imagined she would try to take her own life! She needs someone to give her a boost. Not for our relationship. That's over. Just for facing her problems and getting on with her life. That's all I'm here for."

"You're a good man, Rick. Call me when you get back."

I told her I loved her and we ended the call.

I caught a cab for the hospital in the gray light of a Seattle dawn. I identified myself to the ward nurse and asked her what had happened. She told me it was an overdose of sleeping pills. The EMTs had found a note. The nurse would not show it to me, but told me that it basically said "I have messed up my marriage and my life. Nothing seems to be working for me. I am sorry. This seems the best way." I asked when I could see Justine. The nurse said she was still in a deep sleep, but should be awake in a couple of hours. I bought a Seattle Times and took the elevator to the hospital cafeteria to have breakfast. I kept wondering what I could say to Justine and I could not concentrate on the paper. My watch showed ten-forty when I finished my third cup of coffee and went back to the ward. The nurse said Justine had just awakened and gave me her room number.

"Hello, Justine," I said to the pale, enervated woman in the bed.

"Rick! I'm so sorry! I was foolish … very foolish."

"They tell me you're going to be just fine. You must never think like that, Justine. There are bumps in the road. Everyone hits a couple in their lives. But there are lots of people who care about you! You –"

"Are you one of them, Rick? A person who cares about me?"

I was certainly concerned for her well being and I wanted her to know that. But I also wanted to be fair to her and that meant not saying anything she might misinterpret. "Of course I am. I wouldn't be here if I weren't. And Marilyn cares about you too. She called me this morning. The airport in Cincinnati is snowed in, but she thinks she'll get here tonight. She's coming to be with you."

"Will you stay?"

"I have to get back to Portland, but I'll be with you until Marilyn arrives. I think they may release you to-day and, if they do, I'll see that you get home."

Her eyelids drooped and she seemed to doze for a minute or so. When her eyes opened, she gave me a questioning look. "Do you still think I should go back to Cincinnati?"

"I believe you could be much happier there. I know Marilyn thinks so, too. You'd be back on familiar ground. You'd have old friends to be with until you get your groove back."

She gave a wry smile. "You think I can get it back, huh?"

"Sure you can! You're intelligent. You're a trained technical writer. You're energetic. You just need to re-gain some confidence ... find your old self."

"If I go there, can I call you if I get blue?"

This was not getting any easier. "I'm not sure that's a good idea. I'm the same old me. I have a new profession, but I'm still working crazy hours, still plugged into the job. If the failure of our marriage is a big part of what's bothering you, the best thing would be to live a new life, a life with new possibilities ... a new job ... perhaps a new relationship. When you are back on your feet, send a note or a card and tell me the good stuff. But you have to use your own resiliency to fight the blues."

Her eyes got heavy again. "The best thing ... a new life," she half mumbled. She fluffed her pillow and man-aged a smile. "You always were a straight talker, Rick. It was sweet of you to come up here. Oh, I'm getting so sleepy." She relaxed and was immediately asleep.

I came back to have lunch in her room. The at-tending doctor had informed me that she would be discharged in mid-afternoon. I told him I would take

Justine to her apartment and make sure there were no sleeping pills lying around. I called the airline and arranged to catch a late-evening flight instead of my scheduled eight-thirty plane. Justine's color was much better when we left the hospital. Her apartment on Capitol Hill was clean and airy. I snuck into her kitchen and wrapped all her sharp knives in a towel and hid the lot. Justine called her sister and told her that she was planning on returning with her to Cincinnati. Marilyn said she had made it to Indianapolis and had booked a flight from there that should put her into Seattle at seven in the evening. She also said that she would stay and help Justine wind up her affairs in Seattle. I gathered that Marilyn had even offered Justine a place to stay for a while until she found her own place.

As soon as Marilyn arrived at the apartment, I told Justine that, with the extra time needed for airport security checks, I had to get going. She gave me a kiss on the cheek and thanked me again. I thought how fragile and fateful our lives could be with a lucky break here, a crushing disappointment there, and, for her, a bit of a workaholic spouse. And we only have our own fortitude to keep us going.

※ ※

Saturday, very early morning in Antigua

Baruda had been waiting in the doughnut shop for twenty minutes. He had started checking his watch every couple of minutes when the custodian walked in. Baruda ordered them maple bars and decaffeinated coffee.

"Do you have it?"

"Yeah," the man said and placed what appeared to be a lunch sack on the counter. "There were no problems. I was alone in the room both times."

"Very good. Here's something for you." Baruda passed him the two hundred dollars inside an unmarked envelope. "Drink up. The less time we're seen together, the better."

Baruda rang Hollister's number as soon as he reached his car. By pre-arrangement, he would leave a simple message on her answering machine if the keylogger operation had been pulled off successfully.

"The photos you ordered have been developed," he said and then hung up.

━┼┼━

Saturday, Mid morning in Antigua

Baruda was short on sleep and was not quite his usual, amiable self when he rang the door chime at Hollister's house. She answered the door wearing a light-blue silk sweater and levis. He handed her the keylogger.

"That was quick work," she said. "If your guy connected it properly, I should have the password I need. This could take me an hour or so, possibly even more if the bank's system architecture is unusually complex. Why don't you go down to the harbour and have some lunch? I'll call you on your cell when I have what you want."

Baruda knew he was not welcome to look over her shoulder and would not understand what she was doing even if he had been welcome. He waved good-bye and drove down to the small community hugging the shoreline.

Hollister entered the system using the password captured by the keylogger. She spent the next thirty minutes getting familiar with the file structure the bank used. She found an alphabetic table of depositors and their account numbers. She wrote down the account number for Portino. The charity turned out to be "Helping Kids" rather than "Kids Help". She added that number to her list. Then, she navigated to the server that contained transaction details and to the subdirectory that accessed the data on incoming wire transfers. She guessed, correctly, that all the data in that portion of the server would be encrypted. Over her career, Hollister had learned the workings of many encryption algorithms. And, she had managed to add most of their routines to her personal library. Choosing the one she judged was most likely to decipher the encryption used by the bank, she went to work.

Hollister keyboarded the variables she knew: the amount and the destination accounts. She added two additional variables that Baruda had not been sure of: that the originating nation was the United States and the most likely date. Her first attempt failed. She moved the date back one day and tried again: another failure. She switched to the charity account. After some seconds, her monitor flashed a validation message and a line item came up in clear text. She saw "OMBKUSPDO:US$40000" followed by "TCBKANTSJ" and the account number for "Helping Kids". She could have captured the image with her screen-shot utility program, but she wanted no traces left on her hard drive so she copied the codes by hand.

Hollister exited the bank's system and browsed the web to find the home page of the Society for Worldwide Interbank Financial Telecommunications. This organization was the one that issued the standardized transfer instructions known by the Society's acronym, the SWIFT codes. She found the necessary link on the Society's home page and soon learned that "OMBKUSPD" referred to a transfer from the Oregon Merchants' Bank in the United States and, more specifically, in Portland, Oregon. "TCBKANTSJ" turned out, not surprising her, to refer to the transferee bank, The Caribbe Bank in Antigua located in the city of St. John's. She picked up her phone and called Baruda. She had what he had asked for.

EIGHTEEN

Saturday morning, Portland

I got home Friday night too weary to do anything but pile into bed. The next morning, with strong coffee in hand, I heard my phone chirping. It was Tommy Baruda in Antigua.

"Baruda? Ah, good morning or good whatever-it-is down there. I hope you have what I need. Or were you just calling to tell me that you've spent five-thousand dollars already?"

"Ha, ha, ha! Well, let us say it's both," said Baruda in his rich patois.

"Let's hear what you found out first."

"Very well. Your man Maitland does have an account here. In the Commonwealth Bank."

"Yes!"

Baruda continued, "And he has recently received a large deposit into that account. To be exact,

Mr. Conwright, forty thousand US dollars-worth about five weeks ago."

"That sounds like the type of transfer that I'm interested in. Could you find out the source of the deposits?"

"Only up to a point. But whoever they are, they're covering their tracks very carefully. The deposit to Maitland's account was made in cash by an individual: an individual whom the teller at Maitland's bank did not recognize and who gave no name."

"That's possible?"

"This is Antigua, Mr. Conwright. Many things are possible here. In any case, I began to wonder if the depositor could have been Maitland's old partner, Jerry Portino. Using an old photo, I got a positive ID from the teller."

"Good thinking!"

"Thank you. Then, you see, I had to locate Portino's account. That turned out to be in a different bank, The Caribbe Bank. I guessed that Portino may have only been a conduit. So I needed to examine his account information."

"Were you able to *see* his account!"

"Well, let's just say I know certain things about it. Using some, ah, acquaintances to assist me in this whole endeavor entailed some costs, however. Forty-four hundred American dollars to be precise. In any case, we found an identical deposit into Portino's account by wire transfer from the United States. The date of the transfer was the day before the deposit at Maitland's bank. Incidentally, it was not Portino's personal account. It was the account of a charity, called 'Helping Kids,' that he runs."

"That would be pretty risky in the States. The state has oversight of charities and misuse of donated funds often gets discovered."

"Yes. It is the same here. I checked with the government office where charities have to register. They told me there was no such charity registered there. But I can tell you for a fact that this organization does have fundraisers and does receive donations and does support children's causes. So they must ignore the law to gain more flexibility, shall we say, in their operations. Portino is known as a... I think you call them 'wheeler-dealers', eh?"

"So his donors can't take the gifts they make off their taxes?"

"I would think not, but I suspect many of his donors don't pay taxes anyway."

"I see. This wire transfer you mentioned. You have the transfer information?"

"I have the international bank codes ... they call them SWIFT codes. The sending bank was ... ah, yes ... was the Oregon Merchants' Bank in Portland, Oregon."

"Excellent. Do you know whose account the transfer was charged to?"

"No. That information is not included in the transfer data. I think you can assume that the funds came from someone with an account at that bank, however. My understanding is that a bank isn't like Western Union where you can just walk in with cash and make a wire transfer without even opening an account."

"I get it. In any case, you did well! Were your methods such that we could get a subpoena – or whatever court order acts like a subpoena in Antigua – to get copies of those records?"

"Ah, I would not say you could use my efforts to establish grounds for a subpoena. No, I would not say that. You wanted results quickly and the information you sought was sensitive and protected by bank policy. In fact, it was encrypted. Do you understand?"

"Yes. If it comes to that, we will have to come after the information some other way. But you got me the information I needed. You can send me your bill."

"I will do that. Unfortunately, the bill will be a little over my high estimate. Say sixty-eight hundred total, so another forty-eight hundred American. You can send the money as you did with the retainer: to the Commonwealth Bank in St. John's. And in my bill, some things will simply have to be described as 'miscellaneous out of pocket expenses'."

There were two messages on my machine. The first one was from Justine's sister, Marilyn, telling me that Justine seemed to be returning to normalcy. The second call had been from Bill Ellison at Great Western Bank. He left me both his office and his home phone numbers. As it was Saturday morning, I called him at home.

"Mr. Ellison, this is Rick Conwright."

"Yes, Rick! I can tell you where Mrs.Caughlin maintains an individual account here in Portland."

"Thank you. That will be most helpful."

"The account is at the Oregon Merchants' Bank. It's over in St. John's on Lombard Street. As for Carl Maitland, he has a checking account at U.S.Bank's Lloyd Center Branch. I did manage to learn that it's a small account. It has never been over three figures."

I again told Ellison how grateful I was for his help. More and more of the pieces were starting to click into place. The bank GeorgeAnn used was the same bank that transferred the funds that eventually reached Maitland's account in Antigua. I was not ready to believe that to be a mere coincidence. And her bank was in the neighborhood in north Portland known as St. John's. Maitland's bank had its main office in St. John's, Antigua. That certainly *was* a coincidence but, even so, it seemed like a good sign. Now, I had to find out if the account from which the transfer was made belonged to GeorgeAnn Caughlin.

I called Baruda back.

"Keep your billing open. I have a little more work for you. I have just discovered that my suspected co-conspirator up here *does* have an account at that Oregon Merchants' Bank. It's a small, one-location bank, but we still need to tie that transfer to her particular account. Her name is GeorgeAnn Caughlin." I spelled it for him. "I have an idea how you could help tie that in for me."

"I'll do what I can. What's your idea?"

"You said they ran the money through a charity of some sort. If you could say you were working for the charity and had to –"

"Had to verify the donor who made a forty-thousand dollar contribution?"

"Exactly! You'll have to polish your act. Banks don't like to confirm details to strangers and very rarely do."

"Quite so. I'll make an appropriate inquiry Monday morning. I'll let you know right away if they will confirm the 'gift'."

⚊⚊

Angie had Sunday off and she had come to the houseboat a little after noon. I filled her in on my trip to Seattle and told her that Justine's sister had arrived and was going to help Justine move to Cincinnati. Angie agreed that that was a good solution and said she was relieved that I could disengage. Despite the slightly territorial shading, I took that to mean everything was just fine between us.

Angie had been wanting me to teach her how to row on the river. Sunday was a dry, calm-water day and this was our first chance to have her try it out. I borrowed a single scull from a neighbor and got my own scull down from the roof of the houseboat. We practiced close to shore for over an hour until Angie felt somewhat comfortable balancing in the slender craft and getting her oars in and out of the water smoothly. After our afternoon on the water, I played a CD of the Woody Herman band from the sixties and made us Margaritas. Our conversation turned to the Caughlin case.

"I used that PI that your friend, Beth, told you about. Between him and a banking friend here in Portland, I've had good luck following the money. I know now that Maitland was paid off to the tune of forty-thousand dollars. The funds came to his bank in Antigua on a deliberately obscure pathway, but they originated from an account in a Portland bank. And GeorgeAnn has an account at the very same bank."

"So she sent the money?"

"I can't prove that yet. The transfer codes don't include the originating account number, so we can't come at it that way. But I suspect that she sent the money to Maitland via some kind of a flakey charity that his former partner runs. This PI that I'm using in Antigua is going to try to get the bank to confirm that GeorgeAnn made a specified contribution to that charity. If that works, we have her linked to paying off her hit man. She will likely have some explanation of why she transferred so much money to an obscure charity even if we can show that the money came from her account. And she will probably try to claim she had no idea it was moved from the charity to Maitland."

Angie swirled her drink thoughtfully. "Is there any way I can help?"

"Yeah, I think there is. In fact, you could be the key to 'phase two' of my plan. But, we won't get to phase two unless I can get confirmation that she sent the money."

"So what *is* your phase two, lover?" Angie asked with a smile over the top of her glass.

"We have to rattle both of them ... get them to feel the pressure and do something rash ... something that will unequivocally show they murdered Sean Caughlin. Since the money was ostensibly sent to this charity, Helping Kids, my idea is that you go interview her. Tell her you're investigating a series on scams involving Portland donors and overseas charities. Tell her you know she's made a substantial contribution to a charity in Antigua and that you've learned it is unregistered and that its operations appear to be unaudited."

"Won't she ask how I found out about her 'donations'?"

"Yeah, she probably will. You could hide behind that time-tested journalistic tradition of not revealing your sources. You can say you're about to launch an in-depth investigation in Antigua. Between that and the 'unrevealed source,' we ought to make her very nervous."

"This next week, I'm pulling the mid-day newscast, and then I'm through for the day. I can help you with this tomorrow afternoon if you get the account confirmation. I like it, Rick! I think our producer would even agree to provide a cover story on the scam series in case she checks with the station."

"Great! Don't mention her by name, though. Just say you'll be contacting some local people and that your investigation will go best if you can use that modest subterfuge."

"This will certainly get my producer's curiosity up, but he'll probably let me play it my way."

"You'll be great at pushing her buttons, Angie. Just be careful not to turn your back. If she has had her own husband killed, she has deadly instincts."

"Right! I'll figure out a way to slip it in early on that the studio knows exactly where I've gone. But, if I pull it off, she won't have any reason to connect me to your investigation. My guess is that she'll either come up with some gushy story about the poor kids in Antigua or else will fake concern about being swindled. Either way, she won't make any move against me. Well, maybe she'll make some threat about me invading her privacy if she were to be named in the series, but that's the worst."

She finished her drink and stood up. "Are you ready to bake that halibut? All that rowing made me hungry!"

⇒⊹⇐

It was a little after nine-thirty Monday morning, Pacific Coast Time, when Tommy Baruda placed his call to the Oregon Merchants' Bank. He asked for the person handling wire transfers. A man who introduced himself as Dick Romberg came on the line.

"Hello." Baruda said. "This is Nelson Truback. I'm calling from Antigua. I'm a management trainee with a charity here called Helping Kids. I have a big problem. I'm kind of embarrassed to tell you the situation, but here's what happened. I'm in a probationary period and one of my assignments is to generate and send out thank-you letters and receipts to our donors. My boss gave me the list of last month's contributions to work off of. I was shredding a bunch of papers laying on my desk and, Lord help me, I accidentally stuffed the donor list into the shredder. I have photocopies of checks, but all I have for wire transfers are the SWIFT numbers and the amounts. My boss is very strict and I'm afraid he'll wash me out if he finds out I destroyed the list."

"So you think one of the transfers came from us?"

"Yes. I know that much. And I have a vague memory that the donor from Portland was a Mrs. Kaufman or Coffman." He spelled them out. "Could you possibly tell me if she sent the forty-thousand dollar donation? She is obviously an important donor and I can't afford to screw this up."

"Well, giving out information like that would be quite irregular. Can't you use your computer database to get the name and address?"

"No. I thought of that. But she's a brand new donor and, believe it or not, we're not fully computerized.

Most of our records are still done by hand. And if I ask other people, it will for sure get back to my boss! For all I know, the list I shredded may have been the one and only for that month."

"We're really not supposed to verify account information … but …well, maybe I can help you out this once. You said you're at Helping Kids?"

"That's right."

"What's the account number and bank?" Romberg asked.

Baruda checked his notes from Joyce Hollister and gave the number. "We bank at The Caribbe Bank."

"And you think the donor's name was Coffman?"

"Yes, or something close to that."

"Hold on." There was a pause and Baruda assumed the man was checking his database. Baruda hoped it was that and not that he was calling Helping Kids on another line. He came back to the phone after several minutes,.

"Alright. Yes. Forty thousand. It isn't quite the name you remembered, however. She spells her name C-A-U-G-H-L-I-N. Her first name is GeorgeAnn, all one word and capital A."

"Thank you so much! You probably saved my job! I'm very grateful."

Baruda dialed Conwright's number.

⇒⇕⇐

Tommy Baruda called me in mid morning.

"Conwright, it's Tommy Baruda. I got through to the bank in Portland a few minutes ago. They bought my little story and I have what you wanted to know. Your Mrs. Caughlin *did* initiate that wire transfer to Helping Kids. It was confirmed at forty-thousand dollars by a man in charge of transfers named Dick Romberg."

"You ought to be a con artist! Good work! You must've laid it on pretty thick!"

"Oh, yeah. In our line of work, you know we have to play a role now and then."

GeorgeAnn did not just lie to me about knowing Maitland, she fed him forty-thousand dollars of blood money!

NINETEEN

Monday afternoon

Angie and I agreed that she would approach GeorgeAnn in late afternoon. I called Julio back and asked if he and Ricardo could help me with the surveillance and possible tailing of Maitland starting in late afternoon. They were both willing, despite my calling off the previous stakeout, and we decided that Julio would use his car and Ricardo would be on his motorcycle. I spent the rest of the day paying bills and finishing my final report to the client on another case.

⇒⊹⊹⇐

Angie realized she would have a problem getting past the security man in the lobby of the condo high-rise where GeorgeAnn lived if she arrived uninvited. Her research revealed that GeorgeAnn had served as a trustee of the Oregon Symphony Foundation. Angie called ahead, saying she was working on a story about prominent Portland women and charities.

"I don't know, Ms. Richards. I enjoy your newscasts and specials, but I've just recently lost my husband and I'm really not up for being interviewed."

"Yes, I know about Mr. Caughlin's passing. You certainly have my condolences. I was thinking you would be one of the central figures in my piece. Your carrying on in the face of great sorrow would be so inspiring."

"That's flattering. I do enjoy helping."

Oh, right, Angie thought: getting real involved by using your pen to write checks donating your husband's money.

"But," GeorgeAnn continued, "I really need my privacy at a time like this."

"I understand. Well, perhaps you could just give me some background and a quote or two. We can leave out your bereavement if you wish. I still think you would make a wonderful central figure."

Angie thought her best chance was to play to the woman's vanity. She was right.

"Very well. When would you want to come by?"

"Let's see. It's a quarter to five now. I have the rest of the afternoon open. I can be there in fifteen minutes and it shouldn't take more than half an hour. I won't bring a camera-person until after you and I edit my notes of our conversation."

"That sounds reasonable. I appreciate that. Alright, then. I will see you here around five."

Angie was punctual and the lobby attendant at The Elizabeth said she was expected. In the penthouse, GeorgeAnn greeted her wearing minimal makeup and a simple, black Donna Karen dress. Angie thought the lack of makeup and the dress were affectations for the role of the supposedly grieving widow. She guessed it would have been a little different had she brought a camera-person along. They chatted for a few minutes about the late Mr. Caughlin and work on a television news desk. When the polite preliminaries were over, Angie opened her notebook to signal that she was ready to begin the interview.

"So the central theme of this story is going to be the increasing fraud related to charitable giving."

"Oh! Well, we never had a problem with *that* at the symphony!"

"Of course not. No, I meant the scams that seem to be connected to some Caribbean charities. We think it's possible that prominent people in Portland may have been taken advantage of."

"Again, I would not know anything about that."

"But that's really the heart of the problem, isn't it? The better the scam, the less likely the victim is to realize they've been swindled."

"I suppose so, but why are you asking me about things like that?"

"Well, because of your recent generosity to Helping Kids, of course."

GeorgeAnn visibly paled, then rose and walked over to a wet bar concealed behind louvered doors.

"May I offer you a drink?" she asked.

"No thank you,"

GeorgeAnn nodded and poured herself a stiff Canadian Club and soda. "I don't make a point of publicizing my charitable support. How did you find out about that?"

"My source in St. John's has concerns about how Helping Kids has been run. He tells me that you have made a large five-figure donation in recent weeks."

"I resent that Ms. Richards! That someone would be snooping around about my gifts!"

"Please understand, Mrs. Caughlin. *I* did not do the snooping. My informant simply suspects that all is not as it should be with that charity. When he heard of the subject of my piece, he simply came forward with things he knew. If he's right, it seems you should be grateful to him, perhaps even to me for the warning."

"Possibly. But it still seems like an invasion of my privacy even if you aren't the one who snooped."

Angie ignored the barb and kept going. "I've learned that Helping Kids is not even registered with the Antiguan authorities. It isn't my intention to portray you, or anyone else who has given, as gullible or careless. I was thinking more of 'you just can't be too careful ... these unscrupulous people could be exploiting children to take your money'."

GeorgeAnn gave Angie a penetrating stare. "So you think I've been swindled?"

"I can't say that just yet. I certainly hope not. We'll be doing a lot of follow up investigation down there, alerting the authorities, checking records ... that sort of thing, before we can be sure. If the charity does turn out to be not on the up-and-up, we'll follow the money. It should be a very helpful story for our community and it might even help to get your money back."

"This is all very distressing! I hope it's not true and that Helping Kids is completely legitimate. The children are adorable and I'm sure they really *do* need help. I trust you will keep me informed. I intend to contact my attorney, just in case this *does* turn out to be some kind of a scam. And I think, in any case, she will want to know the name of your 'informant'."

Angie had to give her credit. In the short time it took her to fix herself a drink, GeorgeAnn regained her composure and became the indignant, worried victim. She even had the presence of mind to pretend she knew about the poor children.

"If we have any breakthroughs, I'm sure you'll be informed. Tell me, why did you pick this particular charity to be helped by your generosity?"

"I don't see that's any of your business, Ms. Richards," GeorgeAnn snapped. Then she seemed to think that taking that tack could be a mistake. She continued in a calmer tone, "All I can say is they must have sensed how their message resonated with me: the terrible poverty ... the need. They kept coming back with more pitches. Finally, I just felt compelled to help."

"It seems you alone made the contribution. Was your late husband not as enthusiastic? Did he have reservations about the charity?"

"Really! I think this interview has gone far enough! Our family decisions are surely none of your business."

"Well, I noticed that your gifts to the symphony, for example, have always been from both of you, so I –"

"Enough, Ms. Richards! I feel that you came to see me under false pretenses. You never said anything about fraud or Caribbean charities when you called me. As I said, we are through. Will you please see yourself out?"

Angie called Rick as soon as she reached her car. She told him that the widow seemed tense and angry at the end of their conversation. He said he would be in position to watch GeorgeAnn's building within fifteen minutes. Angie sat in her car reviewing the notes she had taken. She had parked almost across from the opening to the underground garage in the condo building. She finished looking through her notes and was about to start her engine when she saw a black Jaguar speed up the ramp. Rick had mentioned that GeorgeAnn drove a black Jaguar. It was clear to

Angie what she had to do. She did not hesitate. She let one car get in between them and then began following the black Jag.

After four blocks, the Jaguar pulled to the curb in front of a restaurant called Bluehour. A woman got out and walked into the restaurant. Angie believed the woman was GeorgeAnn, but could not be sure. She drove half a block ahead, parked in a loading zone, and hurried back to the Bluehour. She did not want to show herself inside, so she planned to cross the street and watch from behind a delivery truck. Before she stepped off the curb, she glimpsed the woman through the window. The woman was definitely GeorgeAnn. She was talking on a phone not far from the hostess's podium. Angie pulled up the hood on her jacket and remained standing in front of the window. GeorgeAnn was gesturing vigorously with her arm to the person on the other end even though he or she could not see her. Their apparently emphatic conversation ended after GeorgeAnn had taken pen and paper from her purse and scribbled intensely. GeorgeAnn hung up the phone and turned toward the door. Angie closed the hood more tightly around her face and walked briskly toward her car.

＝╪═╪═

I had just reached The Elizabeth. I was heading for the shadowed place where I intended to stand while watching the garage exit when Angie called.

"Rick, I hadn't even driven away when GeorgeAnn left in her car! I followed her to the Bluehour on Thirteenth, but all she did was use the phone. I'm guessing she called Maitland. I watched through a window and it looked like a tense call. She seemed very agitated. Toward the end of the call, she wrote down something fairly complicated ... maybe directions for them to meet somewhere. Now she's heading west toward four-oh-five. I'm two cars behind ... now we're at a southbound on-ramp ... oh, shit! The light's changing. I'm stuck behind another car and she got through!"

"Try to catch up!"

"This light is taking forever to change. Okay, I'm moving onto four-of-five. Oh, oh. I can't see her anywhere!"

"Damn! Great work though! You've obviously spooked her. I've got Julio and Ricardo watching Kleidaeker's place to see if Maitland leaves. I'll check with them. If they were setting up a meeting, let's hope Julio can tail them from that end!"

"Call me, if they see him leave. Can I come with you?"

"No dice, Angie. They're dangerous people. If we *do* catch them doing something incriminating, there's no telling how they would react. I don't want you anywhere near them!"

"I guess you're right, Rick, but there's a great story cooking here. You know I want in on the wrap up."

"Sure, and you know you'll get a scoop when it's over. Pull off the freeway and give me the nearest intersection. I'll join you for a few minutes and you can tell me about your talk with GeorgeAnn."

On my way to rendezvous with Angie, I called Julio. He said they'd been watching for about twenty minutes and no one had left the house.

"All right. Stay with it. There's a chance that a woman driving a black Jag will come to him. If that happens, call me right away."

I saw Angie's car at the curb. There was a small parking lot signed "customers only" across the street. I pulled in there and walked to Angie's car. She had finished giving me a blow-by-blow report of her questions and GeorgeAnn's answers when my phone chirped. It was Julio.

"Rick. A fairly tall man just left the house. He wasn't limping so I figure he's your guy."

"You have that picture I gave you. Did the guy look like the photo?"

"We're not that close. Even through the binoculars, it was hard to be sure. But, yeah, he looked pretty much the same. He's driving a white Ford Taurus. We're ready to trail him if you give the word."

"Do it! It's got to be Maitland. Keep calling in to let me know where you are and I'll try to catch up."

TWENTY

Monday, early evening

Kleidaeker's house fronted on the park in the desirable Laurelhurst district. It was due east of my location, but on the other side of the Willamette River. I got on Burnside and headed east. As I crossed the river, I noticed an evening fog was settling in. Julio phoned to say they were headed south on Cesar Chevez Avenue. There were enough stoplights on that street that I could not catch up unless I could anticipate where they were heading. I could not. Cesar Chavez ran south for almost four miles. They could be heading for the 205 freeway that would take them northeast or southwest. They could be heading for the Sellwood district. They could be heading for the semi-rural industrial area where the sprawling factory-campus of Precision Castparts was located. Until Maitland chose a different street, I had no choice but to stay on

Burnside and turn south on Cesar Chavez far behind the rest of them.

Soon after I turned, Julio called again to say they had turned west on Powell. Now, Maitland could be going downtown or staying on the eastside and heading for the Westmoreland neighborhood. Or, he could be about to get on I-5. The rush-hour traffic was going east on Powell so I was able to make good time westbound. Julio called back to say they had followed Maitland onto I-5 southbound and into the congestion of the early-evening traffic. The fog had thickened and everyone had to slow down. Julio reported from time-to-time and said they were having some difficulty staying behind Maitland with all the on-ramp traffic and Maitland's constant lane changes. He said Ricardo had moved in, one car behind Maitland because it was easier for him to hold position on the motorcycle.

I had joined the southward flow on the freeway when Julio next called.

"Rick, I've lost them! The damn fog! I thought I saw Ricardo take the Highway Ninety-nine exit. I followed, but it turned out to be a different motorcyclist. I'm getting back on I-5, but now I have no idea where Maitland is. I hope Ricardo is still with him!"

"Damn! I've made it as far as the Terwilliger curves. Let's both stay on I-5 and hope that Ricardo can call us."

Almost ten minutes went by before Ricardo called.

"Rick, he got away from me! He took the Durham exit and got in the right lane. The light at the end of the off-ramp turned red and everyone stopped. Your man was the front car on the ramp. There was one car between us. I figured he was going to head west into the Bridgeport Village shopping area. Then the son of a bitch ran the red light and turned *left* toward Lake Oswego! I was going to run the light myself, but just then, two semis came rolling out of the fog westbound. I couldn't risk getting in front of them, so I had to wait. I got myself into the left lane and made the turn as soon as the light changed but, by then, he was gone."

I cursed as Ricardo told his story. "Did you look around on that road heading east?"

"Sure, man. I went down that Lower Boones Ferry Road past two stoplights and the railroad tracks, but no sign of that white Taurus. I even went a little further, but nothing doing … nada!"

"Okay. Isn't there a Fuddrucker's near that freeway exit?"

"Yeah, there is. On the northeast side of I-5"

"Okay. Let's meet there. Julio got fooled in the fog and followed the wrong motorcycle. I'll tell him to go there too and we'll figure out what to do next."

I slammed my fist onto the steering wheel. Our plan had worked. We had scared them into action … they were probably going to meet to compare notes and figure out how to explain the lies and the money. But then our plan went off the rails because of rush hour, the weather, and stoplights. The fog closed in on my car like a smothering presence. We had lost the physical trail, so I had to project ahead … had to deduce where they were heading. By the time I reached the Durham exit, I had just about concluded that that was impossible. Then I remembered something Kleidaeker had said when I first interviewed him: that Maitland sometimes worked remodeling an unoccupied rental house Kleidaeker owned in Rivergrove.

I entered the hamburger palace and waved to Ricardo who was sitting at a table by the window. I opened my notebook and paged through until I found Kleidaeker's phone number.

"Mr. Kleidaeker, this is Rick Conwright. You said something to me about a rental house you had in Rivergrove. Can you give me the address?"

"Why should I do that? What's going on?"

"I told you we have strong reasons to believe that Sean Caughlin was murdered. It is very important that I talk to Carl Maitland again. Am I correct that he is not at your house?"

"Yes. He asked for two or three hours off. He said a friend from Chicago was in town and had just called him. They wanted to get together. What's that got to do with my rental?"

I had to decide right then whether I still considered Kleidaeker a serious suspect. He was an odd guy.

He had reasons to dislike, maybe even hate, Caughlin. But I could not see him paying Maitland to kill anyone.

"I don't think he has any friend from Chicago in town, Mr. Kleidaeker. I think he is deeply implicated in Caughlin's death. I think he is meeting a conspirator in the Lake Oswego area as we speak. It could be that the meeting is at your unoccupied rental."

"Dear God! I hired the man to protect me and you're saying he may be a killer!"

"I could be wrong, but the safest thing for you to do would be to spend the night in a hotel somewhere. Think up some excuse to stay away from him, until this all gets straightened out. But please, can you give me that address?"

"Alright." He gave me a street number on Childs Road. "Make the turn at that gas station onto McEwan and then turn off on Lakeview to get to Childs."

"If I have to, will you give me permission to enter?"

"You're laying an awful lot on me out of the blue! But, yes, if you have to, I give permission."

"If everything is normal at the rental, I'll call to let you know. Do you have a cell phone? Give me that number and then you must leave your house!"

He gave me the number and I said goodbye to a shaken Kleidaeker. I saw Julio arriving as I finished the call. The three of us huddled at a table.

"I really want to see who Maitland is meeting and what he's going to do. Okay, we lost the Taurus, but I have one last idea. I might be completely off base, but there's a chance I know where he went. His boss owns a rental house very near here, in Rivergrove. It's empty at the moment and Maitland's been doing some remodeling there. I'm going to go by and check it out. I have the owner's permission to enter. You men can go there with me if you're willing, but you can go home if you'd rather. If he isn't there, we're done for the night anyway."

"Hey man, we'll watch your back," said Ricardo.

Julio nodded vigorously. "Si, amigo. We're going with you."

TWENTY-ONE

Monday evening

Rivergrove is an older community of modest homes and apartments. But, due to its proximity to affluent Lake Oswego, it is gradually becoming gentrified.

I followed Kleidaeker's directions and saw the address on a roadside mailbox. We drove past the house and parked on the narrow shoulder. Childs was the last street before the Tualatin River. The house was an older, craftsman-style bungalow with shake siding. It was on the river side of the street and I guessed that meant it had river frontage. I told Julio and Ricardo to stay in Julio's car while I scouted the layout. The house appeared to be on a deep lot, but it had narrow set-backs on the sides. A tall laurel hedge ran the length of the property on the east side and a six-foot-high wooden fence bounded the west side. I could see no lights on in the front of the house, but there was a glow of light from farther back.

I crept along the east side over a rangy lawn with long, dew-sodden grass. When I came to the room with the light, I saw the window was covered by a sheer curtain. I could see through the curtain if I stood close to the window. I moved to the near side of the window and peered inside. The walls were stripped to the studs. The carpet had been removed and hand tools lay on the subfloor. The light was coming from a powerful work-light on a long extension cord that disappeared into some other room. I risked leaning in front of the window a little further and saw GeorgeAnn lying on the floor. Her ankles and wrists were bound with duct tape. Her mouth was covered with the tape. She writhed and struggled futilely against her bonds. I leaned a little further and saw Maitland bending over a coil of electrical wire.

I stepped back into the shadows and reached for my cell phone. DeNoli answered my call and said he was in his car driving home.

"Paul, I'm in Rivergrove." I gave him the address. "The house backs on the Tualatin River. Maitland is inside the house. It belongs to his employer, Marshal Kleidaeker. He's got GeorgeAnn Caughlin in there, bound and gagged!"

"Holy shit! You must have spooked them for sure. But why has he turned against her!"

"I don't know! Can you get the sheriff out here fast? With a hostage situation, they better bring a SWAT team and a negotiator."

"Right! Are you alone?"

"I have a couple of guys with me, waiting out on the street."

"Okay. Stay outside. I'll call the sheriff and come there myself as fast as I can."

I went back to the window. Maitland had pulled on gloves. It looked to me like he was getting ready to kill her. She surely had ordered her husband's death, but I could not stand by and watch Maitland commit murder. I ran toward the back of the house. I rounded the corner and saw that the back yard sloped gently to the river. I could make out a small dock through the fog. It looked like an outboard skiff was moored to the dock. I had turned toward the steps that led up to a back door when I slipped on a moldy leaf. I gyrated like a dervish as I regained my balance. Suddenly, I was a human statue in glaring light.

An outdoor floodlight was mounted over the back porch. It must have been activated by a motion sensor. I knew that if I was going to get inside the house, I had to get away from the light. I sprinted back around the corner of the house and waited for it to turn off. A minute later, there was darkness again. I leaned against the shakes waiting for my night vision to return. I called the Portland police emergency number.

Speaking softly, I gave my name to the sergeant who answered and said that I was a PI working closely with DeNoli on a case.

"Paul is on his way to join me at a location in Rivergrove. This is a hostage situation at best and, worst case, it will turn into a homicide! I'm going to leave my cell phone on. Put me on a recorder, but do *not* have anyone speaking. Let it act like I'm wearing a wire."

The sergeant sounded dubious, but granted my request. I put the phone in my breast pocket and moved at a sloth-like pace as close to the foundation of the house as I could get. I took the stairs two at a time in ultra-slow motion. The light stayed off and I stepped under the porch roof and out of the range of the motion sensor. I had my Beretta and a set of picklocks. I practiced with the picks from time to time and was confident that I could use them to get in if the back door was locked. I tried the door knob and the door opened easily. There was no indication that the SWAT team had arrived. Every second mattered. I could not wait for them. I stepped silently into a dark kitchen.

I started as I felt cold steel at the base of my neck.

"Nice and quiet, mister. Now throw your gun to the side and walk slowly ahead. There's a door to the right. Go through that."

I tossed the gun and he marched me forward. We entered the lit room with GeorgeAnn still on the floor. I realized, too late, that the unlocked door had been an invitation to an ambush. Maitland had known I was out there. In the light, he saw whom he had captured.

"Conwright! You just can't help sticking your fucking nose in where it doesn't belong! Brace against that door!"

I leaned on the door as Maitland patted me down. He took the cell phone, my little Maglight, the picklocks, and my wallet. He dropped them in a pile next to the wall.

"So you were packing tonight. No bear spray. Terry's lawyer told me all about your moves with the bear spray."

"Terry?"

"Oh! You haven't figured that out, huh? My half-brother Terry Radich."

Terry, the diamond smuggler. No, I thought, I had not figured that out. "So you're in the blood-diamond business too?"

"Get down on the floor on your stomach, Conwright," he ordered.

I lowered myself to the floor beside GeorgeAnn, but I stayed on my side so I could face him. "The diamonds?" I repeated.

"No. Not the diamonds," he said. "I put Terry's friends onto Bacon's little airstrip and they gave me a stone for my trouble. Terry said they might bring me in if they moved the transfer point to Antigua from Jamaica. For now, I'm just a flunky for gimpy old Marshall Kleidaeker."

I knew I had to keep him talking to give the SWAT guys time to get into position. "How did you know I was there?"

"Don't be a dumbass, Conwright. Kleidaeker had me install a security light in the back yard. You tripped it and you're thinking I didn't notice! I must admit you interrupted my work here, but better to know you were snooping around, than not. Eh, sport?"

"So what happened between you and your girl-friend here? She paid you well."

"Shit she did! This way, I'll only get a part of it. She was going to pay me another sixty thousand after her old man's estate cleared."

"But why this?" I pointed to GeorgeAnn.

"The bitch was losing it. She was out of control. I couldn't trust her to keep quiet. I tried to tell her how to handle all this, but she was too panicked. So she's going to swim with the fishes."

He still held the silenced pistol in his hand. "You can't drown her," I said. "You'll get soaking wet and –"

"Fuck off, Conwright! Don't tell me how to do this. She's going to be a *body* by the time we get to the river. You're going to load her into a boat that's down by the dock. She's going to have that vise over there strapped around her waist." He nodded toward a sturdy vise clamped to the edge of a temporary work table. "She'll stay down for a long, long time."

"So how'd you think of using the magnet to kill Caughlin?"

"GeorgeAnn here told me about his pacemaker. When I worked concerts, there was a guy on our stage crew with a pacemaker. Once the power was on, he'd always ask me to adjust the speakers so he wouldn't have to expose himself to the field. I did a little research on the internet and figured it out from there."

"You and she were going to hook up and live off of her inheritance?"

"Maybe, maybe not. But it's time for you to shut up, Conwright. I need to wrap this up."

I saw that GeorgeAnn had stopped struggling and was lying still. There was still no sign of the SWAT unit.

"You can't go back to Kleidaeker, you know. I've told the police what I've discovered. They'll come for you!"

"You think I didn't plan for something going wrong! I have a new identity. Good old Terry helped out there. They'll never find me!"

He had already cinched a length of insulated electrical wire around GeorgeAnn's waist with enough left over to secure the vise. I saw that her hair was matted at the back of her head and there was a swollen, bloody knob under the dark-blond locks. Once he decided she was panicking, he must have come at her with a blow from behind.

"So enough chit chat," Maitland said impatiently. "Stop playing detective and pick her up! Take her down those steps to the back yard. I'll be right behind you."

I knew damn well that once I had hauled GeorgeAnn outside, he would kill her. And once I had loaded her body into the boat, he would shoot me too. If I was going to save myself, it had to be then and there. I looked around as I got to my feet. A snapline and a chalk bottle to refill it lay on the floor beside GeorgeAnn's head. On my other side, I saw a steel carpenter's square. I looked at Maitland fifteen feet away. The extension cord for the work light ran across the floor toward us and he was unknowingly straddling it.

"Pick her up, Goddamn it!" he yelled.

I bent over her and turned so that my face and my right hand were out of his line of sight. I whispered in her ear to stay still. I felt for the squeeze-bottle of powdered chalk.

"She's stopped moving. I think you've killed her!"

He came closer and peered down at her. I lurched around, aimed the bottle at his face and squeezed it as hard as I could. A cloud of orange dust enveloped his head. At the same time, I yanked on the extension cord. The cord snapped taut up to his groin. He coughed at the dust, took two steps back, and dropped his hands instinctively to his crotch. I flung the metal square at him like a boomerang. It hit him in the ribs and he staggered backwards. I lunged forward and hacked at his gun hand, karate fashion. The gun crashed to the floor and skidded away. My momentum carried me into his body and we both careened into the stud wall.

I lost my balance and went down to one knee as we hit the wall. Maitland kept his feet and ran across the room. He would have reached the gun before I got there, but the gun was nowhere to be seen. Then I noticed that GeorgeAnn had rolled over onto her stomach. He figured it out at the same time I did and we both dove at the woman on the floor. We were like a couple of football players in a pile-up trying to recover a fumble. It was a vivid image as it flashed through my brain, but the problem was that the result could be fatal to me if I could not come up with the gun. We rolled onto GeorgeAnn and spun her over in the process. The gun *had* been under her. I grabbed for it and felt my fingers close on the grip just as Maitland landed a roundhouse right hand on my jaw. I slumped against the stud wall, but kept the gun pointed toward Maitland. I was woozy and nauseous. I knew that if I passed out, it would be all over. I tried to focus my eyes and saw Maitland's back as he piled out the door on the dead run.

It was a good twenty seconds before I got back to my feet and navigated my way to the back door. I had fallen for the ambush-at-the-door once already and was not about to make that mistake again. I brought the work light over to be sure he was not in the kitchen or waiting on the porch. Then a swirl of fog parted and I saw him on the dock untying the boat.

I ran down the sloping back yard toward the dock with his gun in my hand. I was still fifteen yards from the riverbank when Maitland jumped into the boat. He gave a mighty shove with his foot as he got in and the boat glided backwards into the current. I saw him bending over in the stern and heard the starter trying to kick the outboard motor into operation. The boat was facing me as I got off two shots at the hull. Both missed. Then the current began to slowly swing the bow to face downstream. He was far enough out by then, that I could hardly see him through the fog that hugged the surface of the water. Maitland pressed the starter twice more and, the second time, the motor caught. He steered in a sharp starboard turn as soon as the boat was under power. The turn brought the boat in closer to me. I could see it well enough to get off two more shots. The hull was the largest and easiest target in the fog and I thought sinking the boat would put Maitland swimming in the river. I thought I hit the boat with at least one of my shots, but it had vanished in the fog, the sound of its motor quickly tapering to nothingness.

I ran back to the house to grab my cell phone and gun and to make sure GeorgeAnn was still alive. I saw that her eyes were open and that she was breathing normally. I did not know the layout of the house, so I left by the back door. I almost ran over Ricardo who was running along the side of the house toward the back yard.

"Rick, what the hell is happening? Did I hear shots?"

"He was in there. He's got the woman bound up on the floor. He ambushed me as I tried to get inside, but I ended up with his gun. He got away in a little skiff with an outboard. I took some shots at the boat, but I don't know if I hit anything. He went down river."

"Madre de Dios! How are we going to chase him on the river?"

"We aren't. I want you to stay here, out in front. Sheriff's deputies are on the way. Wait until they get here. Tell them that the woman inside is injured. And tell them that she is guilty of murder! Paul DeNoli is coming and he can explain it to them when he gets here. And tell them where Maitland went. Julio and I will try to follow him on the streets along the river in case he tries to get back on dry land."

"In this fog, he'd be smarter to keep going in the boat and put some distance between himself and here," Ricardo said.

"You're probably right, but we've got to try everything. Maybe the sheriff has a police boat that can come up the river to intercept him."

We had come back to the street and Julio materialized out of the fog from the other side of the house.

"Julio, he *was* in there, but he got away in a boat. Ricardo will stay here until the police come." I placed Maitland's gun in my handkerchief and handed it to Ricardo. "Give this to DeNoli. It's the gun I took away from Maitland. Julio, you get in your car and follow me. I'm going down a mile or so and then I'm cutting back on foot to the river. Go past me a ways and do the same thing. Maybe we'll get lucky or at least see him go past. Use your cell phone and stay in contact. I'll do the same."

"I'm on it, Rick!"

"Be careful! If you should see him, don't approach or try to stop him. Call me and I'll pass it on to the cops."

He nodded his understanding and we ran to our cars. I sped down Childs and turned back toward the river on a cross street called Marlin. The odds were, as Ricardo had said, that Maitland would keep going down river to where it entered the Willamette. Even if he wanted to get back on land, he would probably beach the boat on the opposite bank so we could not follow. I just wanted to catch sight of him and report his location to the police. I skidded to a stop in front of a riverside home and ran across the property toward the river. I was stopped by a cyclone fence. Then I saw a gate and dashed through it. I was almost to the river's edge when I heard the snarling bark of a large dog. I tried to go left to get off his property only to find more fencing. It was a German shepherd and he was closing fast. He may or may not have been a trained attack dog, but I did not want to find out the hard way. I jumped into the river and found myself waist deep in icy water. I waded around the fence and, holding my gun and my cell phone above water, and clambered toward the next lot. I had to clench the phone in my teeth so I could free a hand to grab the fence and get enough purchase to climb the muddy bank. The dog stayed on the bank on his side, still snarling, and lunging at the fence.

It was then I saw Maitland's boat nosed up against the bank. I quickly checked it out. There were holes where two of my bullets had passed through the aluminum hull and there was a good six inches of water inside. So he had *had* to beach the boat. I looked back toward the street and saw a galloping figure fading into the mist.

There was a large two-story house on the property. I raced past the house on the opposite side from where Maitland had run. I did not think he had seen me. He was either running to speed up his escape or because he thought the dog that chased me was after him. There were no fences or gates on this property and I was pounding down alongside the driveway toward the street in a matter of seconds. I saw Maitland thirty yards ahead. He was still galloping and I realized that he had injured his foot … or maybe I had plugged him with one of my shots. He still did not seem to know I was behind him. I holstered my piece and sprinted even faster.

He must have heard me as my feet hit the pavement. He looked over his shoulder and started to turn around. In the heat of the chase, I lost my resolve to simply call in his location. He had been quite ready to kill me. I wanted the son of a bitch badly! I'm no football player, but I made a tackle that would have made any linebacker proud. I knocked him off his feet. He went over backwards with me on top of him. Unfortunately, his survival instincts were first class. He got his hands around my throat. I landed a couple of blows to his head and his grip loosened. He jabbed me in the eye and I flinched enough that he rolled out from under me. I regained my feet first. I could only see out of my right eye, but I kicked at him with all I had as he tried to rise. I heard a snapping in his rib cage and he crumpled to the ground. I backed off a step or two and covered him with my gun.

A man came out of the next house over and stared at us. I yelled at him to call the police. I gave him DeNoli's cell number and told him to give his address and say we had cornered Maitland. The man ran back inside.

Maitland sat up and raised his palm to me. "Don't shoot. My foot's bleeding … maybe broken. You fucking shot me! And broke my ribs! I'll sue your ass!"

"Sure you will! You and your ladyfriend are going to have plenty of time to practice jailhouse law."

I kept a close watch on Maitland as I called Julio and Ricardo to tell them I had him and to bring the SWAT unit to Marlin Street. My left eye was now swollen shut. I hoped to God that Maitland's finger had not permanently damaged it. Two minutes later, I heard the squeal of tires as several vehicles screamed around a corner. A couple of patrol cars and the SWAT van wheeled out of the whiteness and skidded to a stop, bookending us on the pavement.

TWENTY-TWO

Monday night

DeNoli arrived while I was explaining what had happened and the sheriff's deputies were cuffing Maitland. Then, two Lake Oswego police cars thundered in. DeNoli had waved me over but, before I got to him, I saw Angie getting out of her car. I ran over and wrapped my arms around her.

"Rick, honey! You're safe!" She kissed me and then saw my face. "Oh! Your eye!"

"I'm okay, Angie. Got a shiner is all."

"And you're soaking wet!"

"Well, yeah. I did a little wading in the river along the way."

"Chasing Maitland you fell in the river?"

"Not exactly, but close. How the hell did *you* get here!"

"I know you told me to stay away, Rick. But, you know me: a newshound!"

"You're incorrigible! How did you find the right place?"

"Now don't get mad. I have to admit I followed you over to the east side and back to I-5."

I thought, great Rick! That's the second time in the last ten days when you have been tailing someone and were being tailed yourself!

"Then I lost you in the fog a little south of Portland," Angie continued. "I gave up the chase, but I was hungry so I stopped at Stanford's in Lake Oswego for some dinner. I had just placed my order when I remembered that I had left my police-band scanner on. I went back to the car. Before I could turn it off, I heard all this radio traffic about getting a SWAT unit out to an address in Rivergrove. It was kind of a long shot, but I went back into the restaurant and canceled my order. Then I drove to the address the dispatcher had called out. By the time I got there, Maitland and you were gone and the sheriff's SWAT unit was just arriving. I saw Ricardo and he filled me in."

"Looks like you've got a hell of a story!"

"I've already called my camera person. It's too late to get something on the late news, but I'll have a great piece for tomorrow."

DeNoli walked over and greeted Angie. Then he asked if he and I could talk privately for a few minutes.

He looked a little steamed up. I could guess what was coming. Angie left us and DeNoli started in.

"Do I have to put a collar and a leash on you, Rick! What were the last words I said to you? 'Stay outside the house,' I said. So of course you go right on in and get in a fight with a guy who's holding a gun on you!"

"He was somehow going to kill her, Paul! He had her bound and gagged and he was pulling on gloves. I thought maybe he was going to strangle her … or dump her off the dock. I didn't *see* that he had a gun!"

"He works as a bodyguard for Christ's sake! Of *course* he had a gun."

"Okay, point taken. But what else could I have done?"

"For starters, you have one murderer trying to kill another. You could've just waited it out and saved the state the cost of the needle. Or you could've banged on the front door and made him jittery enough to run off without taking the time to off her."

"That's a lot of hindsight and speculation and you know it!"

"Maybe, but you've got to stop being such a damned cowboy!"

"So I'm in PPB's doghouse again?"

"Let me put it this way. Your style of doing things won't go unnoticed. I'll stick up for you because you *did* uncover Caughlin's murderers and probably got the D.A. evidence to convict. Hopefully, that will give you enough brownie points that the suits will look the other way."

"Message received, Paul," I said as I hung my head and tried to look sufficiently abashed.

The homeowners along the street had come outside to see what the commotion was about. The deputy sheriffs were securing the back yard and preparing to carry the boat up to the street to be impounded as evidence. DeNoli had finished his obligatory lecture and went off to coordinate matters with the deputies. He had called out his police criminalists to check Kleidaeker's rental for forensic evidence. He told the EMTs to take GeorgeAnn to an emergency room. A Portland police officer would ride with them. His partner would take the patrol car and would meet them at the hospital. Later, they were to take their prisoner on to the Justice Center jail.

Angie's camera person arrived and she asked the homeowner and the deputies for permission to go into the back yard to video the officers getting the boat out of the water. Angie did a voice-over and then told me that she and the camera guy were going back to the rental house in hopes of filming GeorgeAnn as she was taken away. Angie whispered that she would be working through most of the night, but would come by in the morning to get whatever more details I could give her. DeNoli came over to tell me that an Assistant District Attorney would very likely contact me in the morning.

"Mostly she'll want your story of what you've uncovered and what you witnessed this evening. But remember, you shot Maitland. She'll want to go over that with you too."

"I should be okay on the shooting. Citizen's arrest, escaping felon, potential harm to others … all that good stuff."

"Maybe so. And it will help that you actually witnessed his having her tied up and ready to kill her at the rental house."

"Besides, Paul, I was aiming at the damn boat. I only hit him by accident."

"Okay, but you still have to take it very seriously and be careful how you explain it to her."

I was ravenously hungry and I needed to get out of my wet clothes. I drove back to the houseboat for a hot shower and a lasagna dinner heated in the microwave. By the time I had finished eating, it was eleven o'clock. I wanted my client to know what had happened before she saw it on the morning news. Amanda Nelson's husband answered the phone sounding a little irritated by the lateness of the call. I told him I had news for Amanda about the case.

"Amanda, it's over. And there was nearly another death. Maitland convinced GeorgeAnn to meet with him at an unoccupied house on the Tualatin River that he was remodeling for his boss. I don't know exactly what happened between them, but he decided he could not trust her to keep quiet and was getting ready to kill her when I got there."

"Why would she agree to go to such a place?"

"They were probably afraid to be seen together in public or to talk about the situation over the phone. By then, they knew I had uncovered most of it. I imagine he told her they had to meet to get their act together. Or, maybe he was ready to cut and run and had already planned to kill her when he set up the meeting. In any case, he talked her into the rendezvous."

"How did you know they were there?"

"I wanted to panic them into doing something self-incriminating. It seemed to work. When they each left their homes, I had my team follow them. As it turned out, we lost both of them in the fog, but I remembered Marshall Kleidaeker had this rental house near where we lost Maitland. I pulled a rabbit out of my hat on that one."

"Did the police arrest them?"

"Ultimately they did, yes. GeorgeAnn was bound and gagged. It looked as though he had bashed her on the head, but she'll survive to stand trial. Maitland and I fought, but he got away in a boat on the river. I found him about a mile down stream. I had taken his gun away from him and I used it to shoot holes in the boat. I saw later that I had hit him in the foot at the same time. He and I had another tussle and then the cops took over."

"My God! I'm so sorry you had to get involved in all that violence."

"Yeah, me too. But that sort of thing sometimes happens. Since we caught the people that killed your father and the worst I got was a black eye, I'd say that was a reasonable price to pay."

"I suppose so, but it wasn't my intention to put you at personal risk. Please send me your bill. You don't need to do a written report, but perhaps you could bring the bill in person and tell me more about how it all fits together. How they planned it and why."

"I'll do that. Maybe the end of the week or early next week? Once I get caught up, I'll call you to see what would be convenient."

"That would be fine."

"There's something else you need to be aware of. I don't need to tell you that your father was a wealthy man and he owned a fairly high-profile local company. This whole story will make the media in a big way. My friend Angie Richards on the TV news will surely break it tomorrow morning and the rest of the pack won't be far behind. They may ask you for comments. In any case, your father's life will be open to public scrutiny."

"I see. I'll be thinking about what to say. Will they interview you?"

"They will probably try. Except for Ms. Richards, I'll decline. I'll remind them that a private investigator working for a client doesn't discuss his findings. There will also be state and federal criminal proceedings and a lot of facts will have to be kept back until the trials are over. Angie Richards is a little different. I've shared with her some general things about my investigation

– not about your father – but about some of the others. Ms. Richards and I 'spooked' the two suspects, particularly GeorgeAnn. Angie was the key to that. As an established newscaster and investigative journalist, she was the perfect one to take an interest in GeorgeAnn's affairs. Our plan succeeded – though we did not foresee that Maitland would turn on GeorgeAnn."

"Well, I've told you before that I was never so naïve as to think of my father as some kind of a saint. I knew he was a pretty hard-nosed business man. But he *was* my dad, and nothing he ever did would conceivably justify killing him. So long as *we* don't supply unflattering information, I guess I'll have to trust the media to be responsible."

"I know you can trust Angie," I said, "and I hope you're right about the rest of them."

⚊⚊

I was in the middle of that dreary job of checking my neglected mail and e-mail the next morning, when DeNoli called.

"Rick, our criminalists raised a print on that steel rod that was part of the magnetic-field generator. It was on the butt-end of the rod. A nice thumb print. It's a match to Maitland's thumb print. Despite his wiping it down or wearing gloves when he handled it, this must have been from when he first assembled it. So he's locked into that little killing machine!"

317

"Excellent! Did my cell phone pick up anything?"

"What I was getting to next, fella. It was faint and, at times a little muffled, but we have plenty enough for him to be looking at first degree."

"That's great. I think I told you, when he got the jump on me, he dropped the phone in the corner, but he never checked to see if there was an open line."

"The phone was a smart move on your part. The techies are going to do a computerized enhancement and we'll hear even more."

"Don't they have to be careful messing around with the original?"

"They do. They're pretty aware of the protocol and the ADA is looking over their shoulders so whatever additional stuff they hear should all be admissible. You did a damn good job of getting him to talk!"

"Yeah, for a while he was cocky enough to answer my questions and boast a little. And, hell, I had to stall him any way I could!"

"Well, the cavalry *was* a couple of minutes late arriving but, basically, your stall worked."

"Maitland said he was going to get away without a trace. Did he have another identity?" I asked.

"He sure as hell did! A driver's license, a passport, and almost a thousand dollars in cash."

"I told you last night about his half-brother, Terry Radich. Maitland implied he got his new identity from Radich."

"Yeah, I'm sure we'll be working with the feds on that aspect. But those smugglers weren't really connected to Caughlin's death were they?"

"No. The smuggling was connected only in the sense that Caughlin's snooping around to gain some leverage on Bacon led me out on that tangent. If the smugglers had *realized* Caughlin had hired someone to watch the airstrip and take pictures, who knows? Then they might've come after him. How about your two prisoners? Are they ready to rat each other out?"

"They both have lawyers now. The early version from her was that he was blackmailing her about their affair. She sent him the dough only as hush money. Says she didn't know about any plans to kill her husband. Says maybe Kleidaeker was behind it."

"Yeah, I can see her trying that. She'll try to get some 'reasonable doubt' in the minds of the jury. But she'll have to explain why Kleidaeker would have a motive. It's not too likely her late husband told her how he had treated Kleidaeker in the past, years ago. Besides, how can she explain Mailtand trying to kill her last night?"

"I know," DeNoli said. "A blackmailer wouldn't kill the goose that was laying golden eggs for him. I think it's like you said: she's just trying to muddy the waters."

"What about Maitland?"

"He has too much moxie to talk this early. But when he sees how strong the case against him is, I'm betting he'll implicate her in a New York minute. I'm not sure the DA will want to cut deals with either one of them, however. Maitland's a loser and he's guilty of premeditated murder. They won't have quite as strong a case against her, but she's the more evil of the two … a gold digger, a cheating bitch, and a person who would hire someone to kill her own husband!"

"You said something about an Assistant District Attorney wanting to talk to me?"

"Oh, yeah. They've assigned Darlene Tennyson. She said for you to call her. She's spending the morning with the criminalists, but she wants to see you in mid-afternoon."

De Noli and I finished our phone conversation and I called Kleidaeker to tell him what happened and that it was safe to go home. After that, I kept on with the mail and paperwork until noon when I turned on the TV. Angie had come by for breakfast at my place. I clarified a few facts for her in areas where I was comfortable explaining things and she tightened up her story. The mid-day newscast had a spot introduced as "breaking news." Angie laid the foundation of a prominent business man's death, thought originally to be due to natural causes, now declared a homicide. She sketched the relationships between GeorgeAnn and Maitland and said they had both been arrested for murder. Then they showed the footage of the boat with the bullet holes and the arrest of GeorgeAnn at the rental house. It was a good, hard-hitting teaser with the promise of "details at six".

That evening, at the regular news desk, Angie did a great job of developing the story further. I got plenty of credit as she described the final hour of the drama. The money transfers to Antigua added an exotic touch. As I had anticipated, the DA ordered her to hold back some of the details of the magnetic-field generator and the money trail. Nevertheless, the story had legs and it was obvious that she had more compelling segments to come.

⇒⊢ ⊣⇐

On Friday, I called Marilyn to ask how her sister was doing. She said Justine had already lined up a job and was going to join a support group for persons combating depression. Marilyn ended by telling me that Justine seemed to be making good progress and was happy to be back in Cincinnati.

A little later, I got a call from Agent Masters. He told me that the FBI, Customs, and the Canadian Mounties had made more arrests and that they had effectively shut down the British-Columbia-to-northwestern-US link in the blood-diamond smuggling chain. The Mounties had discovered a farm with an airstrip not far from Nelson, B.C. that had been the plane's takeoff point. He said that a couple of numbers on the plane's

tail had been repainted each time it started on or returned from its trans-border trips. That way, the plane
had its legitimate registration in Canada and a slightly different, non-traceable tail number if it was ever
spotted in the States. He said Radich's short accom-
plice, Sam Hostings, was singing like a canary and that
would lead to still more arrests. Masters said the effort,
now, would be to close the net on retailers who had
knowingly bought the diamonds from the smugglers.

DeNoli called later that same day to tell me that
Maitland was starting to cooperate, in hopes of avoiding a death sentence even though no deals had been
offered. DeNoli wanted me to know that one of the
statements Maitland had given was that Kleidaeker
had nothing to do with it. That was the way I had it
figured, but I was glad to know that I had not missed
something important.

My last phone call was from Angie. She said the
story would likely keep her busy all weekend, but she
would come to the houseboat Sunday night. We made
plans to splurge the next weekend by having an ocean-
side getaway at the Stephanie Inn in Cannon Beach.

I met with Amanda Nelson and her husband on
Saturday. I presented my bill including the invoice
from Baruda. Amanda did not question a thing and
wrote out a check on the spot. I thanked her and

tucked the check into my wallet. Then, I told them how Julio's crew had canvassed the high-fidelity stores and how Julio and Ricardo had helped trail Maitland to the rental house and had watched my back as we closed in on him. I explained how I came to know Julio and why he helped me from time to time. Then I gave them more specifics about Julio's foundation.

"That's a really inspiring story!" Amanda said. "I'd like to meet your Julio and learn more about his foundation. Del Crocker tells me that when GeorgeAnn is convicted, the pre-nup will almost certainly be void. So, once the estate is sorted out, I guess I'll be pretty comfortable financially. I would very much like to make a donation."

"That's great! Julio's a fine person and his foundation, unlike the one we found in the Caribbean, is totally legit."

"Thank you for telling me about Julio and for everything you've done on this investigation. I hope I *never* need to use a private investigator again, but – if I do – you're the one I'll call!"

Her husband grinned in agreement and asked, "Will you stay for lunch? Some soup and a ham sandwich?"

"Thanks. That would be nice."

"There's another thing I'd like to say," Amanda began as we walked toward her kitchen. "I've been thinking on some things you hinted at about my father and Stanley Bacon. You've always been discreet about it, but I've read between the lines that Mr. Bacon thought my father had used one of his ideas, perhaps an invention that was important in the business?"

"That is what Bacon believed. It was about a patent for the long-lasting vulcanizing process. I heard some things suggesting that could be the case, but I never took it any further. Besides, I'm no patent attorney so I can't say how valid his belief was."

"I understand. But I'm afraid that I think there was at least some truth to it. And now Stan Bacon has been killed and his widow has been left with a shaky business. Once I'm the sole owner of Rubber Master, I intend to have Del Crocker draw something up so that Mrs. Bacon can have some kind of an ownership interest in the company."

Her husband nodded and my jaw dropped. The soup was hearty and the sandwiches hit the spot. We sat around the breakfast-nook table and watched the beginning of the last regular-season football game for the Oregon Ducks. All this had started with a poker game. Now the last hand had been dealt, and I felt like an aces-full winner.

ACKNOWLEDGEMENTS

I wish to thank Joyce Swan for her patience and suggestions; Del Thomas and the late Bob Miller for their careful and helpful reading of early drafts; author Dean Ing for an early read and good suggestions; Kathy Brault for reading a late draft and making suggestions; Ian MacMillan for reading the manuscript with his keen medical eye; Carlyne Lynch for an early critique and helpful advice on data-base security; Don Lefler for his interest in creative writing and early support.

Made in the USA
San Bernardino, CA
02 August 2014